SUPERNATURAL™

CARVED IN FLESH

SUPERNATURAL™

CARVED IN FLESH

TIM WAGGONER

SUPERNATURAL created by Eric Kripke

TITAN BOOKS

Supernatural: Carved in Flesh
Print edition ISBN: 9781781161135
E-book edition ISBN: 9781781161166

Published by Titan Books
A division of Titan Publishing Group Ltd
144 Southwark St, London SE1 0UP

First edition: April 2013
10 9 8 7 6 5 4 3 2 1

Visit our website: www.titanbooks.com

Did you enjoy this book? We love to hear from our readers. Please email
us at readerfeedback@titanemail.com or write to us at Reader Feedback
at the above address.

To receive advance information, news, competitions, and exclusive
offers online, please sign up for the Titan newsletter on our website:
www.titanbooks.com

A CIP catalogue record for this title is available from the British Library.

Printed and bound in the United States.

HISTORIAN'S NOTE
This novel takes place during season seven, between
"Time After Time" and "The Slice Girls."

ONE

"I'm surprised they haven't left for the winter yet."

Joyce Nagrosky glanced sideways at her companion. He stood at the edge of the pond, tearing small pieces from a slice of wheat bread and tossing them into the water. A half dozen ducks had gathered close to shore, and whenever a morsel landed close to them, they extended their necks, heads darting fast as striking snakes, and snatched up the snack in their rounded beaks. When the bread was gone, they stared at the humans, eager and alert for the next offering.

"Not all ducks fly south for the winter," Joyce said. "As long as it doesn't get cold enough to damage their feet, they can make it to spring just fine."

Ted turned toward her, an amused smile on his face. "I thought you retired from teaching. Besides, you taught English, not biology."

She couldn't help laughing. "Once a know-it-all, always a know-it-all, I suppose."

Even in his sixties, Ted Boykin was a good-looking man,

with a full head of thick white hair, a trim goatee to match, and the most striking blue eyes. Back when he'd been principal at the school where Joyce had taught, he'd been clean-shaven, and while she was normally indifferent to facial hair on men, the beard gave him a roguish air that she liked. She'd worked alongside the man for more than twenty years, but while she'd respected him, even in some ways counted him as a friend, she hadn't been attracted to him. But now here they were. Life sure was funny sometimes. In fact, it could be downright hysterical.

It was dusk in early November, and although it had been on the warm side throughout the day, now that the sun had dipped toward the horizon it was getting cold. Ted seemed comfortable in his brown jacket, but Joyce had donned a blue windbreaker before leaving her apartment, and it didn't do much to ward off the chill in the air, especially since she wore only a T-shirt beneath. She wished she'd at least thought to grab a hat or scarf before walking out the door.

Why so addle-pated all of a sudden, my dear? she asked herself. *Could it be that you were a wee bit nervous to rendezvous with Mr. Boykin down by the duck pond?* She wanted to tell herself that it was a ridiculous thought. She was a grown woman, for god's sake! *Over*grown, truth be told, if not vertically then at least horizontally. And the pond was hardly lover's lane. Even so, she had to admit to a certain uneasiness at being there. She'd been alone since her husband had died a few years back, and while she still missed him, in all that time she hadn't felt the need to seek out a replacement. But then a week ago she'd bumped into Ted—almost literally. She'd been backing her Volvo out of the parking space in front of her apartment at the same moment Ted had been passing in front of her building. He'd barely managed to stop his Bronco in time to avoid ramming her rear end—*And isn't that a phrase rife with naughty possibilities?*—and that's when they'd discovered that after the deaths of their respective spouses, they'd both sold their homes and moved into Arbor Vale Apartments. In fact, Ted lived in the building next to Joyce's, and had for almost two years, without either of them knowing the other was there. Small world, and all that.

The next day they'd met for lunch, and the day after that, dinner. They'd seen quite a bit of each other over the past seven days, and in that time, Ted had been a complete gentleman, not trying to kiss her or even hold her hand. She was, quite frankly, getting tired of it. She wished he would go ahead and make a move already. She was far from shy and would have made the first move herself if he hadn't been so tentative toward her. The last thing she wanted to do was scare him off by being too direct: *Don't you think it's time the two of us had sex? It's not like we're getting any younger.* Somehow, she didn't think that would work.

She brushed her black hair over her ear, even though there was no need. The air was still, and as short as she kept her hair, it rarely got mussed. Since childhood, she'd been something of a tomboy, and now that she no longer had to dress for work, that tendency had reasserted itself. She preferred simple clothes like T-shirts and jeans and wore no makeup. She'd recently taken to collecting jewelry that she picked up at auctions and estate sales, for reasons she couldn't articulate clearly even to herself, but she rarely wore any of it. She wished she'd put some on today, though. Maybe if she seemed more feminine to Ted, he wouldn't keep her at arm's length. *Maybe he hasn't gotten over the loss of his wife yet,* she thought. *Or maybe he still sees me as one of his teachers instead of a woman.* She was surprised by how much this latter possibility depressed her.

The pond lay behind Arbor Vale's buildings, at the bottom of a gently sloping grassy hill. On the other side were woods of oak, elm, and ash trees, their leaves a splendorous mix of yellows, reds, and browns. Most of them hadn't fallen yet, but Joyce knew it wouldn't be much longer before they began drifting to the ground. A week, maybe two. Autumn was her favorite time of the year, partly because it was when school began, but mostly because of the energy that filled the crisp air. It was a delicious paradox that even as the world prepared for the temporary death brought by winter—to be followed by resurrection come spring—it seemed, at least to her, to be the most alive.

To hell with it, she thought. *Life is for living.* She took a step closer to Ted, reached out, and took his hand.

She felt him tense and feared he would pull away, but then he relaxed and clasped her hand firmly. Joyce didn't look at him, and he didn't look at her, but they both smiled and gazed at the water. Ted tossed in the last of the bread, and once it was gone, the ducks milled about, hoping for more, but doomed to disappointment. Joyce admired the way the reflections of the trees on the opposite shore rippled on the water like shadowy ink.

She was wondering what the chances were of Ted kissing her later, and perhaps doing more than just kissing, when she heard a low growling sound. Fear jolted her, and she tightened her grip on Ted's hand.

The ducks let out a series of alarmed quacks as they reared back, spread their wings, and one by one took to the sky, flapping with frantic urgency as they fled.

The sound came again, a deep rumbling like a truck engine in dire need of repair, only it was louder this time. And closer. The sound came from their right, and when Joyce and Ted turned in that direction, they saw a large dark shape emerge from the woods and come toward them, walking on all fours.

It moved with the slow, menacing deliberation of a predator, and at first Joyce thought it might be a coyote. In recent years, the animals had moved into Ohio, and while they were by no means common, there were more of them around than most people thought. Joyce had never seen one outside of TV and the zoo—not alive, anyway. The animals were masters of concealment that preferred to avoid humans whenever possible, and the only time she'd seen one was when it lay dead on the side of the highway after being struck by a vehicle. She had been surprised by how much larger it looked than she expected. Ohio coyotes had shaggier coats than their desert-dwelling cousins, which likely accounted for the seeming disparity in their sizes. But Joyce quickly discarded the possibility that this creature was a coyote. There was something wrong about it. The gloom of dusk cloaked it, rendering it a mobile shadow that moved with a lurching, uneven gait, as if it were injured. Its growls weren't sounds of pain, though, but rather of hunger combined with almost human anger. Could it be a wolf? As far as Joyce knew, no wolves lived in Ohio, at least not in the wild. Maybe this one had been someone's pet that had escaped or been turned loose for some reason. Yet its form lacked the feral grace of a wolf, and seemed more canine than lupine.

Then the smell hit her, a thick miasma of musk and rot that made her gorge rise.

Sweet Jesus, what was *that thing?*

"It's okay," Ted said. His voice was shaky, but he didn't hesitate as he let go of Joyce's hand and stepped between her and the approaching whatever-it-was. Normally, she would have hated having a man—any man—treat her as if she were some delicate thing that needed protecting, but something about this… this *creature* triggered a deep atavistic fear in her, and she was grateful for Ted's gesture. She thought, too, that perhaps his actions were as much for his benefit as hers. As a former principal, he was used to being in charge and dealing with problems head on. It was his default setting, a comfortable role that he could fall back on in a time of crisis.

Still, as much as she appreciated what he was trying to do, her instincts told her it was a bad idea. *Very* bad.

She put her hand on his shoulder. "Please, don't."

Ted gave no sign that he heard her. Instead, he took a step toward the creature and drew himself up to his full height, arms held away from his sides, hands balled into fists.

He's trying to make himself look larger, Joyce realized. *More threatening.* She wondered if he'd done something similar in high school when dealing with potentially violent teenage boys. But hadn't she read somewhere that directly facing a canine and making eye contact was a form of challenge to them? In that case—

The creature rushed forward, mismatched limbs moving with surprising speed, growl so loud it was nearly a roar. It moved so swiftly that in the dimming light of dusk Joyce could only make out the most basic details of its grotesque form: different-sized legs, a single ragged ear, bare skin alternating with patches of fur, and worst of all, a crooked muzzle filled with sharp teeth, far more than the mouth of a simple dog should have been able to hold.

When it was within a yard of Ted, the beast leaped into the air, discolored tongue lolling from the side of its misshapen mouth. Its front paws hit Ted on the chest, its weight driving him backward, slamming him against the ground. The impact drove the air from his lungs, and she heard a crack that she guessed was the sound of one or more ribs breaking.

Joyce had managed to sidestep in time to avoid being knocked down, and she now stood less than a foot away from Ted as he struggled with the freakish dog, which was roughly the size and bulk of a St. Bernard, although it didn't resemble the breed otherwise. It snarled and snapped, intent on fastening its teeth around Ted's throat, and Ted wrapped his hands around its neck in an attempt to hold it at bay. The dog-beast's rear legs—one larger than the other—scrabbled at the ground as it fought to get close enough to sink its teeth into its prey. Ted grimaced, his arms trembling with the effort of trying to hold off the animal. Considering the massive size of the thing, it would have been too strong for most men to handle, and whatever physical strength Ted had possessed in his youth was long gone. He was relying on adrenaline and sheer force of will right now, but Joyce knew they wouldn't be enough in the end. She feared he had only moments, if not seconds, before the monster dog overwhelmed him, fastened its jaws around his throat, and crushed his windpipe in a spray of blood.

Part of her—the primitive animal part that was only interested in self-preservation at all costs—wanted nothing more than to turn and run away as fast as her less-than-svelte legs were capable of carrying her. In fact, without fully being aware of it, she had already half-turned and taken a step away from the pond. But she forced herself to turn back. She would never forgive herself if she ran off and left Ted to die. She had to do something to help him, but what? She wasn't about to try and grapple with the damned beast, and the closest thing to a weapon she had was her sometimes too-sharp tongue, which had filleted many a lazy student over the years. So, without anything else in her arsenal to rely on, she drew in a deep breath and, using what one of her fellow teachers had once referred to as "The Voice of Irresistible Authority," she shouted a single word.

"Stop!"

The word sounded harsh as a whip crack on the chill autumn air, and it echoed across the pond. The dog-thing stopped snarling and turned to look at her, confusion and perhaps a touch of fear in its eyes. Joyce had the feeling that with that one word she had reached something deep inside the beast, an inner core which recognized that humans occupied a higher rung on the evolutionary ladder, and thus were its masters. The creature lowered its gaze and its tail—a hairless appendage that looked like it should have been attached to a giant rat—drooped between its legs. It let out a soft whine.

Ted, who'd been just as surprised as the dog by Joyce's command, loosened his grip on the animal's neck. Instantly, the grotesque canine's upper lip curled away from its teeth, and the confusion in its eyes was replaced by blazing fury. The creature tore free from Ted's grasp and lunged forward with a snarl.

Joyce screamed as the monster-dog sank its teeth into Ted's throat and began shaking him back and forth, as if he were nothing but a toy. Ted's eyes widened with fear and pain, but although his mouth gaped wide, no sound emerged. An instant later Joyce understood why, as thick blood geysered upward. It ran down the sides of Ted's mouth and turned his white hair crimson before soaking into the ground beneath.

She opened her mouth to scream again, but the sound died in her throat. Something strange was happening. She thought at first that it was a trick of the waning light, but Ted's pale pink skin was losing its color, becoming a dull slate gray. More than that, his skin was drawing in on itself, tightening against his bones, muscle and fat shrinking as he transformed into an unwrapped mummy before her eyes. Crazily, Joyce was reminded of one of the last trips she'd taken with her husband before the cancer spread to the point where he was unable to travel. They'd gone camping in Hocking Hills, and instead of sleeping bags, they'd taken a king-sized inflatable mattress with a battery-powered fan that inflated it within moments. The fan had a reverse switch on it that also deflated the mattress, so that when it was finished, it was completely flat, curled slightly at the edges and crisscrossed with wrinkly lines. That's what Ted looked like now: a deflated gray air mattress with a skeleton inside.

The monster-dog held its grip on Ted's throat a moment longer, and Joyce watched as the blood smeared on Ted's face and the creature's muzzle dried and flaked away. Like the monster had absorbed Ted's life energy, drawn it into itself, and was determined not to let go of him until it had gotten every last bit. When it was finally finished, it withdrew its teeth from Ted's desiccated flesh and turned its attention to her.

She heard someone whisper, "Run," and it took her a moment to realize she was the whisperer. Hearing her own voice broke her paralysis, and she turned and ran.

The hill that led back up to the apartment complex wasn't steep, but she was hardly in the best of shape. When she'd been younger, her idea of exercise had been a leisurely stroll in the park, and now most of her physical activity involved walking around antiques stores. Adrenaline could only do so much to compensate for a mostly sedentary lifestyle, and her heart pounded an uneven rhythm in her ears, and her lungs burned as if they were aflame. Her legs felt heavy and shaky, and they became more so with each step she took. Finally, something gave way in her right knee, her leg buckled, and she went down. She landed on her side and slid several feet down the hill before coming to a stop. She lay there, pulse thrumming, lungs heaving, knowing there was no way she could hope to escape the monster-dog now—if she'd ever had a chance in the first place. She closed her eyes and waited to feel the creature's teeth sink into her throat.

But she felt nothing.

She opened her eyes and pushed herself to a sitting position. She turned to look back toward the pond, wondering what had happened. Had something scared the dog-thing off? Or had it simply been too full for another meal? For an instant she allowed herself to hope that she might survive this, but then she saw the creature. It sat next to Ted's corpse, looking at her, head cocked to the side in a very doglike fashion. She understood at once what had happened, and the realization filled her with despair. The monster-dog hadn't chased her because it hadn't needed to. She was too slow, old, and overweight to get away. The creature had only needed to wait for her to bring herself down, and she had done so.

As she watched, the great misshapen beast came lurching toward her on its mismatched limbs, crooked mouth open, discolored tongue hanging out, eyes burning with horrible, inhuman hunger.

She screamed, but not for long.

TWO

"I hate this damn car," Dean said.

"You hate every car that's not the Impala," Sam countered.

"Yeah, well, this one's especially sucktastic. And it smells like feet."

They'd picked up the brown "crapmobile"—just one of Dean's nicknames for it—behind a bar in Canton, Ohio. Dean would have preferred "borrowing" something with a bit more class, or at least something that didn't drive like a turd with tires, but ever since they'd gone off the grid in order to avoid registering on the Leviathan's radar, they'd been forced to keep a low profile, which meant no Impala. It also meant starting a sideline as reluctant car thieves—all for the greater good, of course. If the brothers failed to kill Dick Roman and ended up as human happy meals for him and his fellow monsters, the rest of the planet would be next on the menu. They were careful to take cars that no one would miss much, junkers that would be easy for their owners to replace and which the cops wouldn't work too hard to find. Dean had his hands full keeping the rust heaps they stole running, but there was only so much he could do. He constantly kept his fingers crossed that they wouldn't find themselves in a high-speed pursuit. As rough as the crapmobile was running, if he tromped on the gas, the rods would probably shoot out of the engine like friggin' missiles.

"Here we are," Sam said, pointing to a wooden sign on the side of the road. "Brennan, Ohio, which, according to the sign, is home to the Battling Brennan Brahman."

Dean frowned as they drove across the town line. "Brahman? Aren't they a kind of water buffalo or something?"

"Sort of. They're a type of cattle named after the sacred cow of Hinduism."

"Lousy choice for a school mascot, if you ask me. Alliteration only goes so far, you know?"

After they'd dropped in to the local sheriff's department as a "courtesy" to let them know that two FBI agents were in town and to glean any additional information they could about the deaths, they drove through Brennan to get a feel for the place. Not that they really needed to. They might have gone from Northeast Ohio to Southwest, but for all the miles they'd driven, they might as well have stayed in the same place. After all the years he'd spent on the road, most Midwestern towns looked alike to Dean, and Brennan was no exception. A downtown consisting of small local businesses housed in old buildings, suburbs dotted with mini malls and chain restaurants, and a decaying industrial section, which in Brennan's case was a closed bicycle factory on the south edge of town.

"You need a whole factory to make bikes?" Dean said. Sam just shrugged.

They found a cheap no-tell motel not far from the factory called the Wickline Inn, although Dean had no idea who or what a wickline was. They parked in front of the main office, and Sam went inside alone to register them. They always asked for a room as far from the main office as they could get, preferably one with empty rooms on either side. They'd been attacked in hotels more than once over the years, and the last thing they wanted to do was endanger any innocent lives.

Once Sam came out of the office with their room key, they pulled around to the back of the motel, parked, removed their stuff from the car—a couple backpacks with clothes and toiletries, Sam's computer, and a couple duffle bags containing weapons—and entered the room.

Once they were inside, Dean wrinkled his nose. "Man, this place smells like mothballs and ass."

"No argument there," Sam said.

They put their stuff on the beds and gave the room a quick once over, checking the bathroom, looking under the beds, and testing the window locks. Only when they were satisfied the room was clear did they lock the door. Every hunter worth his or her rock salt-filled shotgun knew better than to cut off a possible exit until they were sure they didn't need it. The brothers didn't bother unpacking in case they needed to grab their gear and get the hell out of there in a hurry. Not for the first time, Dean thought how much his life resembled that of a criminal on the run. He'd never told Sam, but for a while now, whenever they settled into a hotel room, he thought of his time with Lisa and Ben, and how damned nice it had been to go to sleep and wake up in the same place day after day.

The room had a small desk by the window, and Sam set his laptop on it, raised the lid, and booted up the machine. When the screen came to life, he said, "Once again the Winchesters are open for business." He sat down in front of the computer and started typing.

Dean sat down on the end of one of the beds, removed Bobby's flask from the pocket of his brown leather jacket, unscrewed the lid, and took a drink. He didn't take much, just a sip for maintenance. When he finished he replaced the lid, but instead of putting the flask away, he held it in his hands and looked at it for several moments. He remembered finding the bullet hole in Bobby's cap, remembered turning around in the van and seeing the corresponding hole in Bobby's forehead, remembered the blood…

"This is bull crap, Sammy."

"What is?" Sam didn't turn away from the computer screen. Once he got absorbed in the virtual world, he was harder to distract than a soul-starved demon intent on making a deal.

"*This*," Dean insisted, gesturing to take in the room. "Screwing around in Ohio when we should be nailing Dick Roman's hide to the wall."

Sam stopped typing and turned to look at his brother. "I know how you feel. I want to get Dick as much as you do." He frowned. "Wait, that didn't come out right."

"Ha ha. That's friggin' hilarious. Quit fooling around, Sam. I'm serious."

"So am I. Well, not about the dick joke. But I want to stop

the Leviathan, too. Not only to keep them from turning the human race into quarter pounders, but because I want justice for Bobby. Just like you."

Bobby Singer had been shot in the head by none other than Dick Roman himself during a scuffle with the Leviathan, and he'd died in a hospital not long after.

The Leviathan were among God's first creations, predating humans and even angels, but the beasts proved too wild and uncontrollable, concerned only with sating their savage hunger, and God banished them to Purgatory. *Good work on that one, God,* Dean thought. Their friend and ally Cass— also known as the angel Castiel—had inadvertently released the Leviathan when he absorbed all the souls in Purgatory in order to gain the power to defeat the archangel Raphael. Once free of their ancient prison, the Leviathan began planning to take over the world, intending to keep humanity alive solely as a food source. Among other things, the creatures possessed the ability to analyze a human's DNA and transform into an exact physical duplicate of their target. So the leader of the Leviathan assumed the guise of billionaire businessman Dick Roman, and used the man's considerable financial and political assets to build a secret empire around the world.

The brothers knew that the Leviathan's ultimate plan was the subjugation of humanity, but exactly how they intended to accomplish this—and how the Winchesters could stop them—they didn't know. That lack of knowledge gnawed at them like rabid rats, especially in Dean's case. Bobby had been more than an encyclopedic source of information, an endless fount of useful contacts, and a perpetually grouchy pain in the ass. He'd even been more than a close family friend. Bobby had been like an uncle to Dean and Sam. Hell, he'd practically been a second father to them, especially since their own dad had been on the road hunting and killing monsters much of the time while they were growing up. Both brothers missed him like hell.

There wasn't anything in this life that Dean wanted more than to take down Dick Roman, and every second he and Sam spent doing anything other than bringing the pain to that shark-toothed son of a bitch was a second wasted as far as he was concerned. But they were here, so they might as well get to work.

He remembered something he'd been told recently. *Hunting's the only clarity you're gonna find in this life. And that makes you luckier than most.*

Preach it, Brother Ness, Dean thought. He could use a double-shot of clarity right now. Make that a triple. Besides, their detour to Brennan might not be a complete waste of time. *Who knows? There might even be a decent strip club in this town.*

"All right." He sighed and took another hit from Bobby's flask. "Anything new since we left Canton?"

Sam looked at him a moment longer, and Dean thought his brother was going to say something about his drinking, but instead he turned back to face the laptop. He typed for a minute, stopped, then leaned forward and stared at the screen. Dean had seen him like this a thousand times before, and he knew what it meant.

"You got something."

"Yeah. Looks like there's been two more deaths, an older man and woman this time. According to the local paper— *The Brennan Broadsider*—they were found near a pond in back of the apartment complex where they lived. It happened two nights ago."

Dean stood, slipped the flask back into his jacket pocket, and went to look at the screen over Sam's shoulder.

"Does it say if they were getting their freak on when they died?"

Sam gave him a look.

"Hey, if you gotta go, you might as well go out smiling."

Sam turned back to the screen. "They were mummified like the others. Literally nothing left but skin and bones."

"We ganked Chronos, so we know he didn't do it, but it sure sounds like his style."

"Yeah, but the pattern's different. Chronos killed in groups of three over a period of years. So far four people have died in Brennan, all in the last week."

"And I assume they all ended up looking like they were on the diet plan from Hell."

"Yep." Sam continued reading. "The town officials are pretty spooked. They're worried the deaths are the result of some kind of toxic chemical or exotic disease. They've even sent tissue samples from victims to the CDC."

"Unless those guys have doctors who specialize in Weird with a capital W, I don't think they're going to find anything useful."

Sam closed his laptop. "Looks like it's up to us then."

Dean gave his brother a wry smile. "Isn't it always?"

* * *

"You sure we don't need protective suits? You know, like the kind they wear in those movies about plagues and stuff?"

Sam regarded the kid from the rental office. He was in his early twenties, probably fresh out of college and working his first real job. He was medium height, thin, with neatly trimmed black hair and an angular goatee that made him look kind of douchey. He wore a semi-expensive tie and highly polished shoes—both looked brand new—along with a dark blue windbreaker. Back at Arbor Vale's main office, he'd introduced himself as David Something—Stephenson maybe. Although Sam wasn't sure. His brain wasn't exactly firing on all cylinders these days, and every once in a while it slipped a gear. *Beats total insanity,* he thought.

After he and Dean had defeated Lucifer and prevented Armageddon, Sam's body and soul had been separated. His body remained on Earth, while his soul was trapped in the pit with Lucifer and the archangel Michael. Sam's body retained his memories, but without a soul he was the equivalent of a sociopath, devoid of all human feeling. In many ways, being soulless had made him a more efficient hunter. He was more decisive, quicker to act, and completely ruthless. Unfortunately, he also didn't care if he caused any collateral damage during his hunts. If innocent people died while he was killing some monster, so what? It was simply the cost of doing business.

Meanwhile in Hell, Lucifer and Michael played with his soul like two bored cats sharing a single ball of string, and those cats had some damn wicked claws. They shredded his soul as if it were tissue paper, and when it was finally

rejoined to Sam's body—thanks to Death himself, no less—
the damage done threatened to drive him insane. Death
established a psychic wall to protect Sam from the madness
that dwelt within him, but that wall had fallen, and it was
now up to Sam to hold the insanity at bay on his own. Most
days he did a good job hiding the crazy, but it took a lot out
of him, and he wasn't always certain he could trust his senses
and memory.

So maybe the kid's name was Stephenson, maybe not. At
least he was sure the kid was real. Well… reasonably sure.

"Not in this situation," Sam told Maybe-Stephenson.
"We're confident that the danger is minimal."

"But there *is* danger," the kid insisted. "Right?"

Sam and Dean were wearing their best "We're government
employees" monkey suits, and had introduced themselves
as agents Smith and Jones. They'd flashed their faux FBI
credentials at the kid and claimed they were there to assist
the CDC in its investigation. He bought it, and now he was
leading them, reluctantly, to the duck pond at the rear of the
apartment complex.

Dean glanced sideways at him. "If there was any chance of
contamination, don't you think my partner and I would be
wearing…" He trailed off and looked to Sam for help.

"Biohazard gear," Sam supplied.

"Right," Dean said. "That stuff."

"Maybe," the kid said, "but don't you guys get special
shots or something to inoculate you against deadly diseases,
radiation, and other nasty crap? You know, A-level medicine,
the kind of drugs the government pretends don't exist."

"Let me guess," Dean said. "You spend a lot of time surfing conspiracy websites, don't you?"

"Yeah. So?"

"Nothing. Just a hunch." He gave Sam a look that said, *We got us a real genius here*, and Sam suppressed a smile.

Arbor Vale was an older complex, built sometime in the seventies, Sam guessed, but it was clean and the grounds were well maintained. It didn't look like a place where supernatural evil lurked, but if his life as a hunter had taught him anything, it was that appearances meant jack. While monsters, demons, ghosts, and other nasties tended to be drawn to darkness and decay, they were just as likely to be found sniffing for prey in a well-to-do suburb as an abandoned graveyard. Evil—real Evil, the kind with a capital E—could be anywhere at any time.

The pond lay at the bottom of a gently sloping hill, and the Brennan PD had erected a crime-scene tape barrier at the top of the hill to warn anyone from getting too close. The tape was wound between a series of metal stakes driven through orange traffic cones, but despite the officers' best efforts, the tape drooped low enough for them to step over.

"Seriously?" Dean said as he eyed the tape barrier. "Do the Deputy Dawgs in this town really think that's going to keep anyone out?"

"I guess they don't get many major crime scenes here," Sam said.

The Winchesters stepped over without hesitation, but the kid hung back.

"Do you really need me to go down there with you?" he asked.

Dean gestured toward the pond. "You see those ducks swimming down there? Do you think they'd stick around if there was any toxic goo in the area?"

"Ducks could have a natural immunity to whatever it was that killed those two old people." The kid's eyes narrowed. "Or maybe whatever got them was genetically engineered to only be fatal to humans."

"Man, you really need to lay off the Internet," Dean said.

"Besides, I don't want to go anywhere near those woods."

Sam and Dean exchanged a glance.

"Why not?" Sam asked.

"Feral dogs," the kid explained. "Rumor is the woods around town are full of them. I haven't seen any myself, but lots of people have. There's one that's supposed to be an especially scary bastard. Big and black."

"A black dog." Dean shot his brother another look. "You don't say."

"You can go back to the rental office," Sam said. "If we need you for anything else, we'll find you there."

The kid reached into his shirt pocket, removed a business card, and handed it to Sam, who was gratified to see the last name on it was Stephens. Close enough.

"Tell you what, you need me, call me. Nothing personal, but I don't want to catch anything from you guys. I don't want to end up a human-sized prune, you know?"

Without waiting for a reply, Stephens turned and started back toward the rental office, almost but not quite running.

Sam stuck the card in his inner jacket pocket, and together he and Dean started down the hill toward the pond.

"Can you say paranoid?" Dean said.

"You can't blame him. Something bad *did* happen here."

"You think that bad had anything to do with the black dog Braveheart mentioned?"

Sam shrugged. "I don't know. Could be."

Sightings of spectral black dogs went back centuries—it was the legend Arthur Conan Doyle based *The Hound of the Baskervilles* on—but there was no definite answer to what the creatures were. Most hunters tended to believe one of two possibilities: either they were creatures of demonic origin or they were forms taken by shapeshifters. Sam didn't see any reason why both explanations couldn't be true. After all, the ecosystem of the supernatural world was just as varied in its own way as that of the natural one.

"Could be something living in the pond," Sam continued.

"Maybe," Dean allowed. "But if there is, the ducks don't seem to be bothered by it."

As they drew near the pond, they saw two smaller taped-off areas, one close to the water, one a bit farther uphill, both arranged in roughly rectangular patterns.

"Looks like the local PD believes in being thorough," Dean said. "I'm surprised they didn't put up a great big I'd Turn Back if I Were You! sign."

"A musical reference?" Sam asked. "I would've expected something from *The Texas Chain Saw Massacre* or maybe *Porky's II.*"

"Just trying to broaden the repertoire."

The brothers swept their gazes back and forth as they bantered, senses alive and alert. A big part of being a hunter was paying attention to your environment. Sights, sounds, and smells could all provide clues to the presence of a supernatural manifestation, but the most important sense of all was one that didn't have a name. It wasn't psychic, exactly. More like heightened instinct. Hunt long enough, *survive* long enough, and you developed the ability to know when something wasn't right. It was a subconscious process, not a cognitive one, but both Sam and Dean had learned long ago to trust it, and right now that sense was telling Sam that whatever had happened here to cause the deaths of two people, it hadn't been natural.

They reached the tape rectangle on the hillside first. Sam removed his EMF detector from his outer jacket pocket, turned it on, and held it close to the ground. The electromagnetic readings in the area were normal, and he switched the machine off and placed it back in his pocket.

"So we know that whatever did this wasn't a ghost," Dean said.

"It's been two days since the deaths," Sam pointed out. "Any electromagnetic energy left behind might've faded in that time."

"I suppose."

Both brothers squatted to get a closer look at the ground. They didn't break the tape, though. They preferred not to disturb crime scenes any more than necessary, just in case it turned out that an ordinary human scumbag was responsible instead of a thing that went bump in the night.

"According to the *Broadsider*, this is where the woman's body was found." Sam pulled a small notebook out of his shirt pocket and opened it to the most recent entry. "Her name was Joyce Nagrosky, and she was a retired high school English teacher. The other victim was Ted Boykin. He was retired, too. Used to be the principal at the school where Joyce taught."

"Think they came down here for a little extracurricular workout?" Dean asked. "Just 'cause they were enjoying their golden years doesn't mean they couldn't enjoy each other, too. I mean, the guy's last name *was* Boykin. *Boink-ing*. Get it?"

Sam just looked at him.

"I thought it was funny," Dean muttered.

Despite his brother's lousy joke, Sam knew there was a serious question behind it. Supernatural creatures preyed on humans for a variety of reasons, but the most common one was to feed. Some, like the Leviathan, fed on humans literally. Vampires drank human blood. Some ate only certain parts of the body, like kitsune, which fed on the pituitary gland.

Amy's face flashed through his mind, and for a moment he thought he heard her voice whispering in his ear. *All the coolest people are freaks…* He shoved the memory of her aside, along with the pang of guilt that came with it. He had work to do.

Some monsters drained life energy. Some, such as succubi and incubi, fed on sexual energy. If Joyce and Ted had been doing the wild thing by the pond, they might have attracted the attention of something even wilder.

"I don't think so," Sam said after a moment's consideration. "They may have been a couple—the paper didn't say anything about that—but this area's a little too close to the apartment complex for them to have any privacy."

"Maybe they were into the whole thrill-seeking thing," Dean countered, but without much conviction. "I don't smell anything weird. No scent of sulfur, rotting fish, or decayed flowers." He sniffed. "No demon dog stink, either."

"The area's not cold," Sam said. "Well, not any colder than normal for this time of year."

"The ground's pretty well torn up," Dean said. "The locals could've done it. Like you said earlier, they're probably not used to handling a real crime scene."

"Could be," Sam allowed. "But a dog could've done it, too."

"Size of these marks, it would've been a big one."

"Yep. No blood, though. An animal that big, if it attacked someone, it would've made a mess."

Dean pressed his index finger to the ground and pushed the tip into the dirt. "Hasn't rained recently. So if there had been any blood, it wouldn't have been washed away."

The brothers stood, and Dean wiped his fingertip off on his pants leg.

"Let's go check out where they found the principal," Sam said.

The brothers walked down to the edge of the pond and examined the second cordoned-off area. There was less grass there, and the ground was softer. There were obvious prints, mostly from the police and paramedics, probably, but there were also a number of what appeared to be claw marks in the ground, along with a single clear paw print. A damn big one.

The brothers stood thinking for a moment, the ducks on the pond keeping their distance and eyeing them warily.

After a bit, Dean said, "Here's how I think it played out. Ted and Joyce walk down to the pond. Maybe they're taking a stroll, feeding the ducks, thinking about getting busy later, whatever. Then our killer dog approaches from over there." He pointed to the woods. "It attacks them and Ted, being the stand-up guy he is, tries to slow it down long enough so Joyce can get away. She runs, but Cujo makes quick work of old Ted, chases after her, and that's all she wrote."

Sam nodded. "That's how I see it, too. But how exactly did it kill them? The paper didn't say anything about their bodies being ravaged by an animal."

"Yeah, I know. They were mummified. Hey, you don't suppose they were just really, *really* old?"

"I think we need to take a look at those bodies."

As Sam and Dean headed back up the hill, neither of them noticed a shadowy figure step out from between the trees at the edge of the pond and watch them depart.

THREE

A couple hours later, Sam and Dean returned to the pond. They'd ditched their monkey suits for their normal street clothes, something for which Dean was profoundly grateful. He wore his leather jacket, Sam wore his blue coat, and both of them had hoodies and flannel shirts underneath. Even when it was cold outside, the brothers rarely wore anything heavier. Thick clothes could slow you down, and a slow hunter was all too often a dead hunter. Layers were the way to go. You could strip them off as needed, and ditching your outer jacket was a good way to quickly change your appearance in case someone—like the cops—was looking for you.

Dean never felt comfortable in a suit, with the possible exception of his 1940s threads, although he had to admit they had their uses. Not only did they make it easier to get cops to talk to you, they worked magic on hospital employees. They had no problem getting the morgue attendant to grant them access to the bodies of Joyce Nagrosky and Ted Boykin. Better yet, since the county's medical examiner suspected some sort of contagion was at work in their deaths, he hadn't conducted full autopsies. He was waiting for the CDC to report on the tissue samples he'd sent, which meant that Sam and Dean had a pair of pristine bodies to check out. Sometimes the key detail in a supernatural death was subtle, and a doctor might destroy an important piece of evidence without meaning to. But they hadn't had to worry about that this time.

Both bodies had been the same. They reminded Dean of the empty husks that cicadas left behind when they changed into their adult forms. *Damn creepy things, those bugs!* According to the ME's preliminary findings, the bodies still possessed all their internal organs, but it was as if every drop of moisture had been drained out of them. Not just blood, either. All fluid was gone—water, spinal fluid, gastric juices, you name it—leaving Joyce and Ted looking like skeletons covered in thin gray parchment paper. *Corpse-a-gami*, Dean thought. The bodies shared one other salient feature: vicious gashes on the throat. The ME postulated that the injuries had been delivered post mortem by some sort of scavenger. But the way he and Sam figured it, the wounds had been caused by the monster dog, which Dean had consequently taken to calling Dogula.

Their examination of Joyce and Ted's bodies hadn't provided any clues as to the nature of the creature that had killed them, and a follow-up Internet search hadn't yielded anything of use, so the brothers had brought a variety of weapons with them. Pistols loaded with silver bullets, a Winchester 1887 shotgun filled with rock salt—which Dean carried—a knife of cold iron dipped in holy water, and a demon-killing blade. Like the Boy Scouts, hunters believed in being prepared. Or, as Bobby used to put it, *Better to haul some extra hardware than to end up as little chunks of undigested meat in a pile of monster scat.*

"This isn't right, Sam. I know something's not kosher in this town, and I know I agreed to look into it, but I can't help feeling that we're dishonoring Bobby's memory by putting off going after Roman. And don't tell me that we have a responsibility to help the good people of Brennan. The world is filled with monsters, and no matter what we do, we'll never get them all. There are just too damn many of them, and there are only two of us. We have to take care of family business first, and that's what Dick Roman is—not to mention that he and his army of pet piranhas are a threat to the whole freakin' world!"

They'd continued walking the entire time Dean spoke, and had reached the edge of the woods. They stopped and Sam turned to face his brother.

"You think Bobby would want us to walk away from this case?" he asked. Then added, "Or any case, for that matter?"

"No," Dean said, "but that doesn't mean—"

"Before you go any further, hear me out. After our run-in with Chronos, I started thinking."

"Started?" Dean snorted. "Do you ever stop?"

Sam ignored him and went on. "The magic Chronos used to travel through time was pretty powerful stuff. Makes sense, because he was a god, right?"

"Yeah. So?"

"So even though the bodies we saw today didn't look exactly like Chronos' victims, there were some striking similarities."

Dean frowned. "You think we might be dealing with another god here?"

"Too early to tell. But like I said, our run-in with Chronos got me thinking. If we're going to have any hope of ganking Dick Roman and stopping the Leviathan, we're going to need some serious firepower. A case like this, where big-time mojo is involved…"

"Wait a minute. Are you saying that you want to capture the monster, spirit, god, or whatever it is and use it as a weapon against the Leviathan?"

Sam shrugged. "Whatever the Leviathan are exactly, we know they were the first beings God created. That means they're alive, right? If that's the case—"

"Then they could be killed by draining their life force."

Sam nodded. "Possibly. So if we can learn how Joyce and Ted were killed, along with the two others who died before them, maybe we'll be able to find some way to use it against the Leviathan."

"I'm not sure that's a good idea, Sammy. Fighting fire with fire hasn't always worked out so well for us. Two words: demon blood."

Sam lowered his gaze to the ground, but otherwise didn't reply.

Despite his misgivings, Dean could feel his excitement building. He surely wouldn't mind having the supernatural equivalent of a backpack nuke to shove down Dick Roman's slimy throat. There was also a certain symmetry to the idea that he liked, and which he thought Bobby would appreciate. The Leviathan—creatures that lived solely to feed—would be destroyed by a power that devoured their life energy.

"So you're saying this case isn't so much about ganking some random monster as it is about, what? Research and development?"

"Something like that. And if we get to kill a monster in the bargain, so much the better."

Dean thought about it for a moment. "Okay, I'm in. Let's go find Dogula."

The brothers entered the woods. Oak, elm, and ash trees predominated, and the ground held only a scattering of leaves. Good. They'd make less noise that way. The last thing they needed to be doing was crunching leaves underfoot and giving away their position when there might be a life force-sucking monster running around. Dean found himself wishing that it had rained recently. The ground was too hard for there to be any tracks, and while the underbrush showed signs of something having passed through recently, Ohio had a deer overpopulation problem, and there was no way to tell if it was Dogula or a herd of Bambis. Joyce and Ted had died two days before, and there was a chance that the monster responsible had moved on, but Dean doubted it. The things he and Sam hunted tended to stick to one location, more often than not, whether because their particular species was territorial or because they were mystically bound to a specific area.

Dean spoke in a soft, low voice. "So how did you miss the reports of a black dog running around town? You losing your research-fu?"

"I guess no one made the connection between the black dog and the deaths. No reason why they should."

"Yeah. Sometimes I forget Joe and Jane Normal don't know all this stuff exists."

That was one of the reasons Dean enjoyed horror movies so much. Sure, they were hilarious because of how screwed up their lore was, not to mention how many insanely dumb decisions the characters made. But also, when he watched them, he could imagine what it was like to be an ordinary person, enjoying horror flicks for nothing more than a fun scare, knowing all the time he was safe because ghoulies, ghosties, and long-leggedy beasties were only make believe.

The sound of a branch snapping broke the silence like a gunshot, and the brothers froze. Dean's senses, honed from hundreds of battles, screamed at him that they were about to be under attack, and he knew better than to question them. He shoved Sam to the side and dove in the opposite direction an instant before a large black form hurtled through the space where they had been standing. The brothers hit the ground, rolled, and came up on their feet in time to see the creature spin around to face them, jagged teeth bared in a snarl. Even by monster standards, the thing was one ugly son of a bitch. Its body was twisted, its features distorted, and none of its legs matched in length. It had patches of bare skin, as if it suffered from mange, but now that Dean got a good look at it, he saw that its fur wasn't black—at least, not entirely. It *was* black in places, but it was also brown and gray, and its different-colored fur had different consistencies, longer and thicker here, shorter and thinner there. The creature's sections were separated by thin lines of red scar tissue, as if it weren't a single beast but rather a conglomeration of different canines.

"That's thing's not Dogula," Dean said, "it's Frankenmutt!"

He dropped the shotgun to the ground. Rock salt wouldn't be worth a damn against something corporeal. He drew his trusty Colt .45, aimed at the spot between Frankenmutt's eyes, and squeezed off a round. Sam had drawn his Beretta at the same time and he fired as well, aiming for the same target.

Frankenmutt was roughly the size of a St. Bernard, and ungainly as the creature looked, Dean expected it would move with all the speed and grace of an iron anvil. He was confident their bullets would hit the beast. But instead of Frankenmutt's brains exploding out the back of its head to decorate the tree behind it, the monstrous canine became a dark blur and a split second later it crouched three feet to the right of its previous position. Bullets ripped chunks of bark from the tree, but Frankenmutt was unharmed. A good result if he and Sam were looking to start new careers as unorthodox lumberjacks, but not so good if they wanted to actually kill the goddamned monster.

Frankenmutt lowered its head and glared at them with mismatched, rheumy eyes. It growled deep in its throat, a strange sound, with separate pitches overlapping, almost as if two dogs were growling instead of one. Dean kept his gaze focused on its eyes. You could always tell when a human opponent was going to make a move by watching their eyes, and this was also true for most supernatural creatures. Those that had eyes, anyway. Unfortunately, Frankenmutt's were different sizes and colors, and they worked independently of each other, like a lizard's. Not only was it freaky as hell, it made it impossible to guess the creature's intentions.

Dean was caught off guard when Frankenmutt started running toward them, moving with a weird lurching stride that was surprisingly fast. He managed to get off another round from his .45, but the bullet went wild and struck the ground near the dog's right paw. The near miss only pissed it off, and it swerved toward Dean, leaping for him, jaws wide and flecked with foam, discolored tongue lolling from the side of its mouth. Dean dropped his .45 and raised his hands in time to grab hold of the dog's throat as it slammed into him. He maintained his grip as the creature's weight bore him to the ground. The underbrush softened his landing somewhat, but the jolt still knocked the wind out of him. Frankenmutt snarled with savage rage, jaws snapping as it tried to sink its teeth into Dean's throat. He managed to hold the creature at bay, but it wasn't easy. The damned thing was a hell of a lot stronger than it looked. Its teeth were only inches from the soft flesh of his neck, and they were edging closer with each second. If the beast bit him, it would start draining his life force, and once the process began, Dean didn't know how long it would take. Maybe minutes, maybe only seconds. Dean wondered what he'd look like if he got prune-ified, and the resultant mental image wasn't pretty.

Sam stepped forward, assumed a shooting stance, leveled his Beretta, and fired three bullets into Frankenmutt's side in quick succession. Dean felt the creature jerk with the impact of each round, and blood issued from the wounds. Not red, though. This stuff was black, thick, and slow-moving, more like syrup. The black goo made him think of the gunk that poured out of Leviathan when they were wounded, but this ichor was darker and it stank like rotten meat. Despite its injuries, Frankenmutt didn't appear to be in any pain. If anything, it seemed more enraged. It tore free of Dean's grip, jumped off him, and lurched toward Sam, growling and snapping.

Sam held his ground and fired twice more as the monstrous canine bore down on him. The bullets took out hunks of flesh and made more ichor flow, but the creature barely slowed as it lunged toward him. It fastened its teeth on Sam's right leg just above the ankle, and Sam let out a cry of pain and fired point blank at Frankenmutt's head. Part of the dog's skull was sheared away, taking an ear with it. The beast let go of Sam, staggered backward, and then shook its head back and forth rapidly, as if its head was wet and it was trying to dry itself. Blood and bits of brain matter flew through the air, and then the creature turned and ran off into the woods, swerving as it went, almost as if it were drunk.

Sam sat on the ground and took in a hissing breath. He placed his Beretta next to him, and gingerly began to inspect his wound. Dean got up, retrieved his .45, and walked over to Sam, scanning the area for any sign that Frankenmutt was planning to double back and renew its attack.

"How bad is it?"

"I'll live." Sam's sock was wet with blood, and when he peeled it away from the skin, a ragged wound was revealed. "It's not too deep. I think most of the damage was caused when I shot him in the head. The impact caused him to jerk away from my ankle, and his teeth tore the skin."

"All right. Let's tape you up and get you back to the car." Dean knelt next to his brother, reached into one of his jacket's outer pockets, and pulled out a roll of silvery duct tape. Their first aid kit was in the crapmobile, but duct tape would make an effective field dressing until they reached the car.

"I'm fine," Sam insisted. "We have to go after the dog."

He tried to stand, but when he put his weight on his wounded ankle, it buckled, and he sat back down, grimacing with pain.

"Frankenmutt can wait until after we've plugged your leak," Dean said. "Now shut up and sit still." He ripped off a length of tape and went to work.

Dean's field dressing was good enough to allow Sam to make it back to the motel. Once there, he went into the bathroom, carefully cut the tape away with a pair of surgical scissors, and threw the blood-smeared mess into the trash. He then cleaned the wound—first with holy water, then with soap and regular water, and finally with alcohol. Afterward, he lathered on some antibiotic cream, then bandaged and wrapped it. Satisfied, he dry swallowed a couple ibuprofen before limping out of the bathroom. The injury was going to slow him down, but not as much as he'd feared.

Dean had tossed his jacket on his bed, and he sat at the table in his hoodie, leaning back in the chair, feet up, staring at the laptop screen.

Sam smiled. "I hope you're not checking out one of those

sites where you have to click 'I verify that I'm eighteen years or older' for access."

He regretted it as soon as he said it. Considering how obsessed Dean had been with Dick Roman in the past few weeks, Sam would have far preferred his brother to visit a few sleazy websites than try to dig up still more information on their least favorite Leviathan.

"I've been surfing the web looking for the skinny on butt-ugly patchwork dogs." When Sam didn't reply right away, Dean added, "What? Like you're the only one who knows his way around a mouse pad?"

"Skinny?" Sam said.

"Yeah, well... guess I picked up some new vocabulary in 1944." He took his feet off the table, sat up, and faced Sam. "Speaking of picking things up, we should probably get you to a doctor before you come down with Franken-rabies."

"You're joking, right? Supernatural creatures don't carry natural diseases."

"Still, better safe than hydrophobic, right? All it'll take is a series of incredibly painful abdominal injections." Dean grinned.

"That's not how they treat rabies. You get a shot of vaccine in the shoulder, then gamma globulin in the wound and in the hips or the butt. They're no more painful than normal shots. But it doesn't matter because I don't need them."

Dean sighed. "What's the point of being the older brother if you can't torture the younger one every once in a while? Besides, who says Frankenmutt is supernatural? You saw those scar lines, right? He looked like something a mad scientist slapped together from spare parts."

"*Frankenstein* was just a novel by Mary Shelley," Sam said. "You ever read it?"

"I've seen all the movies," Dean said.

Sam ignored him and went on. "Shelley wrote her novel in the early 1800s, long before the modern era of science. The procedure she wrote about is pure fiction. It could never work in the real world. You can't make a single body out of a bunch of separate parts. Forget about trying to hook up the central nervous system, the problems with tissue rejection alone..." Sam trailed off when he realized Dean was staring at him. "What?"

"I thought you went to law school, not medical school."

"My point is that whatever Frankenmutt is, it's not a product of science."

"All right, I'll take your word for it, Dr. Dorkwad."

Sam had been standing as they talked, and his ankle was starting to throb. He also felt suddenly tired. Maybe he'd lost more blood than he thought. He hobbled over to one of the beds and sat down. Dean watched him closely as he walked, and although he frowned, he said nothing about Sam's injury, and Sam was grateful.

"Did you find anything on the Net?" he asked.

"Other than stuff about the movie *Frankenweenie*, no." He closed the laptop and sat back in the chair. "Man, I can't get over how fast that thing was. The way it looked, it should've had trouble just walking, but it moved faster than a cheetah on meth."

"Not at the end," Sam pointed out. "After I shot it in the

head, it took off, but it didn't move much faster than an ordinary dog. And it moved in a zigzaggy kind of way, like it was having trouble staying on its feet."

"That's because you wounded it. If you were missing half your head, you wouldn't be moving very fast either."

"It shouldn't have been moving at all, but the injury only slowed it down, and I think I know why."

"Let me guess. It was full of life energy after killing Joyce and Ted, which is why it could move so damn fast, but its needle dropped to E after you shot it, and it had just enough left in the tank to make a getaway."

"That's my take on it," Sam said. A wave of weariness came over him, and he stifled a yawn. What was wrong with him? It wasn't even five o'clock yet, and he felt ready to hit the sack.

"It'll do till a better theory comes along. So whatever this thing is, it's still just your basic supernatural freak show, only with more emphasis on the freak this time. How do you figure all those dog parts came together, though? Maybe we should check the town for a pet cemetery. Or it could be some kind of group ghost, a whole pack of doggie spirits, and I should've blasted it with rock salt after all."

Sam fought another yawn. "It still could be a Frankenmutt, only one created by magic instead of science. I'll see what I can dig up about spells that are supposed to… fuse body parts… together." This time he couldn't fight the yawn, and he fell back onto the bed without bothering to get under the covers. "After I take a nap."

"Hey, Sam, are you o—"

That's the last he heard before a warm, wonderful darkness gathered him up and swept him away.

In the parking lot outside the Winchesters' room, a figure stood. There was no one around, but even if there had been, they wouldn't have seen him. Not unless he wished it. A gentle breeze was blowing, but even though it caressed his skin, he didn't feel it.

Even from here, he could sense the injury that had been done to Sam Winchester, both the physical component and the spiritual. Of the two, the latter was far more serious.

This isn't good, he thought. *Not good at all.* But all he could do was stand here and continue to watch.

For the moment, at least.

Catherine Luss tossed the *Broadsider* onto the kitchen counter. It was yesterday's edition, but she'd been so busy working that she'd had no chance to look at it before. The headline screamed off the front page in large black letters:

TWO MORE FOUND DEAD IN MYSTERIOUS CIRCUMSTANCES!

She'd only gotten partway through the lead story before she hadn't been able to read any further. She hadn't known either Ted Boykin or Joyce Nagrosky. Both had retired before Bekah started high school, and neither had been among her patients. She also hadn't known the two previous victims—a gas station attendant named Randy Neff and a teenage girl named Angela Bales. She thought Bekah might've known Angela, or at least been aware of her, as they'd been close in age, but she didn't know, and it wasn't as if she could ask her daughter. Not anymore.

She'd poured herself a cup of coffee with half-and-half and artificial sweetener before sitting down at the counter for what she'd hoped would be a relaxing—and badly needed—break from work. The time readout on the microwave said it was 5:12, but until she'd looked out the window, she hadn't known whether that was a.m. or p.m. She wondered how long she'd been down in the lab this time, and was surprised to discover she didn't know. Twenty-four hours? Forty-eight? Did it even matter?

What did matter was that headline, or rather the four lost lives behind it. The story was short on facts and long on hysteria-fueled supposition, speculating that the deaths were caused by anything from a previously unknown super bug to toxic waste or radiation—despite the fact that Brennan had no industry that could have produced either of the latter. She was surprised the reporter hadn't blamed the deaths on UFOs while he'd been at it. But she knew exactly who was ultimately responsible for those poor people's deaths.

She was.

The temperature in the kitchen seemed to drop several degrees. Catherine was wearing a white lab coat over a gray pullover sweater with a thick collar, but she still shivered. She felt the cold as much inside as out.

"It's not your fault."

The voice was soft, little more than a whisper, really, with a slight accent that she thought might be German, although she wasn't sure. A subtle odor drifted to her on the air, a musty smell like a just-opened cedar chest that had been closed for a very long time. She took a sip of her coffee and half turned on the stool to face Conrad.

Even though she'd been working with him for the past few months, she still had to struggle to keep an expression of distaste from showing every time she looked at him. It wasn't that he was hideous. He was rather pleasant-looking, actually, if on the plain side. A thin man in his early sixties, he stood no more than five-foot-five and had a large nose contrasted by small, almost feminine lips and a narrow chin. His hairline had receded well past his forehead, but the hair that remained to him was brown and thick, without a hint of gray. His most striking feature, however, was his large penetrating eyes. They rested beneath thick black eyebrows, and their color was indeterminate, seeming to change depending on the light. Sometimes they were dark blue, sometimes charcoal gray, and other times almost black. As always, he wore a suit, this one brown with an ivory shirt and gold tie—stylish and retro at the same time. It wasn't his appearance that Catherine found distasteful, nor was it the way he tended to remain statue-still until he decided to move. What bothered her was something more indefinable, his… presence, she supposed you could call it. He exuded an aura that she found repellent in the same way that magnets of opposite charge pushed against each other. Whenever he approached, she felt an urge to back away, to keep as much distance between them as possible. He did nothing overt to intimidate her, but she had to fight to hold her ground whenever they were in the same room together—which these days they often were.

She ran her hand through her short blonde hair, suddenly aware of how greasy it was. She was in dire need of a shower. She hated to think what she smelled like, and she probably had the world's worst case of dragon breath from all the coffee she'd been drinking. Working alongside Conrad down in the lab, she never thought about such things. If she did stink, he never gave any sign that he noticed, let alone was bothered by, her body odor. But up here, in what she thought of as the Real World, she was painfully aware of her lack of hygiene.

"Tell that to the families of the four people who died," she responded. "I took an oath, Conrad."

"*Primum non nocere*: First, do no harm," Conrad said. "I am familiar with the Hippocratic Oath." He gave her a slight, almost amused smile, but otherwise stood completely still, his hands at his sides. From the neck down, he might as well have been a mannequin.

"It's my fault it escaped," she said.

"*Our* fault," he corrected. "We both thought the cage you had me purchase would be of sufficient strength to contain the beast. I am only grateful that you were at your practice when it made its bid for freedom. Otherwise, it surely would have attempted to feed on you."

What a mess the damned thing had made in its escape, too. The damage to the lab hadn't been so bad, since the creature headed straight for the stairs after tearing free from its cage, but it knocked down the basement door and raced around the house as it searched for a way out—shredding her furniture with tooth and claw in frustrated rage—before finally crashing through the back door. Luckily, it had happened in the early evening and had been dark enough by then that none of her neighbors had seen the beast as it fled. It also helped that she lived on several acres of land outside town. If she'd lived in a suburb, somebody surely would have spotted the monstrous dog running from her house and called the police. In that case, she'd probably be in jail right now, her medical license suspended. If she'd lived in an earlier age, she'd likely have been burned at the stake. She still could be, she supposed. The people of Brennan weren't exactly the most educated or progressive in the state.

Even though she found being in Conrad's presence difficult, Catherine was thankful for his assistance. He'd taken care of everything, buying and installing two new doors, as well as removing the worst of the damaged furniture and hauling it away. He'd even offered to replace her lost furniture, but she'd declined. She spent most of her time down in the lab, and it wasn't as if anyone else lived in the house. Not anymore.

She held her mug in both hands and looked down at the coffee within. "Maybe it would've been better if I had been here," she said softly.

Conrad stepped forward. For a moment she feared he meant to reach out and touch her, perhaps give her upper arm a reassuring squeeze or lay a comforting hand on her shoulder. She tensed, hoping that if he did she would be able to keep from screaming. As if sensing her discomfort, Conrad took a step back and kept his hands at his sides.

"You shouldn't speak like that," he admonished mildly. "The beast's escape and the lives subsequently lost are regrettable, yes, but I must remind you of the larger concern here. If you achieve your goal, not only shall you reap personal reward, you will change the world forever. Untold billions of lives will be saved, and the human lifespan itself will be extended. It is impossible to say just how long people will live in the new world your work will bring about, but virtual immortality is not out of the question. Isn't the attainment of such a goal—"

"Worth four people's lives?" she interrupted. She looked up at him, jaw tight with anger.

Conrad's eyes narrowed, but his voice remained even as he replied. "Something for which those people would willingly sacrifice themselves."

"Considering we can't ask them, we're never going to know for sure, are we?"

They were both silent for a time after that. Catherine sipped her coffee and tried to ignore how Conrad just stood there, quiet and statue-still.

After a while, he said, "You will not abandon your work." It was part question, part command.

She finished the last of her coffee and sighed. "No, I won't."

Conrad gave her a slow smile.

That's the way a lizard would smile, she thought.

"Good. Now, is there any service I may perform for you?"

Sometimes she found his formal manner charming. Other times, like now, she found it cold and distant.

"We could use some…" She looked down, unable to meet

his gaze. "Fresh supplies."

His lizard smile returned. "It will be my pleasure."

FOUR

After Conrad left, Catherine was able to relax a little. While she was grateful for both the tutelage and assistance he'd provided over the past few months, she was always on edge when he was around. There was something indefinably wrong about him that set off alarm bells in the back of her mind. Beyond his appearance and manner—and aside from what she suspected he did in order to procure more "supplies" for her work—he drew in the energy of his surroundings, as if he were some kind of living black hole. Light, heat, even her own vitality seemed to drain into him, and she felt weary after spending any length of time in his presence. His departure always came as a relief. She was never able to fully relax when Conrad was in the house, and now that he was gone, she knew she should try to lie down and get some sleep. She couldn't remember the last time she'd gotten any decent rest, let alone a full eight hours.

As a doctor, she well understood the effects of sleep deprivation, both physical and mental. Logically, she knew that she couldn't do her best work if she didn't take care of herself. *You have to take care of the machine,* as she always told her patients. Used to tell. The way she'd neglected her practice the last few months, it was all but dead. But that was a small price to pay to achieve her ultimate goal. She would give anything, *do* anything, to make it happen.

Conrad's question—which she'd both interrupted and completed—came back to her.

Isn't the attainment of such a goal worth four people's lives?

She didn't want to think like that. She was supposed to be a healer, for Christ's sake! But despite her protestations to Conrad, she couldn't deny that deep down she *did* think that way. She wasn't proud of the fact, but there it was. However, even though she knew how important it was to get her rest, emotionally she found it almost impossible to tear herself away from her work. About the only time she slowed down was to make a fresh pot of coffee, and she justified that to herself only because she needed the caffeine to keep her alert. She couldn't afford to slow down. She had to keep pushing herself. They were depending on her.

She was no psychologist, but she had done a psych rotation in med school, and she knew that while it was vital to keep pushing herself if she hoped to succeed, there was another, deeper reason she refused to slow down. If she kept her mind busy, she didn't have time to think about anything but work. It was when she allowed herself to rest that she remembered—or worse, dreamed.

She finished her coffee, got up from the table, and poured herself a refill. She headed back to the table, but instead of taking her seat again, she set the mug down, then walked past the kitchen, down a short hallway off to the left, and entered the family room. The lights were off, as they always were these days. She never went in there anymore, so there was no point in wasting electricity. She reached for the wall switch, but couldn't find it. She couldn't have forgotten where it was... could she? This was her *home*. She should be able to remember something as basic as the location of a light switch. She fumbled in the dark for several moments before her fingers finally encountered it and she flipped it with a sharp gesture of irritation, although inside she felt more than a little relief.

The illumination from the track lighting over the couch dazzled her eyes for a second, and she raised a hand to shield them. When her vision adjusted, she lowered her hand and saw that the room looked the same as always, with the exception of a light coating of dust on the cherrywood coffee table and the black leather couch. It almost looked like the room was covered with a thin layer of snow. No, she decided, it was more like she was looking at a faded photograph. A large flatscreen TV hung on the wall above the fireplace. The latter was empty and cold, but there used to be flames in there almost every night, even in summer. On the mantel above the fireplace beneath the television were a number of framed pictures. As Catherine stood there, she experienced the strange feeling that she was somehow trespassing in her own home.

She crossed the crème-colored carpet and stopped in front of the mantel. The first photo she picked up was one of her and Marshall on their wedding day. Both of them were laughing at something the photographer had said—she couldn't remember what. It was her favorite picture of the two of them. The joy they exuded in that frozen moment perfectly captured the essence of their relationship. Love was only part of it, although of course, the largest part. They had genuinely enjoyed each other's company, too. Some couples said they were also best friends, but in their case, it had been true. Marshall looked so handsome in the photo, and so young. They'd been in their early twenties when they married, but even so, the man he would become was visible. Thinner, a bit more hair, but the playful intelligence was present in his brown eyes, and it would only sharpen as the years progressed. And his smile… God, how she missed it.

She placed the picture back on the mantel and picked up another, this one of a pretty teenage girl with long brown hair, dressed in a tie-dyed T-shirt and shorts, sitting on the ground surrounding by flowers. Catherine had taken this picture of Bekah herself in the spring, out in the garden. She and Bekah had spent so many wonderful hours planning, planting, and tending the garden. It had been so long since she'd gone out back, she didn't want to think about the kind of condition it was in. She supposed it was nothing but a tangle of high grass and weeds.

She remembered exactly when she'd taken this picture of Bekah. Eight days before her fifteenth birthday. Nine days before she'd gotten her learner's permit. Twenty-three days before her father took her out for her first night-time driving lesson. That had been four months ago. It was the last time

Catherine had seen either of them alive.

She didn't recall much about the night itself after seeing them off. She assumed the police called her at one point, and she must have called someone after that, because she had a vague memory of sobbing in someone's arms. She thought it might have been Ronetta, her office manager, but she wasn't certain.

The details of what had happened to her husband and daughter, though, those she remembered, or at least could imagine, perfectly.

At approximately 8:40, Marshall and Bekah—in Marshall's BMW, Bekah behind the wheel, excited and nervous— approached a railroad crossing outside of town. They got there just as the warning lights came on and the wooden crossing gate lowered. Bekah braked and together she and her father waited while the train passed. Over the months since, Catherine had wondered what, if anything, they'd talked about. She was certain no music had been playing. As much as Bekah would have loved to cruise to some tunes, her dad would never have permitted such a distraction while she was in the early stages of her driver's education. She thought they might've rolled down the windows so they could better listen to the sound of the train's passage and feel the wind it kicked up. She imagined them looking at each other, grinning and sharing a special moment, just the two of them, father and daughter.

The train passed, the crossing gate lifted, and Bekah took her foot off the brake, gently pressed the gas, and eased over the tracks, looking both ways as the BMW juddered across. Once safely on the other side, Bekah accelerated. An instant later a pickup with its lights off came flying out of the darkness, weaving back and forth, its driver one Earl Fulmer, a local plumber who'd just left a poker game at a buddy's house, running with more alcohol than blood in his veins. Earl hit Bekah and Marshall head-on at what the police estimated was in excess of seventy miles per hour. There were no survivors.

As a doctor, Catherine knew her husband and daughter had died quickly, and despite the horrific injuries they'd sustained, they hadn't suffered. At least, not for long. But even though she knew this intellectually, emotionally she imagined their experience of the accident as very different. She knew that human perceptions became heightened during times of extreme stress, giving rise to the common belief that a person's life flashes before their eyes at such times. She imagined the accident seeming to occur in torturous slow motion while Marshall and Bekah's consciousnesses operated at normal speed. If that were true, every wound they suffered would have seemed to take an eternity to inflict. The agony would have been inconceivable. She knew it was a foolish scenario to imagine, one that had no firm basis in scientific facts, but in her heart she believed it to be true, so she grieved not only for the loss of her loved ones, but for the unimaginable suffering they had endured before finally dying.

She looked at Bekah's photo one last time, brushing the tip of her index finger across her daughter's hair, feeling only cold glass. She replaced the picture on the mantel and walked out of the room, flipping off the light switch as she went. She passed through the kitchen, ignoring the coffee, opened the basement door, and headed down the stairs.

In the first days after the accident, Catherine had wished she'd ridden along with Marshall and Bekah that night. Wished she'd died with them. But that was before the morning Conrad Dippel visited her office, not as a patient, but as what he called a "potential colleague." He said he'd read about her "lamentable loss" in the *Broadsider*, and had what he believed might be a solution to her "profound emotional distress." She'd almost tossed him out on his ass right there and then, but there was something in the tone of his voice, an unwavering confidence that made her want to listen to what he had to say, regardless of how crazy it might sound. Conrad had more than words with which to convince her, too. He'd brought a briefcase filled with the results of hundreds of experiments. The data had been intriguing, but nowhere near as intriguing as the demonstration he gave her in the temporary lab he'd established in the abandoned bicycle factory.

She'd watched him kill a rat by cutting its throat, stitch it up, and then—after administrating a combination of chemicals to the small corpse, in conjunction with some chanted words and hand gestures that she was certain were just for show—bring the animal back to life.

At that point, Conrad Dippel moved from "potential colleague" to a fully-fledged one.

Catherine had left the fluorescent lights on when she'd exited the basement, and had no trouble making her way across the lab. Much of the equipment was Conrad's, transferred from the bicycle factory, but she'd added to it over the previous few months. A stainless steel operating table stood in the center of the basement, an array of surgical equipment laid out atop a table close by. Another table contained vials, jars, and beakers filled with various chemicals, along with other necessary equipment: pipettes, scales, microscopes, slides, and more. Stored on the floor beneath the table were several plastic containers labeled NuFlesh Biotech. Catherine ignored everything and crossed to the large horizontal freezer on the far side of the room. The machine's powerful hum filled the basement, and she could feel its vibrations through the soles of her feet as she approached. She reached toward its metal surface, the cold kissing her skin before her fingers came in contact with the metal.

"I won't rest until we're together again," she said in a soft, loving voice. "I promise."

She lingered there a moment longer before turning away and once more resuming her work.

"Hey, Joe. What's the word?"

Joe Riley sat on the curb outside the Fill 'Er Up convenience store. He'd just finished eating an energy bar, and now was nursing a cup of brown water that the store manager had the gall to call coffee. But it was warm, and that was all he cared about. He looked up as Billy Sutphin approached and gave him a weak smile.

"Sucks is the word. How 'bout you?"

"Same."

Billy settled onto the curb next to Joe with a grunt, knee joints popping.

"Gettin' old," Billy said.

"Aren't we all?"

Joe didn't think Billy was all that old. In his mid-fifties, maybe. It was hard to tell people's ages when they lived on the street. Such a life took its toll, and it was possible Billy could be in his thirties and only looked twenty years older. It didn't help that his thick brown beard was shot through with gray. Joe had only been homeless for four months, and even in that short time, he'd changed to the point where he didn't like looking in a mirror. His face was leaner, complexion sallower, eyes bloodshot, the flesh beneath puffy and bruised-looking. He did his best to keep his teeth clean, but they'd yellowed, and one of the bottom left molars ached all the time. He figured he probably had a cavity. Too bad he didn't have enough money for a dentist.

Joe wasn't well acquainted with Billy, but Brennan wasn't a large town, and its homeless population tended to know one another at least well enough to say hi and shoot the shit now and again. They also tended to keep an eye on one another, make sure folks were doing okay, staying healthy, both physically and mentally. They called this "checking in," and Joe recognized that was what Billy was doing now. There was also a certain kind of networking that went on among Brennan's homeless. Tips were passed along—which church was giving away secondhand clothes, which buildings were vacant and good for a few nights of sheltered sleep before the cops rousted everyone out. Vital information if you wanted to survive on the street.

"Tried my luck at the highway exit today," Billy said.

"Stood there all afternoon holding a 'will work for food' sign." He shivered.

Homeless folk knew to dress in layers when it was cold, and Billy wore a shirt and hoodie beneath an unzipped parka. But even with his limited experience, Joe knew that no matter how warmly you dressed, you could never keep the cold entirely at bay. Hell, he was dressed in layers too, only he had on his Dad's old army jacket instead of a parka, and he felt the night's chill. It was why he'd gotten the coffee in the first place. He offered Billy a sip to warm him up, but Billy declined with a shake of his head. It was too easy to pass germs that way, and homeless folk avoided getting sick at all costs. Joe felt stupid for forgetting that.

"How did it go?" he asked.

Billy shrugged. "'Bout as well as you'd expect. I need to shave off this damned beard. Makes me look too scary, you know? People don't want to stop and open their windows to talk to a guy that looks like some kind of backwoods killer out of a horror movie. You're smart to keep yourself clean-shaven. Men look less intimidating that way."

Maybe so, but Joe's first winter being homeless was approaching, and he figured he'd better start working on a beard if he wanted to keep warm. He finished the rest of his coffee, sat the empty cup on the ground, then lit a cigarette. He offered one to Billy, and this time the man accepted. They sat in silence for a few moments, smoking and watching cars pass by on the street, some of the drivers pulling into Fill 'Er Up to get gas or pick up some items inside. Joe noticed that Billy's hands shook as he smoked, and there was something about the way they trembled that didn't look like it was due to the cold, or at least, not only the cold. As far as Joe knew, the guy wasn't into alcohol or drugs, so he wasn't going through withdrawal. Joe hoped he wasn't coming down with something.

"How was your day?" Billy asked after a bit.

"Not very productive."

"Where did you try? You know what they say, it's all about location, location, location."

Joe thought about lying, but he didn't see any point to it. Pride—foolish pride, anyway—was useless on the street. "I didn't try. I just walked around town most of the day, moving from one place to another. Thinking."

Billy took a last drag on his cigarette, dropped it to the ground, and crushed it out beneath the sole of his running shoe. He then turned to Joe. "I know it's hard, man. I've been homeless for almost four years now, and it still ain't easy for me to ask folks for money. But sometimes we have to do things we don't like to survive, you know? You can't let your pride get in the way. It's like a Buddhist thing. You have to die to the self in order to reach enlightenment."

Joe had no idea what the man was talking about, but he understood the basic sentiment.

"Sometimes it feels like pride's the only thing I got left." Joe finished his cigarette and crushed it out.

He'd had a good job working for the county, driving a snow plow in the winter and doing road work in the summer. He liked being outdoors—he wasn't the sit-behind-a-desk type—and he liked feeling that the work he did helped make people's lives a little easier. Then the lousy economy forced the county to make some budget cuts, and Joe was laid off. A week later his wife filed for divorce, took their little girl, and moved to her mother's in Ash Creek. He hadn't been able to afford a lawyer, so Sheila ended up with sole custody of their daughter, and he'd ended up paying both child and spousal support. He'd looked for other work—every damned day he looked—but no one was hiring. Eventually his unemployment ran out, the bank foreclosed on his home, he lost his car, and the next thing he knew, he became a resident of the street. He told himself it was temporary, just until he could get back on his proverbial feet. That had been four months ago, and he was still here, a victim not of booze, drugs, or mental illness—just plain old lousy luck. He'd adjusted as best he could, but the one thing he hadn't been able to accept was asking strangers for money. It was one thing to be homeless, but it was another thing to be a beggar. Not that he'd ever use that word in front of Billy. He'd been on the street too long to make judgments about what others did to survive. He had no idea what the man's story was and how he'd ended up living like this. That kind of personal information was kept to one's self on the street, shared only with the closest of confidants. But whatever Billy's story was, Joe knew the man had one. Everyone did.

"Tell you what," Billy said, "I managed to score a few dollars today. How about we head on over to the Foxhole for a couple slices of pie? My treat."

"I appreciate what you're trying to do, but I don't need cheering up. Besides, if I have a hard time taking charity from strangers, what makes you think I'll have an easier time taking it from you?"

Billy grinned. "You got to start somewhere, right? C'mon." He took hold of Joe's upper arm and stood. Joe allowed the man to lift him to his feet.

"Well… it *has* been a while since I've had a good piece of pie."

Billy clapped him on the back. "There you go!"

The two men started walking in the direction of the diner, taking alleys for short cuts. Not only did alleys save time, but you could find some good stuff in them. Discarded or lost objects you might be able to sell for a couple bucks, even cast-off clothing sometimes. Sure, alleys could be dark and intimidating, and they didn't smell all that good, but they were useful, and when you were homeless, that was all that mattered.

They were only a block away from the Foxhole, walking through an alley between a coin-operated laundry and pizza joint when Joe had the feeling they were being followed. Before he'd become homeless, he might've ignored the sensation, figuring it was just his imagination. Who didn't walk through an alley with their guard up? But during his relatively short time on the street, Joe's survival instincts had been sharpened, and he knew better than to dismiss any feeling, no matter how trivial it seemed. He gripped Billy's upper arm to stop him, and then glanced back over his shoulder. He honestly didn't expect to see anything, so it was a shock when he saw the figure standing behind them. It was even more of a shock to see the large, cruel-looking knife clutched in the man's hand. *Was the blade black?* It sure looked that way to Joe.

"Good evening, gentleman," the man said. "My apologies, but you both have something I need, and I'm afraid I'm going to have to take it from you. I assure you, this is nothing personal, and if it's any consolation, know that your sacrifice will not only help further the cause of science, it will also help bring about a most glorious change unlike any the world has ever seen."

Joe turned to Billy. "Do you have any idea what the hell he's—"

That was as far as he got before the man with the knife sprang at them.

Dispatching the men was accomplished easily enough. A pair of quick, deep slices to the throat, and all Conrad had to do was step back as the men fell to the ground and wait for them to bleed out. He had no aversion to cutting into still-living bodies, but he preferred not to get any more blood on him than necessary. It didn't take long for their blood flow to diminish, and then Conrad went to work. He selected the clean-shaven man first, judging him to be younger than his bearded companion and likely in better condition. He raised his obsidian blade over his head, and the runes engraved upon it glowed with silver-blue light.

"In your name, my lady."

Then he crouched next to the body and went to work.

FIVE

Blood was everywhere—on the walls, the floor, the furniture, even the ceiling. It looked as if someone had carried in large buckets of the red stuff and splashed it all over the living room, taking pains to make sure that no surface was left untouched. There was so much blood that at first Sam couldn't see anything but crimson. Then a second later, his eyes registered the two forms on the floor in front of the couch, one lying prone, the other straddling it. Both were covered with so much gore that he didn't recognize them right away. The one on the floor was larger, taller, and beefier than the other. Sam thought it might be a man, but given the state of the figure's face—or rather what little was left of it—he couldn't tell for sure. The flannel shirt and jeans didn't help much, but the large boots were a giveaway. They were Earl's, which made sense, considering the cabin was his as well. His left hand was clenched around a small black object which Sam immediately recognized as a statuette of Anubis, the Egyptian god of the dead.

The figure straddling Earl's chest was thinner, shorter, and dressed in a blood-soaked T-shirt and a pair of cut-off shorts. The long hair was so matted with blood, it was impossible to determine its true color by sight, but Sam knew it was a light chestnut brown. He also knew that the hair normally smelled of strawberry kiwi shampoo. He didn't want to think about how it smelled right now.

Trish.

He hadn't spoken her name aloud—at least, he didn't think he had—but her gaze snapped in his direction. Her blue eyes were as empty and cold as the bottom of an arctic sea, and there was nothing remotely human in them. She had something wet and ragged clamped between her blood-slick teeth, and Sam's stomach did a flip when he realized it was part of her father's tongue. She tossed her head back and swallowed the grisly morsel in a single gulp, and then locked gazes with him once again. Her lips drew back from her teeth in a gesture that was more rictus than smile. She rose to her feet and stepped away from her father's body. She moved toward Sam with the feral grace of a jungle cat, and a low keening sound came from deep in her throat. It was the sound of need, of desire, of *hunger.*

This isn't right, Sam thought. *It didn't happen like this!*

It was the last thought he had before Trish sank her teeth into his throat.

"Sam? *Sam!*"

He sat up and opened his eyes, surprised by how much effort it took. Dean's hands were on his shoulders, and Sam realized his brother had been shaking him.

He pushed Dean's hands away and then yawned. "What's wrong?"

Dean had been sitting on the edge of the bed, but now he stood. "You were moaning and thrashing in your sleep, big time. You must've been having one hell of a serious dream, and not the good kind, if you know what I mean."

Sam rubbed his eyes. He didn't remember falling asleep. "What time is it?" He glanced toward the nightstand and checked the read-out on the digital clock there: 9:13. "Wow, I must've been wiped out. I napped for... what, three hours or so?"

Dean walked over to the window and drew back the curtains. Light spilled into the room and stabbed Sam's eyes. His head pounded as if he had a hangover, and he lifted a hand to block the glare as he averted his gaze.

"You slept a little longer than that, Rip Van Winkle. It's nine in the morning."

He'd slept for fifteen hours. Most of the time, Dean and he were lucky to get four hours a night, but every once in a while the lack of rest caught up with them and they crashed for the better part of a day. "Guess I needed to get caught up on my sleep. Sorry."

He sat up the rest of the way and swung his feet over the side of the bed. He winced as his right foot touched the carpet, and he remembered his wound. That memory brought the rest along with it—Brennan, the mummified corpses, Frankenmutt—and he was jolted fully awake.

He looked around the room, trying to appear casual as he

checked to make sure that everything was the way it should be. He had a hard time telling what was real and what wasn't these days, especially when he'd just awakened, or was tired or stressed. But he didn't see any hallucinations—none that were obvious, at any rate—and when after a few moments the room, the furniture, and Dean remained the same, he allowed himself to relax.

"Any coffee?" he asked.

Dean walked over to the table where a couple coffee cups from a fast-food joint sat. He brought one to Sam, then went back and took a seat. The brothers sipped their go-juice for a few moments in silence before Dean asked, "So what were you dreaming about? And if it *was* the good kind of dream, make sure you don't leave out any naughty details."

At first Sam couldn't remember what he'd been dreaming about, but then the details came flooding back, and he wished they hadn't.

"Trish."

Dean arced an eyebrow in surprise. "Trish Hansen?"

Sam nodded and took another sip of coffee. It seemed sharp and acidic as it went down his throat, and his stomach roiled in response.

"That was a while ago," Dean said softly. "We were teenagers."

"Barely."

They were silent for a few moments after that, both continuing to work on their coffee.

After a bit, Dean asked, "Why do you suppose you dreamed about her?" He didn't look at Sam as he spoke, but there was a clear edge of tension in his voice.

"I don't know. I guess I've just been thinking about death lately."

Dean turned to him, a hard expression on his face that verged on anger. "Lately? In case you haven't noticed, Death could be both of our middle names. If we aren't ganking some monster, we're watching someone we love go belly up."

Someone like Bobby, Sam thought, although he didn't say it aloud. "That's kind of what I mean. Death is so much a part of our lives that sometimes we take it for granted…" He hurried on before Dean could protest. "Until something happens to remind us. In a lot of ways, what happened to Trish was the first time I realized just how close death really is to all of us. Not just hunters, but everybody. It's always there, just a heartbeat away, waiting for the right time, you know?"

Dean nodded gravely. "Yes. Yes, I do."

Of course you do, Sam thought. For a short time, Dean had actually served as a stand-in for Death with a capital D.

Sam went on. "Besides, we were talking about *Frankenstein* yesterday, so that's another probable reason I was thinking about death—at least subconsciously—as I conked out."

"Yeah. Probably." Dean's tone was distant, distracted, and Sam knew that he was remembering Trish. Remembering how she died… and remembering the horrible thing she had become in death.

Sam wanted to take Dean's mind—and his own—off Trish Hansen, so he put his almost-empty coffee cup on the nightstand and stood, trying not to grimace as he put weight on his injured ankle. It hurt, but not as bad as it had yesterday. "So, any new developments regarding Frankenmutt while I was zonked?" he asked.

"Not so fast there, pilgrim," Dean said.

"Pilgrim?"

"Caught a cowboy flick on TV last night while you were off in dreamland," Dean said, sounding a bit apologetic. "Anyway, before we get back to work, I want to take a look at that ankle of yours."

"What for?"

"We don't know exactly what the hell Frankenmutt is, and after the way you passed out last night, I want to make sure that you didn't pick up something nasty when he bit you."

"I didn't pass out," Sam muttered. "I fell asleep."

Dean had eased up on the overprotective big brother bit over the last couple years, but he still got on Sam's nerves whenever he fell back into his old role. Still, Sam couldn't fault his brother's reasoning, and besides, he knew Dean wouldn't let up until he was satisfied.

"Whatever. Let's take a look at that ankle and make sure you didn't catch Frankenrabies."

"Fine."

Sam sat on the foot of his bed and crossed his right leg onto his left. He'd fallen asleep in his clothes, and by longstanding agreement between the brothers, Dean had left him that way. He'd taken his shoes off before bandaging his ankle the night before, though, so all he needed to do was pull up the pant leg a little and begin unwrapping the bandage. Dean rose from the table and walked over to the bed to get a closer look at the wound.

"You're hovering," Sam said.

"Deal with it," Dean replied.

Sam finished removing the bandage and was gratified to see the wound looked greatly improved since yesterday. It wasn't bleeding anymore and scabs had already started to form. The tissue around the wound wasn't swollen, nor was it red, but he probed it with his fingertips to be sure. The flesh was tender, but it felt cool: no infection.

"I gotta admit, it looks pretty good," Dean said.

"So no more worries about Frankenrabies?" Sam asked.

"We'll see."

Sam started to rewrap the wound, but then decided to let it breathe for a while.

"As I was saying, anything new?"

"Not really. No mysterious wasting deaths were reported, so it looks like Frankenmutt didn't drain anyone's battery last night. I researched black dogs some more on the net, but didn't find anything we don't already know. I also looked into Brennan's history, but near as I can tell, until recently nothing even remotely supernatural has ever happened here. When it comes to the wide world of weird, this may be the least interesting town in the whole damn country. Hell, I'm thinking about retiring here some day."

Sam smiled. "Assuming we get rid of Frankenmutt first."

"And the Double-Header."

Sam frowned. "Excuse me?"

Dean grinned, then went back to the table and turned on the laptop. Sam hobbled over, and since there was only one chair, Dean made him take it. Dean looked over his shoulder as the screen came to life and displayed the webpage for the

Broadsider. The headline read Local Unemployment Reaches All-Time High.

"Scroll down," Dean said.

Sam did so, and toward the bottom of the page, he found a smaller headline: Man Reports Encounter with Two-Headed Monster. The headline was only a link, so Sam clicked it and an instant later, the entire article was displayed on the screen.

MAN REPORTS ENCOUNTER WITH
TWO-HEADED MONSTER

Late last evening, Brennan resident Lyle Swanson called 911 to report that what he referred to as a "monster" was raiding the trash containers behind his house. When Brennan police arrived at the Swanson residence, they discovered several trash containers had been overturned and their contents scattered, but they found no evidence of who or what was responsible. When the police spoke with Mr. Swanson, he described hearing noises outside, and when he looked through his back door window to investigate, he saw a creature that resembled a "large naked man with two heads and four arms" going through his trash and "eating all the good stuff." Police took Mr. Swanson's statement and suggested he purchase trash containers with locking mechanisms to prevent a recurrence of the incident.

Dean chuckled. "Man, I don't know what Lyle was drinking last night, but I'll have a double."

Sam looked over his shoulder at his brother. "You don't

think what he saw was real?"

Dean frowned. "C'mon, Sammy. I only wanted you to see this so you'd get a laugh out of it. I didn't think you'd take it seriously." His eyes narrowed as if he was suddenly suspicious of something, and Sam knew he was worried that his little brother's crazy was starting to show again.

"Think about it," Sam said. "Frankenmutt looked like he was a combination of different dog parts, right? So maybe this Double-Header is the same kind of thing, only he's a combination of different *people*."

Dean regarded the computer screen for a moment then turned his attention back to Sam. He sighed.

"You grab a shower. I'll track down Lyle's address."

Sam nodded, rose from the chair, and started toward the bathroom, almost shuffling as he went. He wondered when the coffee he'd had would finally kick in. Despite all the sleep he'd gotten, he felt so damn tired...

Dean listened to the sound of the shower while he worked on digging up Lyle Swanson's address. Sometimes living in close quarters with Sam got on his nerves, and he knew Sam felt the same way about him. What two brothers could spend almost every moment together and not irritate each other? It was normal human behavior, no harm, no foul. But he'd never told Sam that he often found the sounds of someone else close by—say, for instance, a running shower—comforting, even soothing. Footsteps across a floor, the scrape of a chair being pulled away from a table, the tapping of computer keys, the creak of bedsprings, the soft breathing of someone else sleeping. As Sam had pointed out, they spent so much of their time dealing with death. Being surrounded by simple day-to-day sounds, *human* sounds, helped remind Dean that there was life in the world, too, and that he wasn't alone, not as long as he had family.

Dean found his thoughts drifting toward Trish Hansen. He hadn't thought of her in years, but now that Sam had brought her up, Dean was having a hard time thinking about anything else. One year in their early teens, their dad had gotten a lead on a possible location of Yellow-Eyes, the demon that had killed their mother. Supposedly, the demon had been spotted by a hunter in Alaska, and John Winchester was hell-bent on running the bastard to ground and making him pay for what he'd done. But his desire for vengeance didn't cloud his judgment, at least not where his sons were concerned. John wasn't about to take Sam and Dean along on such a potentially dangerous hunt, so he'd arranged for them to stay with a friend in Washington State. Walter Hansen wasn't a hunter himself, but a master forger who provided false documents and ID for hunters to use. He also ran something of an unofficial trading post, as some of his clients paid him in barter. Weapons were the most common alternate currency, but sometimes they paid with other, more… esoteric items that they acquired during the course of their work. Dean hadn't cared much about any of that, however. At his age, the most important thing about Walter Hansen was that he had a teenage daughter named Trish.

He remembered the first time he saw her. Dad hadn't told them that his friend had a daughter, so when Walter let them

into his cabin one early spring evening, both Dean and Sam
had been surprised to see a girl sitting cross-legged in front of
the fireplace. She looked to be around his age, maybe a year
older. Her complexion was light, her features delicate, and
the brown hair that flowed over her shoulders seemed almost
bronze in the firelight. Her gray sweater was big and baggy
on her, but her faded jeans hugged her slender legs, giving
Dean a tantalizing idea of what the rest of her body might
look like. She wore no shoes, and she held her bare feet in
her hands, as if the fire wasn't enough to warm them. Later,
he would take note of the playful intelligence that danced in
her eyes, would feel a strange thrill in his chest whenever she
let out one of her too-loud laughs. But what struck him most
at that moment was the way she turned her head to look at
them and smiled, big and bright, as if welcoming old friends
instead of greeting a trio of strangers. It may well have been
the best smile he'd ever seen on a woman.

"We good to go?"

Startled, Dean looked up from the laptop screen to see
Sam standing by the table, hair a tousled wet mess, motel
towel wrapped around his waist.

"Dude, I thought we had a rule about running around
naked in front of each other."

"I'm not naked."

"Close enough. Get dressed, Towel Boy. I got Lyle's addy.
Found it in an online phone registry." Dean closed the laptop.

"Good. When I was in the shower—"

Dean held up his hands. "Please! There are some things I
do *not* need to know. What happens in the shower, stays in

the shower."

Sam sighed. "I was going to say that I had an idea how we can set a trap for Frankenmutt."

"Oh. Well, that I do need to know. You can fill me in on the way to Lyle's."

As Sam finished getting ready, Dean sat back in the chair and did his best not to think about Trish Hansen.

"We've seen a lot of crazy over the years, but Lyle's got a good shot at winning a special place in the Winchester Hall of Weird."

The brothers were in the crapmobile, heading back to Arbor Vale Apartments after interviewing Lyle Swanson. Sam sipped a latte with two shots of espresso that he'd picked up at a coffee shop on the way. Normally, he was careful to limit his caffeine intake, but the meager boost he'd received from his morning cuppa had already faded, and now he felt like taking a nap. He hoped he wasn't coming down with something. Killing monsters was hard enough without having to do it while coughing, sneezing, and dripping snot.

"It didn't help that he smelled like a distillery, and it wasn't even noon yet," Dean added.

Sam looked at his brother. He wanted to say something about pots calling kettles black, but he didn't have the energy to get into an argument right then. He took another sip of coffee before speaking. "He didn't seem that bad to me."

The Winchesters had foregone their usual pose as FBI agents when visiting Lyle. They didn't think the man would buy a couple Feds dropping by to check on a report of a two-headed, four-armed naked man eating garbage. Even with all their experience creating cover stories to explain their presence at crime scenes, they figured they'd have a tough time selling that one. Instead they'd told him they were staff reporters for *Ohio* magazine assigned to do a feature story on the state's paranormal hotspots. Luckily, Lyle didn't ask to see their nonexistent journalist IDs.

He hadn't been able to tell them much more than they'd already gotten from the article in the *Broadsider*, and when he showed them the place where the multi-limbed monster had rooted through his trash, there were no discernible signs that anything out of the ordinary had been responsible. There were still remnants of garbage strewn across Lyle's back yard: stained paper plates, empty liters of soda, crusty microwave meal trays, crumpled snack chip bags, and wadded-up fast-food wrappers. Lyle was a middle-aged man who proudly told them he was a lifelong bachelor, and from what Sam saw, the guy ate like one. When they asked him why he hadn't cleaned up the mess yet, he said, "I ain't touchin' that crap! You think I wanna get monster cooties?"

Sam and Dean had exchanged looks at the cootie remark. It explained a great deal about why Lyle was a bachelor.

"Sam, his trash got hit by some kind of animal. A raccoon or a possum, maybe even a coyote. Not freaky Siamese twins."

"Conjoined," Sam said. "The proper term is *conjoined* twins."

"Whatever. The point is that there's nothing supernatural going on at Lyle's place. He doesn't need us; he needs a good shrink."

"What about the peanut butter jar?"

"What about it?"

"The lid was off."

"Yeah, I noticed. Are you saying that's proof something with hands—like four of them—raided Lyle's outdoor buffet? He may have thrown it away like that, with the lid and jar separate, and even if the lid was still on, raccoons have got hands, right? They could've gotten it off."

"Maybe," Sam said.

The EMF detector hadn't picked up any energy emissions, and they hadn't found any footprints, human or animal. They'd pretended to take notes, and they promised Lyle they'd send him a copy of the magazine when their article appeared. They left after that, and although Sam couldn't disagree with his brother's assessment of Lyle, he also couldn't escape the feeling that the man was telling the truth. Call it hunter's intuition. Maybe with a little work, he could convince Dean to reconsider Lyle's story, but he'd worry about that later. Right now, they had a monster dog to catch.

They parked in front of the building closest to the pond, and walked down the hill toward the water. Both were armed—Dean's shotgun loaded with regular shells instead of rock salt this time—and Sam carried a plastic shopping bag emblazoned with the logo of a large department store chain.

"I don't know about this plan of yours, Sammy. It seems a little out there, even for you."

Sam tried not to bristle at the implication—which admittedly he might be reading into his brother's words— that his fragile mental state was responsible for him coming up with his unorthodox plan to lure the monster dog. "We know Frankenmutt drains life force, right? And after our encounter with him yesterday, he took a lot of damage. He's going to need to heal, and that means he'll have to feed."

"Assuming he *can* heal," Dean pointed out. "He might be like a movie zombie and just keep on rotting and getting nastier no matter how much he feeds."

"Possibly," Sam said. "But he didn't show any sign of decay yesterday, right?"

"I guess not. He was one butt-ugly pooch, but his meat looked fresh enough."

The brothers reached the pond, turned right, and headed into the woods.

Sam lowered his voice. "So if he needs to heal, he'll be hungry, but he won't be looking for food to eat, he'll be looking for life force to absorb. That's what we're going to give him—or at least pretend to."

"I get the logic," Dean said, "I just don't think that Frankenmutt's going to fall for it. He may be some kind of freak, but he's still a dog, and their senses are too sharp to..." He trailed off and pointed.

Sam looked where his brother indicated and saw the body of a rabbit lying on the ground, partially hidden by underbrush. At least, he thought it was a rabbit. The body had shrunken in upon itself, making the animal look like a skeleton covered with a layer of ill-fitting fur.

"Looks like Frankenmutt had a snack," Dean said softly.

Sam nodded, and they continued deeper into the woods.

They encountered the desiccated corpses of other animals—more rabbits, a couple groundhogs, and a cat. The latter had no collar, and Sam figured it for a stray.

When they came upon a small clearing, Sam said, "This should do."

Dean nodded and kept watch, shotgun at the ready, while Sam went to work. He knelt down and placed the shopping bag on the ground next to him. First he removed the lifelike baby doll they'd purchased from the store's toy department. He'd already removed it from the packaging in the car, and he placed the pink, rubbery thing upon a small pile of leaves.

"Man, look at us, playing with dolls," Dean muttered.

Sam ignored him.

Next, Sam took a container of baby powder—Softness for the Skin You Love was this brand's slogan—and he sprinkled a good amount on the doll. He put the powder back in the bag and then withdrew a can of ready-made formula. He opened it and poured a little of the thick white liquid on the doll's mouth. Not too much, just enough to simulate a baby who's fed and needs its mouth wiped. He then set up the most important part of the illusion. He took his smart phone out of his jacket pocket, cranked the volume up as high as it would go, and activated the audio file he'd downloaded earlier. The sound of a baby crying echoed through the woods, and Sam placed the phone on the ground close to the doll's head. Then he and Dean retreated to a pair of nearby trees and took cover. Sam set the plastic bag and the open can of formula on the ground, drew his Beretta, and together he and his brother waited.

The reasoning behind Sam's plan was simple. Frankenmutt needed life force, and what had more life energy—at least in mystic terms—than a baby? Spiritually speaking, a baby was full of *potential* life energy. It was like a bank account full of money that no one had started to withdraw from yet. That made it a rich source of food for a creature like Frankenmutt. At least, that's what Sam hoped.

When he'd been without a soul, Sam might've used a real baby as a lure. Oh, he'd have done everything he could to make sure the baby wasn't harmed, but if something went wrong and the child died, soulless Sam wouldn't—couldn't have shed a tear. The thought made him sick, and he was glad those days were behind him. When Sam had first told Dean about his idea, Dean had admitted it had potential—even if it was a little on the demented side—but he'd voiced some doubts. *You can make it sound like a real baby, but it'll still smell like plastic and rubber. Once Frankenmutt gets close enough to get a good whiff of Sammy Junior, he'll know something's wrong and turn tail.*

Sam agreed that was a possibility, which was the reason for the baby powder and the formula: to make the doll seem more like a real baby. Sam had no idea if Frankenmutt had ever had a real life as a dog—or separate dogs—before becoming a freakish conglomerate monstrosity, but if he had, Sam hoped that somewhere in his doggy brain resided the memory of what babies smelled like. If not, then he hoped the creature would be so damned hungry that the cries of distress would be enough to lure it, and it wouldn't be put off by the scent of plastic.

He'd set his phone to play the audio file on a loop, and several minutes passed while they listened to the baby's cries without any sign of Frankenmutt.

"Maybe he filled up on animals and he's not hungry anymore," Dean said. "Or maybe he's too far away to hear."

Sam figured either was a possibility. "Let's give it a bit longer before—" He broke off. He'd caught sight of something out of the corner of his eye, and he spun toward it, Beretta raised and ready to fire.

He expected to see Frankenmutt bearing down on them, but instead he saw a man standing a dozen yards away, next to an old oak. Sam couldn't make out his features clearly; almost as if he was viewing him through a sheet of gauze. He was of medium height and dressed in a dark suit. Blue? Black? Sam couldn't tell. His hair color was light, most likely blond, but maybe white. His age was impossible to guess, as his facial features were a flesh-colored shimmer that rippled continuously like water.

"What?" Dean said, turning and bringing his shotgun around.

Before Sam could reply, the figure vanished. One instant he was there, the next—poof!—like he'd never existed. A wave of dizziness came over Sam, accompanied by a deep weariness that he could feel down to the bottoms of his feet. The Beretta felt suddenly heavy in his hand, and he thought it might slip from his fingers and fall to the ground. But he managed to maintain his grip on the weapon, and a second later the dizziness passed and the weariness eased, although the latter didn't leave him entirely.

"It's nothing," Sam said. "Thought I saw something. I was wrong."

Dean scowled at him, and Sam could guess what he was thinking.

"I'm fine," he insisted. "All my marbles are more or less in place."

Dean grunted. "It's the *less* I'm worried about."

Sam said nothing. So he'd had a hallucination, so what? It wasn't his first, and he doubted it would be his last. The important thing was that it hadn't lasted very long, and it hadn't distracted him from—

A branch snapped behind them. Followed by a low, throaty growl.

"It's behind us, isn't it?" Sam said.

"Yep."

The brothers whirled around and fired.

SIX

Lyle Swanson was not a happy man.

Not that this was out of character for him. Even at the best of times, he wasn't the cheeriest of people. His fellow employees at Swifty Print had what they thought was an ironic, and hilarious, nickname for him: Mr. Sunshine. It wasn't that he was foul-tempered. He didn't get angry or frustrated when things went wrong, and he didn't complain about setbacks. He wasn't a particularly chatty man, but he didn't avoid conversations with his coworkers, either. He was just one of those people who seem perpetually gloomy. If he'd been a cartoon character, he would've had a small black raincloud hovering over his head all the time. He shuffled when he walked, shoulders slumped, head tilted at a downward angle, facial features slack and drooping. He rarely smiled, and when he did, it was with the barest upturn of the mouth, the expression so muted that most people didn't recognize it for what it was. And no one could ever remember hearing him laugh, not even so much as a soft chuckle.

There was no reason for Lyle to be a human incarnation of Eeyore, at least none that he could see. He'd had a happy enough childhood, and while he hadn't been popular in school, no one had bullied him. In fact, most of the kids had barely noticed he existed, and the same went for the teachers. His life so far, while wholly unremarkable, had been almost entirely without conflict of any significance. Yes, he was a bit of a germaphobe, the kind of person who's never without hand sanitizer and wipes. And he'd never had much interest in sex. It seemed like too much work and, to be frank, more than a little messy.

His job—you really couldn't call it a career—wasn't the most fulfilling in the world, but it paid his bills, and the benefits, while not outstanding, were sufficient for his needs. He had his own house, a small one just outside the town limits, where it was nice and quiet. When naked monsters weren't digging in his trash can, that was.

His health was good, and according to his doctor, if he kept going as he was, there was an excellent chance he'd live to a ripe old age. There was absolutely no reason on Earth why Lyle should be, as his mother used to put it, a Gloomy Gus. He supposed he'd simply been born that way.

Today, however, he had more than ample reason to be unhappy. It was bad enough that a trash-hungry bare-assed monster had paid him a visit the day before, but what really stuck in Lyle's craw was how everyone had reacted to his story. The police had come out to take his statement, sure, but had they done any real investigating? Had they taken photographs, dusted for fingerprints, taken plaster molds of footprints, or swabbed for DNA? Had they done anything that the crime scene investigators on TV did? Hell, no. They hadn't even bothered to search the woods behind his property. He'd had the feeling that it had taken every ounce of control the officers possessed to keep from laughing the entire time they were talking with him.

As bad as that had been, the story in the *Broadsider* that morning had been worse. Good thing he got the paper delivered or else he might not have seen the article before heading in to work. He'd called in sick because he hadn't wanted to deal with his fellow employees making fun of him all day. Marcy, one of Swifty Print's managers, had answered his call, and when he told her he wasn't coming in, she asked if he was playing hooky so he could spend the day with his new friend. Before he could respond, she'd added. *Just be careful. You never know what a naked man will get up to. The stories I could tell you, honey! Just remember one thing…* And here she'd paused for effect. *Forewarned is four-armed!*

He hung up on her peal of laughter.

Then those two magazine writers had come by. They'd seemed professional enough at first. They acted as if they were genuinely interested in hearing his story, and they listened closely as he went over the details. But when he showed them the mess in the back yard, they'd begun to seem doubtful. They hadn't said as much, but he'd caught the looks they tossed back and forth. Looks that said, *We got ourselves a real piece of work here.* Like the police, they didn't take any photos, and that was when he knew they weren't going to include him in their article. Magazines *always* used pictures with the stories they ran. The fact that they hadn't bothered to take any told him everything he needed to know about what they thought of his... well, he supposed you'd call it a sighting.

Maybe I shouldn't have used the word cooties, he thought.

So now here he was, working in his back yard to clean up the mess left by the whatever-the-hell-it-was. He wore rubber gloves and a surgical mask to protect himself from the worst of the germs. He wished he had a pair of coveralls, too, but he didn't. Instead, he'd donned an old long-sleeved plaid shirt and a pair of jeans, both of which he'd bag up and throw away when he finished with the clean up. Even with the gloves, he didn't want to touch the trash. Maybe monsters didn't have cooties as such, but something had caused those weird deaths where people shriveled up like prunes, and he wasn't about to take any chances. He didn't own a tool designed for picking up litter, so he'd had to improvise. He'd taken a pair of salad tongs from his kitchen, and they did the job well enough. Of course, they'd have to be thrown away too when he was finished, but that was okay. Utensils were easily replaced. A man's life, not so much.

Lyle was bent over and in the process of picking up a torn and empty package that had once contained fudge-covered vanilla-cream sandwich cookies—his only real vice—when he felt a tingling sensation on the back of his neck. He froze there, crouching, salad tongs gripping the cookie package in one gloved hand, a plastic garbage bag for the trash he'd gathered so far in the other. Someone—some*thing*—was watching him.

He didn't consider himself an especially brave man, but he didn't think of himself as a coward, either. He didn't like scary books or movies, but not because they frightened him. He didn't think they were realistic. Sure, bad things happened to people—sometimes *really* bad things, but awful as they were, they were understandable, even routine in some ways. Diseases, accidents, natural disasters, and most common of all, humans being shitty to one another. But to be scared of some horrible unknown thing lurking in the shadows? It had seemed ridiculous.

Now—frozen in mid-crouch in his back yard, the surgical mask covering the lower half of his face suddenly tight and stifling—he knew how the people in those stories felt. They weren't simply frightened, they were *terrified*, breath caught in their throats, hearts pounding a trip-hammer beat, sweat erupting from their pores, stomachs filled with ice water. They felt small and weak, caught between two all-consuming but opposing impulses: to run away as fast and far as they possibly could, and also to stand statue-still and hope to remain unnoticed by the nameless thing that stalked them. Lyle now knew what they knew—what it was like to be prey. He'd never been so scared in his life.

He heard breathing first, heavy and labored, punctuated with a soft whistling-wheezing sound, as if the lungs producing it weren't quite working right. The sound was off to his left, and he didn't want to turn his head to look, he really didn't. He'd rather squeeze his eyes shut and, like a child hiding under the covers in the dark, hope that if he couldn't see the monster, it couldn't see him. But he turned his head anyway, he couldn't keep himself from doing so, and when he did, he saw exactly what he expected to.

The monster had returned.

Yesterday he'd watched the creature from within the safety of his home, peeking through the small white curtain that covered the back-door window. He'd been concealed from the thing's view, protected by a solid wooden door locked with a deadbolt. It had been a strange sight, that was for damn sure, but he hadn't felt threatened. The situation had been so bizarre that it hadn't seemed real. He'd felt like a detached observer, watching the creature on a TV screen. It had seemed absurd with its two heads and four arms, like something out of a child's cartoon. But now, with the creature standing less than a dozen yards away and nothing between them but air, it didn't seem so absurd. In fact, it was downright terrifying.

It stood six feet tall, and its naked body—aside from the extra parts—was that of a normal man. Although it carried a few extra pounds around the middle, it was in relatively good shape, with hard muscle and a light covering of black body hair. Each head had to lean to the side—one right, one left—in order for them to fit on a single body, and Lyle found himself thinking that both of the poor sons of bitches probably suffered from perpetually sore necks. The head on the right had straight black hair that hung in long greasy clumps, and an unkempt beard that was badly in need of trimming. The head on the left had a lighter complexion, and its thick hair was a soft ginger color. It was clean-shaven, with a dusting of freckles on the cheeks. Both heads held similar expressions: eyes wide and wild, mouths slack and open. A thin line of drool ran from the corner of Ginger's mouth and dribbled onto its chest.

It stood hunched forward, no doubt because of the added weight of those extra arms and head. The second set of arms protruded from the front of the creature's shoulders, and were thinner than the other pair, the skin lighter, body hair almost nonexistent.

They're Ginger's arms, Lyle thought, and his stomach gave a flip at this realization.

Right then, all four of its arms were hanging loosely, as if it had forgotten for the moment that they were there.

Lyle noticed another detail, one he'd missed before. At the junctures where Ginger's body parts connected with Black Hair's were patches of skin that didn't look right. The color and texture were strange, artificial somehow, and it reminded Lyle of the Silly Putty he'd played with as a child. Of all the wrong things there were about this creature, that not-skin was somehow the worst, and looking at it made Lyle feel sick to his stomach. Well, sicker.

For a long moment the monster stared at him with its two pairs of eyes, as if it was as surprised to see Lyle as Lyle was to see it. *Maybe he's wondering what happened to* my *extra head and arms,* Lyle thought. The idea struck him as so ridiculous that he couldn't help letting out a short laugh, although it sounded more like a sob. The creature started at the sound, and for an instant Lyle thought it might bolt like a frightened deer and run back to the woods. But instead its two mouths stretched into hideous lopsided grins.

"Hun!" Black-Hair said.

"Gee!" Ginger said.

There was a short pause between the sounds, but when the heads spoke a second time they did so in rapid succession, so the syllables came out as a single almost-word.

"Hun-gee!"

Ice collected on Lyle's spine, and his bowels turned watery. The creature spoke in the simplistic manner of a toddler, but this time Lyle had no trouble understanding what it—they—were saying.

Hungry.

Lyle dropped the garbage bag and tongs, and ran like hell for his house. The creature let out two excited hoots, like those a large ape might make, and gave pursuit.

Lyle heard its pounding footfalls and whistle-wheeze breath, and adrenaline surged through his system, spurring him to run faster. He once again felt a tingle on the back of his neck, only now the sensation seemed to be warning him that the two-headed monstrosity was reaching for him, its fingers—nails overlong, cracked, and split—mere inches from his flesh. The feeling was so strong that he couldn't stop himself from looking back over his shoulder, and as soon as he did, he wished he'd resisted the impulse. The creature wasn't as close as he'd feared, about fifteen feet behind him—which was good—but the *way* it ran… It moved with a spastic, lopsided gait, as if its nervous system had short-circuited and was firing off impulses at random. Instead of reaching out to grab him as he'd pictured, all four of the creature's arms hung limply, the extremities flailing and flopping as their owner continued to lurch after Lyle. It was without doubt the most horrible thing Lyle had ever seen. So why did it strike him as almost funny?

A giggle escaped his mouth, one tinged with more than a hint of hysteria.

As if the giggle was a cue, the creature bellowed its tag-team word again.

"Hun-gee!"

Lyle's giggle became a shriek, and he faced forward and ran even faster.

He'd left the back door unlocked, and even though his hands were sweating something fierce, the rubber gloves kept his grip from being slick, so he was able to turn the knob without difficulty. People at work teased him about being OCD, but he wished they could see him right then.

Who's crazy now?

He threw open the door, lunged inside, and slammed it shut behind him, whirled around, threw the deadbolt, engaged the smaller lock on the knob, and backed quickly away. He moved too fast, stumbled over his own feet, and fell backward, landing hard on his ass. The impact jolted his spine and caused his teeth to clack together painfully. In the process he bit into the tip of his tongue, and blood started to fill his mouth. He tried to spit, remembered the surgical mask, tore it off his face and dropped it on the kitchen floor. He then turned his head and expelled a glob of blood. It splattered onto a lower cabinet door, but he didn't notice, and even if he had, he wouldn't have cared. He had more important things to worry about right now than a little mess.

OCD be damned.

He fixed his gaze on the door and waited.

It won't get in, Lyle told himself. *The lock's strong. I know, because I installed it myself.* Besides, the way those arms were flapping around, they might not function properly. If that was so, even if the door had been unlocked, the creature might not be able to turn the knob. So no matter what, he was safe. He *was.*

The door burst inward without any warning, glass shattering, hinges tearing free, the deadbolt ripping through the jamb. The door slid across the floor and bumped to a stop against Lyle's feet.

The two-headed man stood in the now-open doorway, all four arms held out ramrod straight, palms up.

Guess those arms work after all, he thought.

The creature lurched into the kitchen, double grins widening into twin leers.

"Hun-gee!"

Lyle heard someone laughing, and it took him a moment to realize that the sound bubbled up from his own throat. The whole thing was just too damned messed-up to take seriously.

The creature reached Lyle, knelt awkwardly before him, and placed all fours hand on the sides of the man's face. Lyle's laughter broke off in a gasp. The monster's flesh was cold—so cold it burned.

Then a great heaviness settled on Lyle, and with it came a weariness more powerful than any he'd ever known. He struggled to keep his eyes open, but really, what was the point? His limbs felt as if they'd turned to lead, and although he tried to pull away from the monster's quadruple grip, he was weak as a newborn. He couldn't move, let alone fight. It would be simpler to just give in, let his eyes close, and allow himself to slip away.

So that's what he did.

Just before the endless darkness took hold of Lyle and swept him away forever, he heard a pair of voices speak a single word.

"Good…"

"Is it dead?" Dean asked.

"How should I know?" Sam said.

"Check it."

"*You* check it!"

Dean had pumped every round his shotgun held into that damned dog, and Sam had emptied his Beretta's clip, reloaded, and continued firing. Frankenmutt was down, finally, but neither of the brothers was sure it was permanent. During his years as a hunter Dean had encountered a lot of supernatural entities that were hard to kill, but he'd rarely run into anything as tough as this patchwork pooch. Frankenmutt lay on its side, its flesh a savaged, bloody ruin from all the damage it had taken. Dean almost felt sorry for the thing. Almost.

"Give me a sec."

Dean reloaded his weapon, then stepped forward slowly, lowering the barrel until it was pressed against Frankenmutt's head. He nodded to Sam, who walked over to the monstrous dog and prodded its belly with his foot. When the creature didn't react, he prodded it harder. Still no response.

"Doesn't look like it's breathing," Sam said.

"Since when does that matter in our line of work?"

"True." Sam leveled his Beretta and put another round in the beast's side. Its body bucked with the impact, but otherwise it didn't move.

"I'm voting for dead," Dean said.

"I'm good with that."

Dean removed the shotgun from the creature's head and waited while Sam retrieved the doll and his phone. Sam tucked the doll under his arm and turned off the crying baby sound effect on his phone, tucked the device into a pocket, and returned. The two of them then crouched down to examine the patchwork dog's corpse. As ugly as the thing was, Dean expected it to smell like something that you'd find at the bottom of a slaughterhouse Dumpster, but it just smelled like a normal dog. He sniffed. Make that a normal dog covered in blood.

"The sections all look like parts of regular dogs," Sam said. "Except for the face. That's pretty messed up." He trailed a finger along the line of hairless tissue between the dog's right front leg and its shoulder. Similar lines crisscrossed the beast's body.

"Doesn't look much like scar tissue, does it?" Dean said.

Sam shook his head. "Doesn't feel like it, either. It's kind of... spongy."

A line of the strange flesh circled Frankenmutt's neck, and Dean reached out and touched it. It was firmer than normal skin, and when he pressed it in, it remained that way for a moment before slowly returning to its previous shape. *Weird*.

"I see what you mean. It's almost like some kind of... I don't know, glue or something."

"I was thinking the same thing."

Dean straightened, and the brothers regarded the body of the monster dog in silence for a time.

After a while, Sam asked, "Which end do you want?"

Dean considered for a moment. "Man, there's no good choice here, is there?" He took another look at the creature's distorted face and sighed. "I never thought I'd be saying this about an animal, but I'll take the ass. Try not to get too much blood on you."

They each took an end, lifted, and began carrying Frankenmutt out of the woods. Halfway back to the car, Sam stopped and turned his head sharply to the left.

Dean tensed, senses on high alert, ready for another attack. He looked in the same direction as Sam, but couldn't see anything but trees and underbrush.

"What is it?" he asked.

Sam didn't answer right away. He squinted, as if he were having a hard time focusing his eyes on whatever he was looking at. Finally, he shook his head as if attempting to clear it.

"For a minute, I thought... Never mind. It's nothing. Let's go. Frankenmutt's not getting any lighter."

The brothers continued lugging the dead dog, Dean unable to decide what bothered him more: that Sam's arms were trembling with the effort of carrying his half of the creature—Frankenmutt was a big boy, but he wasn't *that* heavy, not with the two of them sharing the load—or that it looked like his hallucinations were getting worse.

Just once, it would be nice if a hunt went down easy, he thought. *We stroll into town, find the Nasty Whatzit, walk up to it, gank it, and stroll on out. No muss, no fuss.*

Yeah, right. And maybe vampires would quit sucking blood and start chugging energy drinks instead.

He saw me.

Daniel wasn't sure how that was possible. The living couldn't see his kind, not even if he wanted them to. But the younger brother had stared right at him. Daniel had felt the youth's gaze bore into him. For the first time in all his long existence as a Reaper, he'd felt exposed, and he'd slipped behind an ash tree to conceal himself. He'd felt absurd, hiding like that, as if he were… well, mortal.

But once the shaggy-haired youth went back to helping his brother cart the corpse of the dead dog-thing away, Daniel caught the whiff of death coming off him, and realized what must have happened. He waited until they were out of sight, and then followed after them, careful not to make too much noise. Again, he felt ridiculous taking such precautions, but he had no idea how sharp the youth's death-perception had become, and he wasn't going to take any chances.

He found what he was looking for almost right away. The dog-thing's bullet-ravaged corpse had left a trail of blood drops in the brothers' wake, but he wasn't interested in those. It was the other trail that caught his attention. A thin wavering black line hovered an inch above the ground, thready and faint, like ink released in water. Daniel knelt to get a closer look at it. It was fading quickly, and he touched his index finger to a section of the shadow-line before it dissipated. He brought his fingertip, now smeared with a soot-like smudge, up to his nose. He sniffed a couple times before inserting his finger into his mouth. When he withdrew his finger a moment later, the tip was clean.

He was now certain what had happened to the younger brother, and it wasn't good. At least, not for the boy. But as for Daniel… he might be able to make this work in his favor.

He stood and continued following the brothers, amending his plans to take this unforeseen, but not entirely unwelcome, development into account.

Peter Martinez sat in front of his office computer monitor staring at rows of data displayed on the screen. He wasn't reviewing the information, at least not in the usual way. He'd purposely unfocused his gaze to the point where the numbers were blurry, and then he tried to relax and allow his mind to wander. He knew this data forward and backward, and he'd tried analyzing it using every logical method he could think of, without success. So today he'd decided to try a more creative approach. Instead of tackling the problem in a linear fashion, he was going to try turning his subconscious loose on it. As much as scientific advances were a result of step-by-step processes, they also were born in sudden unexpected bursts of insight, the fabled and often sought after Eureka! moment. Today Peter hoped to cultivate a moment of his own.

His office wasn't very large, nor was it impressive. If it hadn't been for the nameplate affixed to the wall outside, no one would have guessed that this was the office of the CEO and Head of Development for NuFlesh Biotech. Though considering that his office was located in a strip mall between a sub shop and a license bureau, and that the business had a total of five employees, including himself, he didn't see much point in putting on airs. He wore a long-sleeved red pullover and jeans, a step below corporate casual, which was fine as far as he was concerned. He was a scientist, not a stockbroker. He wore a full black beard, partially because he thought it made him look more intelligent—and a bit roguish—but mostly to hide the burn scars that covered the lower right half of his face. He did all his "paperwork" virtually, and aside from the computer, the top of his desk was empty. He had a few books on the shelf behind him, none of which he'd touched in who knew how long. His doctoral diploma hung on one wall, while on the opposite was a framed poster—a large black-and-white photo of Einstein sticking his tongue out. The poster was supposed to remind Peter not to take everything so seriously, but today the sight of it only pissed him off. He couldn't afford to let the stress get to him. Not if he wanted to create the optimal conditions for a subconscious breakthrough. And he badly needed one.

Two years, seven months, eight days. That was how long he'd been struggling to solve this particular problem, and at this point, he was willing to try almost anything. The financial state of his company wasn't exactly "robust," as the corporate types would put it, and if he didn't make some progress on the new formula soon… He thrust the thought from his mind. Worrying about money was no way to relax.

He gazed at the screen and allowed his breathing to become slow and even, and before long he felt his body relax against his office chair. That's when it kicked in.

The Itch.

It began on his right shoulder blade, little more than the sensation of a feather brushing against his skin. He could ignore that. But it soon spread across his entire back, his chest, down his right arm, up his neck and across the right side of his face, building in intensity until it felt as if a thousand ants were crawling over his skin. That he *couldn't* ignore.

"Don't scratch," he whispered. He gripped the armrests of his chair tight, fingers digging into the padding. He knew from long, painful experience that not only didn't scratching make the itch go away, once he got started, he wouldn't be able to stop until he'd clawed bloody runnels in his flesh. Even then the itching would continue.

Peter knew it was common for burn victims to experience discomfort like his, even long after their burns had healed and scar tissue formed. In his case, that had been almost three decades before. He'd gotten his scars as a result of a house fire caused by his idiot of a stepfather falling asleep on the couch one night while smoking. Peter and his mother got out of the house in time, but his stepfather hadn't made it. His mother hadn't lasted long, either. She'd died en route to the hospital, not from her burns—severe as they were—but from a heart attack. Peter had only been eleven at the time. Even though twenty-seven years and more operations than he cared to think about had passed since then, the Itch, when it came, was as bad as ever.

The many doctors and specialists he'd seen over the years had prescribed a variety of remedies for the Itch: topical lotions to stretch and loosen the scar tissue, hypoallergenic lotions, anti-itch creams like hydrocortisone, and analgesic creams such as lidocaine. None of them worked except lidocaine, and even that only managed to take the edge off the Itch. There was only one treatment he'd ever found that provided relief, and he'd used up the last of it a couple days before. He'd tried contacting his supplier, but so far the man hadn't responded to any of his voicemails or texts. If he didn't get in touch soon, Peter didn't know what he was going to—

His desk phone rang, and the sound made him jump. He snatched the receiver off the hook and answered the call, speaking through gritted teeth.

"Damn it, Allison! I *told* you I didn't want—"

"I'm sorry, Mr. Martinez. I know you asked me not to disturb you, but Mr. Dippel is here, and I thought—"

"Send him in." He hung up without saying goodbye.

He didn't like being brusque with his office assistant, but he couldn't help it. When the Itch was upon him like this, it took everything he had not to scream. He remembered one of his doctors telling him that while he was certain the itching was real, it couldn't possibly be as intense as Peter reported.

I'm confident there's a somatic component at work here, the doctor had said.

Peter wasn't an MD, but he was a biochemist, and he'd known damn well what the doctor had *really* meant. *Psycho*somatic. Unlike most people, Peter knew that psychosomatic sensations were real, but they were caused by mental processes rather than disease or injury. The simplest example was the stomach pain some people experienced before a stressful event, such as an important exam or presentation at work. The pain was real, the physical processes that caused it were real, but it was triggered by stress. Peter's understanding of what the doctor had said didn't mean he agreed with it, though.

There's a strong correlation between people who experience somatic pain and those who suffer from post-traumatic stress disorder. The fire you survived…

Peter shoved the memory away.

With every fiber of his being, all the way down to the subatomic level, he was certain that the Itch was solely the result of the terrible injuries he'd suffered as a child, and not related to his emotional state in any way, shape, or form.

Normally he would have gone into the outer office to greet Dippel, but he feared that if he took his hands off the chair's armrests, he'd start digging his fingernails into his skin and wouldn't be able to stop. So he sat and gripped his chair even tighter and waited. A moment later there was a soft knock at the door. Peter tried to say, *Come in,* but the words came out as a pained grunting. They were enough to get the message across, though. The door opened and Conrad entered.

"Hello, Peter. As always, it's good to see you. Please, don't get up. I can see that you're… concentrating." Conrad gave him a thin smile as he took a seat in the chair in front of Peter's desk.

Peter was struck anew by the strength of Conrad's presence. Whenever the man was in the room, everything seemed to gravitate toward him. People's attention, for one thing. It was hard as hell to take your eyes off him. It took an effort even to blink. But it was more than that. The air flowed toward him, leaving the rest of the room hot and stuffy, and he drew in light as well, illuminating himself more brightly while deepening the shadows everywhere else. It was as if he exerted his own manner of gravitational pull, one that was somehow more psychic in nature than physical. It was a ridiculous idea, Peter knew—he was a scientist, for God's sake!—but it was one he couldn't shake.

As always, Conrad wore a suit and tie, making him look more like a business owner than Peter. If it was possible, the man appeared even more cadaverous than the last time Peter had seen him, and not for the first time he wondered if Conrad was battling some sort of disease, cancer maybe. But despite his appearance, the man always seemed to be alert and filled with energy. After nearly thirty years of having people look at his own burn scars first before noticing there was a human being attached to them—if indeed they ever noticed—Peter certainly knew better than to judge by appearances. One thing he liked about Conrad, in fact, was that the man never seemed bothered by his scars. It wasn't that he was able to put aside his disgust, which was what most people who considered themselves enlightened did. Conrad was well aware of Peter's scars, but he wasn't repulsed by them. He always met Peter's gaze, and never averted his eyes. Peter even occasionally had the uneasy feeling that Conrad *liked* looking at his scars.

"I'm sorry that I haven't returned your messages," Conrad

continued. "I've been especially busy of late. I had hoped to find you in good health, but regrettably, I see that isn't the case. I take it that your supply of my special unguent has been expended?"

You know damn well it has, you bastard! I left you enough messages saying so!

Out loud, Peter simply said, "Yes."

Conrad smiled. "Then it is indeed fortuitous that I stopped in for a visit today."

He reached into the inner breast pocket of his jacket and removed a glass vial with an old-fashioned cork stopper. The contents was a pale green-tinged yellow, an unappealing color, but Peter didn't care what it looked like. He only cared that it worked.

Conrad placed the vial on the desk top, but when Peter tried to grab it, he snatched it away.

"My usual fee?" he asked.

Yes, yes, YES! Peter nodded.

Satisfied, Conrad handed over the vial. Peter snatched it from him, pulled the cork out with his teeth, and spat it onto the desk. Then, without a scrap of self-consciousness, he stood, pulled off his shirt, and threw it to the floor. Reddish scar tissue covered the right side of his body from the lower half of his face, down to his mid-abdomen, including three-quarters of his right arm, as well as his right shoulder and shoulder blade. The air should have felt good on his exposed skin, but all it did was intensify the Itch, which had already reached maddening levels. Peter dumped some of the thick oily unguent into his palm and began smearing it on, moving as fast as he could.

"Not too much," Conrad cautioned. "A little goes a long way."

Peter ignored him and kept slathering it onto his body. Relief was almost instantaneous. A cool tingling sensation began to spread across his scarred flesh, the Itch receding in its wake. He let out a sigh and collapsed back into his chair, not caring if he smeared any of the goop on the fabric. He must look a sight, shirtless, scar tissue glistening with a sheen of oily yellow-green gunk, but he didn't care. All that mattered was the Itch was gone.

"Thank you," he said.

Conrad acknowledged Peter's gratitude with a slow nod.

"I know I've said it before, but I wish you'd give me the formula for this stuff. I'd pay any price for it."

"I do not wish to be insulting, but given the current state of your business, such an offer can only be hyperbole."

Peter *was* insulted, but he knew he couldn't argue the point. He'd developed NuFlesh—the product, not the business he'd named for it—for people like him. NuFlesh was artificial skin that paramedics could use as a temporary wound patch until they could get an accident victim to the hospital. In that regard, it was successful. It did indeed seal off wounds and burns, keeping them protected and free of infection. Unfortunately, it tended to decay after an hour, two at the most, and tests had suggested it might be toxic, making long-term use impossible. So even if Peter managed to solve the decay problem—which was his current focus— he would then have to turn his attention to the toxicity issue.

All of this added up to a sad bottom line for NuFlesh Biotech, and he and his employees were far from rolling in money. It was the major reason he'd located his business in Brennan. Office space was cheap. If he could make his artificial skin work, he'd change the world of medicine forever—and get stinking rich into the bargain. But that, as the saying goes, was a mighty big *if*.

"Besides, even if I gave you the formula, I doubt you'd be able to replicate it successfully," Conrad said, then smiled. "After all, it isn't as if you haven't already made the attempt, hmm?"

Peter could feel himself flush with embarrassment. It was true. He'd attempted to analyze the chemical unguent on several occasions, and while he'd been able to determine the ingredients and their proportions easily enough, he couldn't make the damned stuff work, no matter how hard he tried.

"You've told me the unguent is an ancient formula once used by the Egyptians to protect their skin from dry heat."

"My own variation on that formula, but essentially, yes," Conrad confirmed.

Peter forced a smile. "Let me guess: the reason I can't recreate it is that I lack the magic touch."

Conrad's smile widened. "Precisely."

Peter scowled. He hated it when he had the feeling that Conrad was toying with him.

The man had approached him a few months before, saying that he'd read about NuFlesh on the company's website and was intrigued by its promise. He'd wanted to purchase fifty pounds of the stuff for his own unspecified research needs. Peter's patent on the most recent version of the NuFlesh

formula was still pending, and he was reluctant at first to
allow someone who might be a potential competitor to have
that much of the material. Then, when Conrad had told
him he had a treatment that would relieve Peter's periodic
itching—although how the man had known about that,
Peter had no idea—he'd been skeptical. But Conrad had
delivered, and Peter had been only too happy to let him have
his pound of artificial flesh, times fifty, in exchange. Since
then, Conrad, who'd always presented himself as something
of an old-world gentleman, had become increasingly snide
and even cruel at times, and Peter would have been happy
to sever their relationship... if he hadn't needed Conrad's
mysterious unguent so damned bad.

"Honestly, I don't know what you're doing with all the
NuFlesh you've... I guess purchased isn't the right word.
Bartered, I suppose. You know it's unstable and potentially
toxic to boot."

"It suits my current needs as is," Conrad said. "And I can,
as people say these days, work around those problems."

Peter burned with curiosity. No matter how many times
he tried to pry details out of Conrad about what he wanted
NuFlesh for, the man never gave away anything. He wondered
if Conrad had found a way to solve the decay and toxicity
issues. He had no idea what the man's educational and
professional backgrounds were—again, Conrad had resisted
his attempts to find out—but he gave the impression that he
was well acquainted with the sciences, especially chemistry.
The unguent was proof of that. Maybe if he offered Conrad a
job? Not that he had any money to pay him. But if he made

him a partner…

"I'd like a hundred pounds this time," Conrad said. "If at all possible."

Peter unconsciously rubbed the scar tissue beneath his beard as he thought. His fingers came away sticky with unguent. "That's just about all I have on hand at the moment. It takes a while to manufacture, you know, and there are experiments scheduled…"

Conrad once again reached into his inner jacket pocket, removed a second stoppered vial, and placed it on the desk.

Peter looked upon it with an addict's hungry gaze.

"You have a deal."

As he reached for it, Conrad grabbed his hand and stopped him. It was the first time the man had touched him, and Peter was surprised by how cold his flesh was.

"A warning. My unguent comes with certain… side effects if used too frequently and in large amounts. It is why I have made sure to parcel it out rather than give you too much at one time. Take care not to use it more than once every two days. Three would be preferable. You must heed my instructions, regardless of how intense your itching may become. Do you understand?"

"Sure. Whatever you say."

Conrad looked deep into his eyes, as if trying to gauge his sincerity, before finally releasing his hand. Peter grabbed the second vial and held it close to his face. The yellow-green contents resembled bottled mucus, but right now it was one of the most beautiful sights he'd ever seen.

Screw you, Itch, he thought.

Although it might have been his imagination, he could've sworn he felt a slight momentary irritation behind his right ear, as if the Itch was saying, *Don't worry. I'll be back—soon. And then we'll really have some fun!*

A short time later, Conrad drove away from the strip mall, ninety pounds of NuFlesh on the back seat of his black SUV, sealed in airtight plastic and packed in unmarked cardboard boxes. It was less than he wanted, but it was all Peter had, so it would have to do. Peter promised to call him when he had more made, and considering how badly the man needed his unguent, Conrad had no doubt he'd make good on his promise.

NuFlesh was amazing material, and although Conrad had no idea if Peter would ever perfect it, it didn't matter as far as his purpose was concerned. As he'd told the man, the current NuFlesh formula was sufficient for his needs—as long as he added a few alchemical touches of his own.

There was much that Conrad didn't like about the modern world—for the most part the people were unrefined and ill-mannered, and they seemed incapable of concentrating on a single task for any length of time—but he found the Internet exceedingly useful. He'd been fortunate to discover the NuFlesh website one evening while doing research, and had been filled with excitement, hoping that at last he'd found the answer he'd been searching so long for. The material had worked better than he'd dared dream, and now, after three long centuries, he was finally on the verge of seeing his vision made reality.

"Praise Hel," he whispered.

In addition to the NuFlesh, there were two metal coolers in the storage area behind the SUV's back seat. In each of them, packed in ice and wrapped in strips of cloth soaked in an alchemical mixture of his own devising, were the other supplies Catherine needed. She'd given him a list, and he'd gone out last night and done his best to procure all the items on it. Unfortunately, the two homeless men that he'd chosen as donors hadn't been in the best of health—he'd seen evidence of cancer in one man's lungs in addition to an enlarged heart, and he'd found cirrhosis in the other's liver along with a surprisingly large tumor in the brain. He'd been forced to leave the affected organs behind, for even with the skilled application of NuFlesh, they would be useless. But he'd managed to obtain most of the items Catherine desired, and he thought she would be pleased. If she needed anything more, he could always go out again that night. Not only was he highly practiced at procurement, no matter how many centuries he'd done it, the work never got old for him.

It's the simple pleasures, he thought, and smiled.

He felt a sudden vibration in his front pants pocket that startled him. He removed one hand from the steering wheel, reached into his pocket, and pulled out his cell phone. As always, he thought he'd never get used to the damnable contraptions. He looked at the screen display, saw Catherine's name, and answered it.

"Hello, Catherine. It's quite a coincidence that you called. Even as we speak, I am on my way to your home to deliver—"

She cut him off, something a well-bred woman would

never have done in his day. "Have you seen today's paper?" she demanded.

At first he thought the bodies of the two homeless men had been discovered, and she was upset. But he dismissed that possibility at once. In all the time they'd been "collaborating," she had never directly addressed the issue of where he came by the raw material he brought her, even though he knew it made her uncomfortable. No, it had to be something else.

"Has the dog struck again? Do not concern yourself. After I have brought your supplies, I will go in search of the beast and—"

"It's not the damned dog! It's something else."

She'd done it again! If he didn't need the woman's medical skills so badly… Her words sank in then.

"Something… else?"

She proceeded to tell him.

SEVEN

"What's the name of this place we're looking for again?" Dean asked.

"NuFlesh Biotech."

They were driving through downtown Brennan, after a stop back at the motel to do a little research, scarf down some fast-food takeout, and change into their suits. Dean had eaten a half-pound bacon cheeseburger with everything on it—and extra bacon, of course—along with a large order of fries. Now the food was lying in his stomach like a lead brick, and he was beginning to wish he'd gone Sam's route and had a salad. Although he would never admit that to his brother. If he did, he knew Sam would see that as an opportunity to convert him to the Cult of Good Nutrition, and he'd never hear the end of it.

"NuFlesh. That sound ominous to you?"

"Only a lot," Sam said. He took a sip of his extra-large coffee. They'd stopped on the way to pick it up, and he'd ordered it black this time, with two shots of espresso.

Dean was frustrated. Despite the fact that Sam had convinced him that dealing with Frankenmutt might lead them to some kind of new weapon they could use against Dick Roman, the longer they spent in Brennan, the more antsy he was becoming. Roman and the other Leviathan were out there, stuffing their fanged faces with human flesh while continuing to advance their plans for world conquest, and the shape-shifting sons of bitches weren't about to put their program on hold while the Winchester brothers tended to other business. The Leviathan were like a deadly disease that would continue to spread unchecked unless something was done about it, and hanging around this podunk town ganking freakshow dogs wasn't doing anything to stop them.

It didn't help that Sam seemed to be even fewer fries short of a Happy Meal than usual. Dean was certain his brother had experienced some sort of hallucination in the woods that he didn't want to talk about, and he was guzzling coffee like it was water and he was a man crossing the Sahara on foot. Dean was no stranger to the concept of self-medicating, but he wasn't sure what Sam hoped to accomplish by loading up on caffeine. It seemed to him that all that stimulation would only make Sam jittery and anxious, which in turn would make it harder for him to keep control of his mental state. Then again, Dean preferred "medicine" that took the edge off rather than sharpened it, so maybe it was simply a matter of to each his own. Still, he was determined to keep an eye on Sam which, he had to admit to himself, was pretty much what he normally did. So in a way, when it came to the Winchesters' screwed up lives, he supposed everything was more or less normal.

It didn't help his mood that Frankenmutt's corpse was starting to stink up the crapmobile big-time. The monster dog was in the trunk, wrapped in a couple motel towels, but its stink had filtered through the car's interior, and was making his already queasy stomach worse.

Definitely a salad next time, he thought. *Maybe a taco salad, with extra meat, salsa, and sour cream.*

"I like it better when the things we kill disintegrate when they die," he said. "Less mess to deal with."

"Definitely less stink," Sam agreed. "I'm not sure, but I think Frankenmutt's decaying faster than normal. Which only makes sense if it was made out of parts of already dead dogs. Once it's dead—or dead again, I guess—whatever force was arresting the decomposition process is gone, and so—"

"It's bye-bye Frankenmutt, hello nasty pile of rotting meat."

"Pretty much. I just hope there's enough left by the time we get to NuFlesh."

"You really think the guy that owns the place can help us?"

"I don't know. But you saw the pictures on their site. The kind of stuff they make looks an awful lot like those weird scar lines on Frankenmutt."

When they had returned to the motel room, Sam had gotten on the Internet and worked his tech geek mojo until he found the NuFlesh website. It had taken him a while, which surprised Dean. Usually Sam could find information on the net as easily as Dean could find beef jerky on a convenience store shelf, but considering Sam's starting point was little more than the search term "weird scars," he supposed it was impressive that he'd come up with anything at all.

NuFlesh was in the business of making artificial skin that, according to the website, had "profound medical applications that could eventually change the world." From what Dean had seen, though, they still had quite a way to go before they could fulfill that promise. The stuff looked more like flesh-colored rubber than actual skin, and when it was applied to a person, it looked far less natural than skin grafts did. Sam had also discovered—buried deep in the site so that it wouldn't be obvious to the casual browser—that the success record of NuFlesh was, to put it kindly, modest. It didn't sound to Dean like the stuff worked well enough to patch a paper cut, let alone hold together a bunch of dead doggy parts. But he had to admit, it did look kind of like Frankenmutt's scars, so he supposed talking to NuFlesh's creator was worth a shot. With any luck, he'd turn out to be the Dr. Frankenstein they were looking for, and they could get the hunt over with and get back to what really mattered: taking down Dick Roman and his army of oversized piranha.

"Speaking of Frankenmutt, how's that bite doing?" Dean asked.

Sam took another sip of his hi-test coffee. "Good. Still no sign of infection." He crossed his legs and pulled up the cuff of his jeans to show Dean where he'd been bitten. True to his word, the skin there looked healthy. The bite marks were scabbed over, and there was no swelling or reddening, not even any bruising. Dean found the latter a bit odd. Frankenmutt wouldn't have won any beauty contests when he was alive, but he'd been at least as strong as an ordinary dog, if not stronger. The pressure of his bite should have left some kind of mark on Sam to accompany the puncture wounds caused by his teeth, but there was nothing. Maybe Dean had overestimated the monster dog's strength—or maybe not. It was one more thing to keep his eye on.

It didn't take them long to find NuFlesh Biotech. Dean was surprised to discover the business was located in a strip mall.

"It's not exactly what I expected," he said.

"What did you think we'd find? A rundown castle with a giant lightning rod jutting from one of the towers and a hunchbacked assistant lurking behind a parapet?"

Dean shrugged. "No, but I figured it would look more… I don't know, sciencey."

He pulled the car into a space in front of NuFlesh and parked.

"It *is* a start-up company," Sam pointed out. "This is probably the best location they can afford."

Dean shut off the ignition. He grimaced as the car's engine juddered and knocked a couple times before cutting out. God, he missed the Impala!

We'll be together again, baby, he thought. *Soon as Daddy kills Dick Roman.*

"Maybe so," Dean said, "but it doesn't have any style. It looks more like a dry cleaner's than the lair of an evil genius."

"We don't have any proof yet that Dr. Martinez had anything to do with Frankenmutt. And even if he did, why would he want to advertise that he's Brennan's version of Dr. Frankenstein? Look at the Leviathan. They might be ancient creatures from the dawn of creation, but they adapted to the modern world right away. They blend in. Maybe that's what

Martinez is doing."

"That's another thing. Martinez—it's not a good mad doctor name. Frankenstein, Jekyll, Moreau, Phibes. Those are creepy names. Martinez, not so much."

They got out of the car. Sam finished off his coffee and tossed the empty cup into a trash receptacle on the sidewalk in front of NuFlesh. As they walked toward NuFlesh's front door, Dean could smell that they'd both been perfumed with *eau de Frankenmutt*. He figured they'd need to get their suits dry cleaned after this was over. For a brief moment, he was grateful that they weren't driving the Impala. He'd have hated his baby getting all funked up with dead monster dog stink.

Inside the small reception area, it quickly became clear they smelled worse than Dean feared. The office assistant—a bird-thin woman in her fifties with braided white hair—pursed her lips and turned her head slightly to the side as she spoke with them in a futile attempt to keep her nose as far away from their stench as possible. They showed her their fake bureau IDs, she made a quick call, and a moment later a side door opened and Dr. Peter Martinez came striding out.

Now that's more like it, Dean thought, and was instantly ashamed of himself. The man had obviously suffered serious burn injuries sometime in the past.

Dean knew better than to judge anyone based on their appearance. At least anyone human. When it came to supernatural predators, however, most of the time you really could judge a book by its cover. If something looked like it wanted to eat your flesh or devour your soul, it probably did.

Even though Dean knew better, he couldn't help thinking

that Martinez's burn scars made him look like a perfect evil scientist. Of course, his clothes could use some work. A flannel shirt, jeans, and running shoes didn't scream *I'm a guy who stitches together pieces of dead people in my lab!* Maybe if he added a white coat with a few bloodstains on it…

"I'm Dr. Martinez." He smiled, the unscarred corner of his mouth rising higher than the other. He shook Dean's hand, then Sam's. "How can I help you gentlemen?"

Dean found himself staring at the man's burn-scarred flesh. He'd seen plenty of scars in his time—hell, he had more than a few of his own, as did Sam—and he wasn't normally put off by them, but now that Martinez stood only a couple feet from them, Dean could see that there was something not quite right about his. They were moist and glistening, as if coated with petroleum jelly, and the flesh sagged. The whole effect made Martinez look as if he were a wax figure that was in the process of slowly melting.

Dean glanced at Sam, and could tell by his brother's expression that he found the man's strange scars equally disturbing. More telling than that, though, was the office manager's reaction. When Martinez had first appeared, she'd gasped, and now her eyes were wide, as if she couldn't believe what she was seeing. Whatever was going on with Martinez's scars, it wasn't normal.

Dean revised his earlier judgment. Dr. Martinez was definitely a candidate for Brennan's local mad scientist.

Sam started to introduce them, but halfway through he broke into a huge yawn.

"Sorry," he mumbled. "Late night on the job."

Dean shot him a look. "As my partner was saying, we've been called in to help with the investigation into the strange deaths that have occurred here in town over the last few days. We think you might be able to help."

Dean watched Martinez closely for any reaction to the mention of the wasting deaths that he'd come to think of as The Pruning, but the man appeared to have none beyond puzzlement.

"I'm a biochemist, not a disease specialist. I'm not sure I can be of much use to you."

"We think the deaths might have a link to NuFlesh," Sam said. "Not the company itself so much as your product."

Martinez frowned. "I don't see how that's possible. Not only doesn't NuFlesh create any kind of side effects that could account for those deaths, the product's still in the development stage and isn't in wide use in the public sector. In fact, I don't know of anyone in town that has a NuFlesh graft."

The man reached up to scratch at the sagging scarred flesh on the side of his face in what looked to Dean like a nervous habit. His fingernails opened thin runnels in the puckered skin that immediately filled with a yellowish fluid, but he didn't seem to notice. Dean's stomach did a flip.

Salad. Next time, for sure.

"We've got something we'd like you to look at," Sam said. "It'll only take a moment of your time, and we'd really appreciate it."

Sam kept his gaze fastened on Martinez's eyes, and Dean knew his brother was trying not to stare at the fluid-filled lines the man had carved into his face.

"Of course. Glad to help."

"Excellent," Sam said. "It's outside."

As the three of them left the office, Dean saw that the office manager had gone pale. Between enduring the stink of Frankenmutt's corpse that clung to them and seeing her boss mutilate himself, she looked like she too was regretting whatever she'd chosen to have for lunch.

Dean's stomach gurgled. *I know just how you feel, sister,* he thought.

Sam would have killed for another coffee right then, maybe with three shots of espresso this time. He was having a hell of a time keeping his eyes open, and he was beginning to think that it was more than simple weariness. Maybe it was his body's reaction to having to struggle against the madness that roiled within him. Fighting the crazy took a lot out of him, and it was only natural that it took a toll on his energy levels. He wondered how much longer he could keep going like this before his system had had enough and went into full shutdown. Maybe instead of just crashing in some motel room for a few hours, he'd slip into a deep slumber from which he'd never awaken. He was surprised to find that the thought didn't scare him. It was actually kind of comforting, in a weird way. He'd read about very old people who looked forward to dying, seeing it as a chance to lay down the burdens they'd carried for so long and finally rest. Given everything that had happened to him already in his relatively young life, he understood that attitude better than most people his age, but he never thought he'd end up feeling that way himself.

Getting a little too morbid, he told himself. Best antidote for that was to concentrate on the job at hand.

One good thing: at least he hadn't hallucinated Dr. Martinez's oozing, sagging scar tissue. He could tell from Dean's reaction that he'd seen and was disturbed by it, too. So, that was a relief. Sam had no idea what could cause the man's scar tissue to ooze like that. As far as he knew, old scars didn't suppurate. He wondered if Martinez had tried using his formula for NuFlesh to repair his face. Though he had said that the product was still in development. If that was the case, then maybe the weird scar lines on Frankenmutt had nothing to do with NuFlesh, which would mean that he and Dean were, to coin a pun, barking up the wrong tree.

They reached the car and Dean opened the trunk.

"This is the best the bureau can afford?" Martinez said as he eyed the ancient vehicle.

"Budget cutbacks," Dean said without missing a beat. "You know how it is."

A truly horrendous stench wafted from the trunk's interior, causing all three of them to take a step backward. Sam was grateful it was November. He didn't want to think about how bad Frankenmutt would have smelled if it had been August.

"What in the hell *is* that?" Martinez said, hand clamped over the lower half of his face in what Sam knew was a futile attempt to block out the stink.

"You tell us." Dean threw back the top of the blanket covering Frankenmutt and exposed the creature's ravaged corpse.

Dr. Martinez stared at the beast, but Sam and Dean kept their gazes focused on him. They were looking for some sign of recognition in the man's eyes, but all Sam saw in his expression was disgust. Either the man was a damn good actor, or he had never seen Frankenmutt before. Then his disgust turned to confusion and then curiosity. He lowered his hand from his face and stepped forward to get a closer look.

"Is this a *dog*?"

"From the looks of it, more like several," Dean said.

Martinez leaned even closer, and Sam was impressed that he could do so without gagging. He reached into his shirt pocket and withdrew a pen. Using it as a probe, he touched the tip to the fleshy line dividing Frankenmutt's rear leg from his body.

"I see now why you wanted to consult me. This material resembles NuFlesh."

"Resembles?" Sam said.

Martinez continued poking at Frankenmutt with his pen. "The color and texture are both somewhat different. It's more pliable than NuFlesh, more like the actual skin."

"But it *is* artificial," Sam pressed.

"Undoubtedly." Martinez gave him a quick lopsided smile. "Whatever this thing is, I think it's safe to say it wasn't born this way."

Dean gave Sam an exasperated look.

Undaunted, Sam continued. "Assuming that this… animal is what it appears to be, could NuFlesh—or something like it—be used to join the separate parts together?"

"Like some kind of meat glue," Dean added.

Martinez straightened and stepped back away from the trunk. Sam noticed he didn't return his pen to his pocket.

Sam didn't blame him.

"Are you serious?"

"Humor those of us without PhDs in biochemistry," Dean said.

Martinez thought for a moment. As he did, he scratched at his face again. The scar tissue broke and oozed more fluid, and sagged another fraction of an inch.

"I designed NuFlesh as an artificial substance for use in skin grafts, though I've always thought it could one day be employed in transplants. But that's only in theory. Such applications are years, maybe even decades, away." He looked at Frankenmutt again. "Even if someone has managed to develop their own NuFlesh formula that's more advanced than mine, the hurdles they'd have to overcome to create a thing like this are staggering. Fusing bone, connecting muscles and nerves... Why the problems with tissue rejection alone—"

"We get the picture," Dean interrupted. "It's not exactly the kind of thing you can do with a junior mad scientist kit and a little old-fashioned elbow grease."

"Hardly," Martinez agreed. "I'm confident in saying that no one on Earth has the capability to make an abomination like this. Although why anyone would want to is beyond me. You believe it has some connection to the recent spate of mysterious deaths?"

"Yeah." Dean drew the blanket back over Frankenmutt's corpse and closed the trunk. "We figured people took one look at it, and died from an overdose of ugly."

Sam gave Dean a warning look, then turned to Martinez. "There's no risk of contagion."

"I assumed that was the case," Martinez said, "or else you would've observed stricter containment protocols." He glanced at the closed trunk. "Or any, for that matter. I mean, not even the federal government could be that stupid, right?"

Sam glanced at Dean, but neither of them said anything.

"When you find out where that thing came from, please let me know," Martinez said. "Professional curiosity, you understand. Now, if there's nothing further, I do have work I should get back to."

"One last question," Dean said. "Could this artificial flesh stuff be used to make a guy with two heads and four arms?"

Peter stood on the sidewalk outside his business and watched the agents drive away in their ancient wreck of a car, taking the corpse of the misbegotten creature—and its horrendous stink—with them. After they had gone, he took his phone from his pocket and keyed in Conrad's number. While he waited for him to answer, he idly scratched his face. The Itch was mild, far better than it had been, but it still bothered him. When he was done speaking with Conrad, he'd go back inside and apply more of the man's special unguent. True, Conrad had cautioned him against using too much, but it was the only thing that gave Peter any relief. Really, what was the worst that could happen?

He didn't feel the viscous fluid that oozed from the furrows he gouged in his scarred flesh, and even if he had, he probably wouldn't have cared.

The embalming room in the basement of Harrison Brauer's

Legacy Center—in plainer language, a funeral parlor—was cramped and clammy, although he preferred to think of it as cozy and cool. The colorless walls and tiled floor seemed to glow in the stark fluorescent light, and if he spent too much time working down here, his eyes would start to water. If it got really bad, he'd don a pair of sunglasses, making him, at least in his own mind, the hippest mortician in town. The air held an iron tang that he'd long ago gotten used to, and which, truth to tell, he'd come to find rather pleasant. A pair of white marble tables occupied the center of the chamber, and above them a metal showerhead hung from the ceiling, just in case Harrison needed to wash away a particularly nasty spill. Set into the floor between the tables was a large grated drain, which he often thought of as a perfect metaphor for the end of life. Ultimately, everything that lived ended up washed down the Great Drain of the Universe.

Next to one of the tables was a gurney, and lying face up on it, naked, was Mason McKelvey, owner of McKelvey's Motorama, Brennan's most successful used car dealership. He'd been brought in less than an hour before, after spending the last nine days of his life in a hospital bed as his kidneys slowly ceased functioning. A shame, really, as he'd only been in his early sixties; not young, but then again, not all that old, either. Harrison had never bought a car from Mason—the funeral business had treated him well, and he could afford to purchase his vehicles new—but he knew the man from both the rotary club and the town's merchants' association. A nice enough fellow, if a bit loud and self-serving. Though as he'd been a salesman, and by all accounts, cold-blooded and ruthless when it came to forging a deal, Harrison figured the man's jovial obnoxiousness was par for the course. When most people came to him, lying naked and statue-still, they seemed diminished somehow; smaller, sunken in on themselves, skin sallow and hard like wax figures. Mason was no exception. A thin man with a surprisingly thick shock of wild white hair, a sharp nose, and oversized ears, he appeared almost comical despite his current surroundings. Down here in the embalming room, there was nothing about Mason McKelvey to indicate the position of power and respect he'd held in life. Not for the first time, Mason thought that death truly was the great equalizer.

Harrison certainly understood how surface appearances didn't always show the person within, for he himself defied the stereotype that most people had of morticians. Instead of looking like Gomez Addams—grim black suit, corpse-white complexion, mad gleam in his eyes—he was tall, ruddy-faced, and rotund, like a clean-shaven Santa Claus. His demeanor matched his appearance. He had a constant smile on his face, and he laughed often and easily, a loud infectious sound that came from deep in his chest, inviting everyone who heard it to join in.

Harrison shifted Mason from the gurney onto one of the marble tables with an ease born of equal parts strength and long practice. He wheeled the gurney into a corner of the room to get it out of the way, and then returned to consider Mason. The first steps in preparing a client for embalming are simple: scrub the skin, clean the nails, shampoo the hair, and then massage the limbs to break up rigor mortis. Then the mouth is sewn shut and the facial features carefully posed before the body stiffens. After that, the process becomes more involved. The blood is drawn, the stomach emptied, and the body filled with arterial firming fluid, which also gives the skin color. Harrison preferred using Index 32 lithol, which he purchased from a specialist supply company.

The tools of Harrison's trade surrounded him: the trocar that emptied out his clients' stomachs, the scalpels he used to dig into their arteries, the Duotronic pump that injected chemicals into their bodies, causing them to give off a vinegar-like scent. But he didn't reach for any of these. Instead, he pulled open a drawer and removed a makeup kit. He placed it on the table next to Mason's head, opened it, and went to work.

Half an hour later, he was finished. Harrison stepped back to admire the results.

He had covered Mason's face, ears, and neck with white, outlined his lips with bright red to create a garish smile, and painted a large black dollar sign over each eye. On the left cheek he'd written the word "Buy" in black, and on the right he'd written "Sell." He'd combed Mason's hair up and back, sprayed it so it would remain in place, and then colored it green to represent money.

He removed a hand mirror from the makeup kit and held it in front of Mason's new face. "What do you think? You've heard of a clown car, right? Well, now you're a car clown!"

Harrison laughed, but evidently Mason didn't get the joke, for he remained silent. *Screw him.* Harrison thought it was funny.

He returned the mirror to the kit, walked over to the counter, and picked up his camera. He then spent the next several minutes taking pictures of Mason from different angles.

"You know you're just going to have to clean all that off."

The voice startled Harrison, but he recognized it almost immediately. Instead of turning to look at the speaker, he continued shooting photos as he answered.

"I'll admit that mine is a transitory art, but that's what makes it so special. I reveal my clients' inner nature, bring it to the surface for perhaps the first and only time since the day they were born, and then I restore the more familiar appearance their family and friends expect. But for a short interval at least, if only down here with me, they become their truest, most profound selves."

Satisfied he'd gotten some good shots for his latest scrapbook—he'd already filled seven others—he lowered his camera and finally turned to face Conrad.

Conrad stepped forward from the shadowy corner where he'd been standing and approached the table where Mason lay. Harrison didn't question how Conrad had managed to enter the embalming room without his hearing him. He knew that he became so focused when practicing his art—which he considered his true vocation—that a bomb could go off behind him and he'd barely notice. Besides, Conrad had a way of moving snake-silent when he wanted to.

Conrad glanced at Mason's altered face. "I suppose it was his ears and nose that gave you the idea to make him up as a clown."

"That, and the awful TV commercials he made for his

dealership. He was one of those car salesmen who always talk too loud and fast when they're on camera, you know?"

"Death shouldn't be mocked like this," Conrad said. "It is sacred."

Harrison didn't attach any mystic or religious significance to death. As far as he was concerned, it was only a biological process, no more important or meaningful than flipping off a light switch when you left a room.

"To what do I owe the pleasure of this visit?" he asked to change the subject. "Should I assume that you're in need of the kind of materials that only I can supply?"

"Thank you, but no. At the moment, I happen to be well stocked."

Harrison frowned. "Nothing personal, but I didn't take you to be the type to make social calls."

"I'm not." Mason's body lay between them, but now Conrad began slowly walking around the table, approaching Harrison. "Do you remember when I first came to you?"

"Of course." How could he forget the day a well-dressed, overly formal man entered his parlor and introduced himself as Conrad Dippel? Conrad—who looked far more like an archetypal mortician than Harrison ever would—had brought with him several containers of a material called NuFlesh and a business proposition.

"I sought you out for several reasons. One was your profession. It is an ancient and noble one which my lady well regards. Another was your surname: Bauer. It means *brewer* in German. My lady has always held a fondness for the Germanic people, and I myself am honored to claim that heritage as well."

Harrison had heard Conrad speak of his *lady* before, but he had no idea who he was referring to. Some sort of supervisor, he supposed.

Conrad continued. "Not to mention the fact that you have access to certain 'materials,' as you call them, along with facilities suitable for working with them. Also, I asked around town about you and discovered you had a reputation for somewhat eccentric behavior. Not an uncommon prejudice when it comes to those who devote themselves to the funereal arts, I admit, but I found the rumors intriguing."

Conrad had reached Harrison's side of the table and now stood only inches from him. Given his height and girth, Harrison rarely felt physically threatened, but even though he outweighed Conrad by a good margin, he felt intimidated by the man, and it was all he could do to keep from shrinking back in his presence.

"However, after working together for several weeks, it became apparent to me that while you have sufficient…" He glanced at Mason's clown face. "…imagination, you lack another quality vital to the success of my project." He reached toward Mason's face, and with his index finger wiped away a portion of white. He then slowly rubbed the makeup between thumb and forefinger, as if taking his time to get a feel for it. "Do you know what that quality is?"

Harrison sensed that something was wrong, but he didn't know what. The emotional atmosphere in the room was like the building electrical charge in the moments before a thunderstorm broke loose, and he didn't like it. Not one bit.

He shook his head.

"Medical training. It's my own fault, of course. In my day, professions were less specialized than they are now, and scientific advances in biology, anatomy, and medicine, meager as they might have been, were often made by those who worked with the dead. I believed that my experience could make up for what you lacked, but I soon saw that this was hubris on my part. I could not fault your enthusiasm for the work, but our progress was slow, and my lady grows impatient. So when another candidate presented herself, one who had the medical training you lack, I decided to change horses in midstream, as I believe the saying goes."

Harrison wondered where Conrad was going with all this. Wherever it was, he doubted it was anywhere good.

"I can't say I wasn't disappointed, but there wasn't much I could do about it. Besides, you continued to pay me for services rendered, so I figured I couldn't complain," Harrison said.

Harvesting organs and even entire limbs from his clients posed little problem. The organs of course were never missed, and as for the limbs and even torsos, mannequin parts were effective substitutes. If necessary, the hands were gloved due to an unfortunate chemical "accident" that took place during the embalming process. Families were extremely unhappy at this—until Harrison offered them a discount to make up for the extra shock during their time of grief.

"But my assessment of your skill level turned out to be premature," Conrad said. "Have you seen today's paper?"

Harrison could now guess where the conversation was heading, and he really didn't like it. "I don't follow local news. Nothing interesting ever happens in Brennan."

"Then it's most fortunate that I happened to stop at a convenience store on my way over and purchase a copy. I discovered an article I think you might find intriguing, and I clipped it out for you." He reached into an inner pocket of his jacket, removed a folded piece of newsprint, and held it out to Harrison.

Harrison didn't take it right away. He kept the temperature cool in the embalming room—not out of any professional need, simply because he was more comfortable that way—but in the last few minutes the air had grown decidedly chilly. It could have been his imagination, but he didn't think so. The drop in temperature felt like a sign of danger, the equivalent of an angry rattlesnake shaking its tail in warning. Because of this, Harrison stood frozen, unsure what to do—or not do—next. In the end he reached out and took the clipping from Conrad. He unfolded it, trying to convince himself that he only imagined the newsprint felt cold as ice, and read. It didn't take long to get through the article, and when he was finished, he looked up and met Conrad's gaze, although he really didn't want to.

"I know you're responsible for this monstrosity," Conrad said, "so don't insult my intelligence with a denial. You're the only person in town, aside from myself and my current colleague, who could've hoped to even have a chance at restoring the dead to life, let alone…" His lips pursed in disgust. "…altering their physiognomy."

Despite Conrad's warning, Harrison nearly denied it anyway, but chose instead to remain silent.

"I had barely begun tutoring you in the alchemical arts, and the instruction I gave you was minimal at best," Conrad continued. "You shouldn't have been able to resurrect an insect, let alone a human."

"He has two heads," Harrison said. "Does that mean he counts as two people?"

"I understand why you did it." Conrad glanced at the clown-faced corpse lying on the marble table. "Perhaps *understand* is too strong a word. I *recognize* that you have a proclivity for the outré in your work. What I don't understand is *how* you accomplished it on your own. Pray, enlighten me."

Harrison didn't see how any good could come from his admitting the truth, but was so thrilled with what he'd done that he had to tell *someone*—even if that someone might kill him for it.

"I paid attention to you as you worked," he said. "Much more attention that you realized. You carry an ancient leather-bound notebook with all sorts of alchemical formulae in it. You left it lying on the counter once, and I was able to flip through it while you were busy with other tasks. I may not have an eidetic memory, but my memory *is* excellent. Plus, I took pictures of the formulae with my phone for later reference. That information was all I needed to begin my search on the Internet. Then, after you moved on to a new assistant, I got to work. Most of the information I found was nonsense, but I knew what to look for, so I recognized it when I came across the real thing. Once I'd amassed enough knowledge about technique, all I needed was some NuFlesh. I paid a call on Dr. Martinez and told him that I was interested in trying out his wonderful new product as an alternative to mortician's putty. He gladly sold me several boxes of the material. After that, it was mostly a process of trial and error. Getting hold of the proper chemicals, mixing them in the right proportions under the perfect conditions, performing the rites without a flaw…" He trailed off and gave Conrad an embarrassed smile. "I'm not telling you anything you don't already know, am I?"

"You must have used fresh corpses. If any significant decay sets in—"

"The resurrected's physical form won't be stable, and will eventually rot away. I know. Despite the fact that I do have access to the bodies of the recently deceased, families would notice if any of their loved ones turned up missing. So I drove my hearse to Crichton—it's fifty miles from here—found a pair of donors outside a bar late one night, and picked them up. It really wasn't any trouble. Ether might be old-fashioned, but it's a wonderfully effective hunting tool."

"You assembled the creature here?" Conrad asked.

"Yes. I've taken to calling him Byron." He paused, but Conrad gave no reaction. "*By*-ron? Bi? As in two? Two heads, get it?"

Conrad looked at him blankly.

Harrison sighed. It seemed neither the living nor the dead appreciated his sense of humor.

"And where is the *creature* now?"

"How should I know? He's like a cat, comes and goes as he pleases. He sleeps in an old shed out back where I used to keep lawn equipment. Which works out well. I mean, I can hardly have a naked two-headed man running around inside when there's a service going on, can I?"

He thought for a moment. "Do you think Byron will eventually become Brennan's version of Bigfoot? I hope so. It would be good for the tourist—"

Before he could say the word "trade," Conrad's right hand shot out and grabbed hold of his throat, cutting off both his voice and his air. Conrad's hand was so cold it burned Harrison's flesh. He gripped Conrad's arm with both of his hands and tried to break free, but even though the man didn't look all that strong, his grip was like frost-covered iron, and Harrison couldn't dislodge it.

"While I must admit to being impressed by your initiative, I can't allow you to interfere with my plans. The last thing I need is any undue attention to be drawn—"

Conrad's phone went off in his pocket. Harrison was surprised to hear it had a musical ring tone, and even more surprised that it was Blue Oyster Cult's "Don't Fear the Reaper." Maybe the grim and oh-so-proper Mr. Dippel had a sense of humor after all.

Conrad maintained his grip on Harrison's throat as he dug his phone out of his pants pocket with his left hand and answered the call.

"Hello?" He spoke that one word and no more. He just listened, scowl deepening and jaw clenching. His grip tightened too, and Harrison began to feel lightheaded, almost as if he was floating, and gray spots danced in his vision. He heard the sound of a vast amount of water—a river or even an ocean—roaring as it circled an unimaginably large drain, one that led down into a darkness blacker than any he'd ever conceived. He knew he'd soon be caught up in the swirling tide and swept down into that endless night. He wasn't afraid, though, was rather looking forward to it, in fact. After working with death for so long, he was finally going to get to experience it for himself. His only regret was that he hadn't specified in his will who he wanted to prepare his body for burial. There were a couple other morticians in town, but Harrison wouldn't trust either of them to stuff a turkey, let alone work on his corpse. He supposed he'd have to take what he could get. It was too late to—

Conrad's hand sprang open. Released from the man's grip, Harrison fell to his hands and knees and sucked in wheezing lungfuls of air. It looked like he wasn't going to die today. He was disappointed, but he consoled himself with the thought that the drain would be there waiting for him when his time came at last.

Into his phone, Conrad said, "You have my gratitude. I shall bring some more unguent by for you later as a thank you. No charge."

He disconnected and put the phone back in his pocket.

"It seems the undue attention I spoke of has already come to us. You are fortunate the call came when it did, for now I have need of you." He smiled. "For a while longer, at least. I want you to find this creature of yours, bring it here, confine it, and then contact me immediately."

Harrison almost said, "And what if I don't?" but he already knew the answer to that question, so he simply nodded.

Without another word, Conrad turned and left the

chamber. As soon as he was gone, the temperature began to rise. Harrison got to his feet, still wheezing. He rubbed the frost burns on his throat. He'd do as Conrad ordered. He'd bring Byron home, and the two—or maybe it was three—of them would wait for the grim-faced prick to return. They'd have a surprise in store for Mr. Dippel. Oh yes they would.

Humming and ignoring his sore throat, Harrison turned his attention back to Mason. He wondered what the man would look like with a purple face. Like an eggplant with hair and eyes, he decided. He couldn't wait to find out.

He withdrew a container of cleansing wipes from the makeup kit and began removing the white from Mason's face.

EIGHT

"Have you guys ever done it?"

Sam's cheeks burned, and he had to swallow before he could talk. "Excuse me?"

Trish rolled her eyes, but she smiled as she did so. "Gone hunting, I mean. Has your dad ever taken you?"

Sam was about to say no, but Dean kicked him in the leg. The three of them had been sitting at the kitchen table for the last hour playing euchre, although Sam had watched Trish more than the cards. During those rare moments when Sam wasn't looking at Trish, he'd been checking on his brother to see if he was watching her, too. Of course he was. Trish was smart, funny, beautiful, with an air of sadness about her that Sam found irresistible. He was sure Dean felt the same way. How could he not? Most of the time Sam didn't mind being the younger brother, but every once in a while, he caught Trish looking at Dean in a way she didn't look at him, and he wished he was the oldest.

"Sure we have," Dean said. "Lots of times."

Sam gave his brother a look, but he didn't say anything. Partly because he didn't want to make Dean mad, but mostly because he didn't want to look like a whiney little kid in front of Trish. He didn't like lying to her, but—he rationalized—he wasn't really. *Dean* was. Keeping your mouth shut wasn't the same as lying, was it? But if that was the case, then why did he feel so lousy about it?

"That's so cool!" Trish glanced over her shoulder at the basement door behind them. Even though it was closed, and had been the entire time they'd been playing, the nervous way she looked at it made Sam think she half expected her father to be standing there listening. Walter's "workshop," as he called it, was set up in the basement, and he'd been working down there for the last couple hours, forging whatever documents his hunter clientele needed.

She turned back to them. "Dad hates it whenever I ask anything about hunting." She lowered her voice, even though there was no way her dad could have heard her from down in the basement. "My uncle was a hunter. He got killed by a werewolf."

"Werewolves are bad-ass," Dean said, almost admiringly. Then he looked at Trish, as if just realizing what he'd said. "Sorry," he mumbled. "I wasn't thinking."

"What else is new?" Sam said with a smirk.

He hoped to score a couple points with Trish by getting a dig in, but when Dean kicked him in the leg again—much harder this time—he let out an *ow!* of pain, and he figured that cost him whatever coolness points he might have gained.

Trish lowered her gaze to the tabletop. "It was the same

werewolf that killed my mom."

"Damn," Dean said. "I'm really sorry."

"Me, too," Sam hurried to say, although he wasn't sure exactly what he was apologizing for. It just felt like the right thing to do.

Trish kept laying down cards as she spoke, and although Sam felt funny continuing to play the game considering the topic of conversation, he kept on, as did Dean.

"One summer my family was on a camping trip. I was only nine. My uncle Ryan—my mom's brother—came along. He'd just gotten divorced from my aunt and was depressed. My parents thought the camping trip might help him get away, clear his head a little, you know?"

Sam didn't know, not exactly, but he nodded anyway, as did Dean, who probably *did* really know—or at least had a better idea of what Trish was talking about.

"We went on a night hike. Dad hoped we'd see some bats, maybe spot some owls. Mom and Uncle Ryan came along, but before long he said he wasn't feeling good and was going to head back to camp and turn in. He left, and after a couple minutes, Mom decided to go back, too. She didn't say anything, but I figure she was worried that he planned to crawl into his tent and drink himself blind. Dad wanted all of us to go back, but Mom told him that it would be a shame for me to miss out on getting to experience the woods at night. Truth was, she probably wanted to keep me away from camp in case Ryan got upset with her for checking up on him and started yelling or something. Dad wasn't worried about Mom finding her way back to camp on her own in the dark. They were both experienced campers and hikers, and they could handle themselves in the wild just fine. Besides, there was a full moon that night, so there was plenty of light to see by."

She glanced at the basement door once again, as if reassuring herself that her father wasn't going to open it any moment and walk through. After the better part of a minute passed, she resumed her story, continuing to play euchre as she spoke.

"I don't know how much longer Dad and I kept hiking. Half an hour, maybe. Whatever it was, it was long enough. When we got back to camp, we found…" She trailed off and looked at the cards remaining in her hand, frowning as if she didn't remember what they were for. "You know how in horror movies people can always hear the monster attack someone in the woods, no matter how far away they are? We didn't hear anything at all. No growls or snarls. No screams. Only crickets chirping and night birds singing, as if everything was normal. Dad figures Uncle Ryan tried to fight off the werewolf and protect Mom, but even though he had a rifle with him, he never got off a shot. The damned thing was too fast. Not that it would've mattered, since he didn't have silver bullets. When the werewolf finished with him, it went after Mom. She tried to run, but she didn't get far from camp before it caught up to her and took her down. She ran in the opposite direction from where Dad and I were. She was trying to lead the werewolf away from us."

She stared at the cards for another moment before tossing them onto the table. A second later, Dean did the same, and

Sam followed his brother's lead.

"What happened to the werewolf?" Dean asked.

"A couple hunters—your kind of hunters, not the regular kind—had been on its trail for several weeks. They finally tracked it down and killed it before dawn. Stabbed it in the heart with a silver blade. If they'd only found it a few hours earlier…"

None of them spoke for several moments. It was Dean who eventually broke the silence.

"It was your aunt, wasn't it?" he said. "The werewolf, I mean."

Trish nodded. "The hunters found us sometime after sunrise. We were still in the camp, both of us in shock. From what they told us, when people change into werewolves they become mindless animals, filled with nothing but hunger, hate, and rage. But some unconscious part of them is driven to prey on those they view as a threat, or who they have some kind of grudge against." She forced a smile. "My aunt and uncle didn't exactly have an amicable divorce." Her smile faded. "I'm thirsty. Do you guys want a drink?"

The brother shook their heads. Trish got up from the table, went to the sink, filled a glass with tap water, and drank it straight down. She then put the empty glass in the sink and leaned on the counter, arms crossed as she continued her story.

"Dad didn't believe the hunters at first. Who would? But they eventually convinced him that what they claimed was true, and they advised him not to say anything about werewolves when he reported the deaths. He agreed and the hunters brought my aunt's body to our camp and… made it look like she was attacked by an animal, too. Dad and I stayed away while they did it. After what had happened to Mom and Ryan, it was the last thing either of us wanted to witness. Then the hunters wished us good luck and left. We got in our pickup and Dad drove us to town to report what had happened.

"The next several days were pretty awful, as you might imagine. Dad told the police that my aunt had come along on the camping trip as a last-ditch effort to fix their marriage. He told them he'd taken me on a hike before dawn so we could watch the sunrise together while the others slept. He said that everyone was dead when we got back, and so we jumped in the pickup and raced to town. The police suspected my dad of committing the murders at first, and I think they might've continued if I hadn't backed up his story. After we'd buried everyone, the hunters stopped by our home to see how we were doing. Dad asked them dozens of questions about what it was like to be a hunter, how many of the monsters everyone thought were pretend were actually real, and how he could become a hunter, too. But even filled with sorrow and anger as he was, it was obvious to the hunters that my dad was too gentle a man to follow in their footsteps. As Dad taught art at a local college, that gave the hunters an idea, though. They said that in their line of work they often needed official-looking documents and identification. They didn't use the word counterfeit, maybe because I'd refused to leave Dad's side since the murders and they didn't want to say anything in front of me that made them look like criminals. They said they had a hard time finding anyone to make such documents, let alone someone who could do it right. That's how Dad started working in, as he calls it, 'hunter support.'"

After she was finished, she swallowed. "I'm still so thirsty. Guess I talked a lot, huh?" She turned around and refilled her water glass.

Sam felt sorry for Trish, but he didn't know what to say or do. His own mother had died when Sam was a baby, so he felt sympathy for Trish's loss, but he couldn't say that he shared it, exactly. He'd never gotten the chance to know his mom, but Trish had been nine when hers had died. Because of that, her mom's death must have hit her so much harder than he could imagine. In a weird way, though, he was jealous of her. At least she'd had nine years with her mom. She had photos of the two of them together, maybe even videos. If so, she'd always be able to watch them and know what her mother's voice sounded like, how she moved, how she smiled. Trish had *memories* of her mom. He didn't have any of his, not a single one.

Trish stood at the sink, her back to them, when the glass suddenly shattered in her hand.

"I know what you're thinking, Sam." Her voice had changed. It was deeper, guttural. "You're jealous of me. You think you had it worse than me because your mom died when you were a baby. You know what? That's makes me angry."

She turned around. Her eyes had become a feral yellow, her fingernails had lengthened into cruel, hooked claws, and her mouth was filled with sharp teeth.

"*Very* angry."

She raised her clawed hands and ran snarling toward Sam and Dean, spittle running from the corners of her mouth, hunger blazing in her eyes.

Sam only had time to think *I'm sorry* before she tore into him.

Sam woke up to what he first thought was an earthquake, but he quickly realized it was just Dean shaking him by the shoulders.

"I'm awake," he said, pushing Dean away from him.

"It's about damn time! I've been shaking you for almost five minutes, but you didn't respond. I was about to give up and haul your ass to the nearest hospital."

Sam glanced around, still foggy-brained. He was sitting in the passenger seat of the crapmobile, seatbelt unbuckled. The passenger door was open and Dean stood outside, looking equal parts worried and pissed.

"Guess I dropped off. Sorry." He hauled himself out of the car and nearly fell when his legs buckled underneath his weight. He managed to grab hold of the open door and keep himself upright, but it was a near thing. His body felt heavy and slow, as if it was filled with wet sand.

"Dude, something's wrong with you!" Dean said.

"I'm fine. Well, no, I'm not, but all I am is tired. Once in a while everything catches up with you. After we've taken care of whatever's going on in this town, I'll zonk out and sleep as long as it takes to get my energy back, all right? Until then, I'll just have to make do."

Dean still didn't look happy, but he didn't protest, which as far as Sam was concerned, was good enough. Trying to look as if he wasn't fighting to stay awake, he glanced around to see where they were. Dean had parked the car on a gravel shoulder. Trees lined both sides of a narrow blacktopped country lane that had no lines painted on it.

Back road, Sam thought. *Probably not too far outside town.*

His dream came back to him then, images and emotions slamming into his mind with sledgehammer force. He drew in a surprised breath, and Dean looked alarmed. He started forward, but Sam waved him off.

"I'm okay. I just remembered what I dreamed about during the drive, that's all."

Dean's eyes narrowed as if he were scrutinizing Sam, trying to decide whether he was telling the truth or attempting to cover up how bad his condition really was.

"It was about Trish again," he said.

Dean relaxed a bit. "Another rough one, huh?"

"Yeah. It started out normal enough. It was about the euchre game when she told us how her mom and uncle died. Remember?"

Dean nodded. "Like it was yesterday."

"But at the end it turned... weird."

For a second, he was afraid Dean was going to ask him how weird, but he was grateful that his brother didn't press him for more details.

They looked at each other for a few moments without speaking.

"Maybe your crazy's starting to affect your dreams," Dean said. "It could be a good sign. Instead of producing hallucinations, your brain is shifting over to having regular old bad dreams. Maybe in time they'll fade, too."

Sam thought about the shadowy figure he'd seen when

they'd carried Frankenmutt's corpse to the car.

"Maybe," he said, trying not to sound doubtful. He changed the subject. "So—why are we here?"

"Maybe you're so tired lately because you're catching a cold," Dean said. "Your nose has got to be clogged with snot, otherwise you'd smell why we're here."

Sam frowned, drew in a deep breath through his nose, and regretted it instantly. Even though they were standing outside of the car, the stink of Frankenmutt was overpowering. Sam wondered if maybe Dean was right and something was wrong with him. How else could he have missed the beast's rank odor of decay? Was it possible for anyone to be *that* sleepy? Maybe it was his crazy again. If his mind could make him think he was seeing and hearing things that weren't there, maybe it could make him unable to perceive something that was. The thought wasn't a comforting one.

"I take it that this is where we say goodbye to Frankenmutt," Sam said.

"Stinkenstein. I changed his name. And yeah, if we don't dump his rotting carcass soon, we'll never be able to get his Frankenfunk off of us."

Sam gave his brother a look. "You're having way too much fun with the Franken-names."

"In this job, you take the perks where you can get them. C'mon, help me haul its corpse into the woods. Then we can go back to the motel and take a couple dozen showers apiece."

"You think we should burn it?"

Dean nodded. "Yeah. So far it hasn't shown any signs that it's going to get back up and start tearing people's throats out, but why take chances? If nothing else, burning it will kill the stink—I hope."

"Sounds like a plan. Fire always works in Frankenstein movies, right?"

"That's what I was thinking. Then again, fire kills just about everything. That's the beauty of it."

The brothers headed to the rear of the car, and Dean inserted the key into the trunk lock, but he didn't turn it right away. "You might want to try and breathe through your mouth for the next few minutes."

Sam nodded and Dean began to turn the key. His phone rang. Leaving the key in the lock, he pulled out his phone and answered it.

"Hello?" He listened, then glanced at Sam. "Yeah, this is he. Who's this?" He listened some more. "Sure, yeah, I'll be there as soon as possible." He disconnected and tucked the phone back in his pocket.

"Who was it?" Sam asked.

"Local police. They found the card we left with Lyle Swanson—on his body. His withered, dried-up body. We got ourselves another victim of The Pruning."

"Think the Double-Header paid him a return visit?"

"That'd be my guess. Whoever's making these monsters, it's like they've got a damn assembly line going. Let's go torch Stinkenstein and haul ass over to Lyle's."

Dean turned the key and the trunk popped open. A stench wave hit them like a solid wall, and both brothers took a couple steps backward.

"Can't we just burn him right there in the trunk?" Sam asked.

"Tempting, but we might blow up the car in the process. Not that it would be any great loss," Dean added. "C'mon, the sooner we get this over with, the better."

Sam nodded, and they got to work. One good thing about the stench: at least it kept him awake.

Conrad knelt naked on the floor of what once was the warehouse for Kingston Bicycles. The facility had no electricity and hadn't for many years, but that didn't trouble him. The warehouse's windows were dirty and streaked, but enough light filtered through for his needs. Besides, electric light was still something of a novelty to Conrad. He'd gotten by for the majority of his long existence with candles or lamplight. Just because the world had changed didn't mean he had to as well. Sometimes the old ways were best.

Case in point: hanging from the rafters in front of him was a piglet. He'd purchased the animal from a local farmer several days before, and had kept it tied up in a corner of the warehouse on a bed of sawdust with straw scattered over it. He'd made sure the animal had plenty of food and water—it was important that it be healthy and strong—and when he'd gotten the chance, he'd even taken it out for short walks to give it some exercise. Now it dangled at the end of a rope, wriggling and squealing, back hooves bound tight, head pointed at the floor. Conrad didn't mind the noises the animal made. On the contrary, he appreciated them, for they were sounds of life, and the more life the piglet had in it, the better.

The tools Conrad had brought with him were simple. A

stone bowl and knife, very old and worn from much use, both emblazoned with ancient runes. If a linguistics scholar had been present, he or she might have recognized the runes as being similar to those used by the Norse people, but these symbols predated those by centuries. The bowl rested directly beneath the squirming piglet, and next to it, the blade pointed north. The bowl was named Hunger, and the knife called Famine.

Conrad closed his eyes, bowed his head, and then spoke in a reverent voice. The language he used was a forerunner of Old Norse.

"Hel, *Frau Holle*, Dark Mother, Guardian of Graves, Queen of Night Unending, I beg you to accept this sacrifice from your most unworthy of servants."

This particular sacrifice wasn't as elaborate as those conducted in the old days, long before Conrad's birth. Back then, entire villages would sacrifice pigs and horses, boiling the meat in large cooking pits, and sprinkling the animals' blood on statues of their deities. The villagers would eat the meat, drink mead, and pray for a good year and peace. In some villages, during every ninth year there was a *blotan*— or sacrificial—feast of nine days, during which nine males of each species, men included, were sacrificed, their bodies hung from the branches of trees near the temple. The most devout villages sacrificed ninety-nine people—men, women, and children—and although Conrad admired their devotion, few villages were large enough to survive the loss of so much of their population every nine years.

Conrad knew rites such as the one he was about to perform

were more symbolic than literal, but he'd served Hel for over three hundred years, and he knew that the dark goddess, while understanding the necessity of a downsized sacrifice in the modern world, still expected her servants to get the basics right, to cross their T's and dot their I's, as it were.

He opened his eyes, picked up Famine, and touched the blade's tip to the sacred nine points of life on his body: the genitals (from which life sprung), the heart (which pumped blood), the nose, the mouth, and both lungs (all involved in breathing), the stomach (which digested food), the forehead (behind which lay the brain), and lastly his right hand (which held weapons and tools with which to fight, hunt, and build). Holding Famine with his left hand, he carved a single rune into the flesh of his right palm. To a modern English speaker, the symbol would have resembled a large X, but it stood for the word *gebo*, meaning gift. Conrad waited until the blood was flowing strongly, and then pressed his palm against the side of the piglet. He returned Famine to his right hand, gripping the stone handle tight so his blood smeared it, then carved the rune for *gebo* into the piglet—the animal now squealing in terror—until its blood mingled with his own, mystically linking the two of them. Conrad and the piglet were now one, and the sacrifice of its life would substitute for the sacrifice of his. That is, if he'd done everything right. If not, Hel would take his life along with the piglet's. After three centuries, he could perform this ritual in his sleep, but that didn't mean he was incapable of making a mistake, and even the smallest flaw might upset his lady. He hoped that if she found his sacrifice wanting, she would forgive him, if for no other reason than because she still had need of him.

He grabbed hold of the back of the piglet's neck to keep it steady, and then with a single swift, practiced swipe, he sliced open the animal's throat. Blood poured from the wound and into Hunger below. Conrad held the blade beneath the flow to wet it, and then flicked it toward each of the sacred nine points of his body, splashing himself with the piglet's blood. He then placed Famine on the floor next to Hunger, pressed his wounded hand over his heart, closed his eyes, and waited. He listened as the sound of blood splatter lessened, became a trickle, then slowed to intermittent drops. When it stopped at last, he opened his eyes.

Hunger was filled with dark blood, but as Conrad watched, the level began to lower. Within moments, the blood was gone, absorbed into the stone. He smiled. Hel had accepted his sacrifice.

He bowed his head.

"My lady, two men have come to Brennan. I believe they intend to interfere with our plans, and I ask for the means to track them, so I might slay them before they can cause us further difficulty."

Someone else might have asked Hel to strike the two men dead, but he knew the dark queen preferred her servants practice self-reliance. The gods help those who help themselves.

For several moments, nothing happened, and Conrad began to fear that his lady had forsaken him. Then he heard a voice whisper in his mind, the words like a midnight wind blowing across the icy surface of a frozen lake.

So it shall be.

The rune he'd carved into his palm erupted with fresh pain far more intense than anything a mere cut could cause. It was a cold pain, but a cold so strong it burned like fire. He gritted his teeth and pulled his hand away from his chest. He watched as the blood that still welled forth from the X he'd carved into himself froze and became crimson ice. The pain worsened and the sensation of cold spread through his body. He began to shiver. Despite the cold sensation, sweat poured off of him as he fought to endure the agony. Finally, just as the pain had become so bad that he was considering snatching up Famine with his left hand and hacking off his right, the sensation began to lessen. Within moments, it was gone, leaving behind only a dull, distant throbbing.

He examined his palm. The blood was gone and the wound healed, leaving behind an X-shaped black scar. Conrad held his hand straight out before him experimentally. He felt the cold return, though far less painfully this time, and only on the left edge of the rune. He moved his hand leftward, and the cold spread farther, until it covered the entire rune. He smiled. Hel had given him the equivalent of a compass to track the two meddlers. The rune was indeed now a *gebo*—a gift—but now a gift from the goddess instead of to her.

He inclined his head in gratitude. "I praise your eternal darkness, my lady."

He rose to his feet, ready to begin the hunt. Then he glanced down at his body, splattered with blood from the ritual. Perhaps he should clean himself up first. He looked at the dead piglet dangling over the empty stone bowl. Maybe he should avail himself of the opportunity for some sustenance, too. He couldn't remember the last time he'd eaten, and he was *so* fond of raw pig heart.

He bent down, picked up Famine, and started cutting.

"Did you see the way those cops reacted to us?" Dean asked. "Now I know why they call it getting the stink eye. We reek!"

"At least our stench will keep them out of the house while we check the scene," Sam said. They'd stopped on the drive over for yet another coffee for Sam, and he sipped it now.

"No need for that," Dean said. "They're already too worried about catching whatever plague they think is responsible for The Pruning. They don't want to spend any more time in here than they have to."

"Whatever works," Sam said, and took another sip of coffee. "I mean, they were in such a hurry to get out, they didn't question the logic of agents posing as reporters to question Lyle."

They stood in Lyle's kitchen. The county medical examiner had already come and gone, but Lyle's body hadn't been removed yet in order to give the "agents" a chance to examine it. He sat on the floor, his back against a cupboard door, a withered husk, parchment-dry skin stretched tight across bone.

"You don't have to be a forensics expert to read *this* crime scene," Dean said. "Double-Header busted down the back door, slurped up Lyle's life energy, then took off. I wonder who reported Lyle's death."

"I heard a couple cops talking outside as we walked up. Looks like Lyle was in the process of picking up trash in his back yard when the Double-Header came after him. He never finished—obviously. Later on, the wind kicked up, started blowing trash into his neighbor's yard—"

"I get the picture. Neighbor comes over, all pissed off and ready to complain, and finds our boy Lyle prune-ified."

"Yep." Sam hit his coffee once more.

Dean wondered how much coffee, with added espresso shots, someone could drink before suffering a caffeine overdose. Though Sam didn't seem to be experiencing any symptoms. So far, all the coffee he'd guzzled hadn't shifted his system into overdrive. Hell, it had barely kept him awake. Still, he'd have to make sure Sam didn't make himself sick.

He had hoped that the smell of Sam's coffee might help to leaven the stench of the late, unlamented Frankenmutt that clung to them, but if anything, he found the mingled scents even more nauseating. The combined smells didn't seem to bother Sam, but Dean didn't know if that was a good thing or a bad thing. Over the years, Sam had suffered a number of experiences that had altered his behavior one way or another, and it had gotten to the point where Dean wasn't sure what normal was for his brother anymore. Not that he was one to talk. He'd lost more than a few of his own marbles over the years. He supposed that was one of the reasons the two of them stayed together. Sure, they were family, but they also kept each other going, almost out of habit. If they were this bad now, he wondered what they'd be like when they were old men. Not that there was any guarantee they'd live long enough to reach their golden years. There was a reason why hunters never bothered to save for retirement. All they needed to save for was the cost of a burial. And even that was an iffy proposition, since when they died—assuming they really did die, rather than being turned into a vampire or something—there might not be enough of them left to put in the ground.

The morbid turn his thoughts had taken—an occupational hazard—inevitably led him to think about Bobby. No condo in Florida for him. At least he and Sam had been able to bury Bobby, first burning his bones so there was no chance he'd come back as a vengeful spirit. He reached into his jacket pocket and touched Bobby's flask. *I miss you,* he thought. For a moment, the flask's metal seemed to warm beneath his fingers, then the sensation was gone, and he dismissed it as his imagination.

"Both the Double-Header and Frankenmutt drain their victims' life force," Dean said. "They might not look anything alike, but they're basically the same kind of monster."

"They're combinations of different bodies," Sam pointed out. "So in that sense they do resemble one another."

"So we're definitely looking for a mad scientist type."

"Or a mad sorcerer. There's no way science alone could create monsters like these."

"Maybe whoever's responsible swings both ways," Dean suggested.

"So we're dealing with what? A sorcentist?"

Dean gave his brother a look. "From now on, leave coming up with the wacky nicknames to me, okay?"

"Fine." Sam thought for a moment. "If what we've got here is some kind of new fusion of science and magic, it could be something the Leviathan have no defense against."

"So we might actually be close to finding Leviathan kryptonite."

"Leviathanite?"

"Dude—seriously."

"You're really quite beautiful, you know. In fact, I'd go so far as to say you're a masterpiece."

Harrison watched Byron take another bite of his—its—their—treat. Each head had two chocolate bars, one for each hand, and they ate in almost perfect unison, raising the candy to their mouths at the same time, biting down, chewing, and swallowing. Harrison had done nothing to connect their brains, so he knew their synchronized movements had no physiological base, which made them all the more fascinating to watch, especially with four hands delivering the chocolate. He was glad to see that the heads had no difficulty swallowing. One of the trickier bits of Byron's creation had been connecting both heads to a single alimentary canal. It would've been impossible without NuFlesh, not to mention the mystical augmentations Harrison had picked up from Conrad. All in all, he was quite pleased. Next time, perhaps he'd try for three heads—a hat trick.

Byron sat cross-legged on the floor of the shed while he ate, and Harrison stood watching near the door, a stun gun held at his side. Harrison had ordered the weapon online before he began working on Byron, just in case his creation decided to get a bit feisty. The charge the gun delivered wasn't strong enough to do any serious damage to Byron, but because his mental level was barely above that of an infant, the pain of the electrical jolt was enough to discipline him. Harrison had rarely needed to use the stun gun, though, not when chocolate produced far more effective results. Byron derived no nourishment from food, and it would do nothing to satisfy the hunger that now burned at the core of his being, but it tasted good, and that made it an excellent motivator. Finding Byron and bringing him to the shed had been child's play. All Harrison had needed to do was wander through the woods behind the Legacy Center, waving an unwrapped chocolate bar in the air and calling out, "I've got a treaty for my sweetie!" until Byron came loping toward him, drooling with anticipation. After that, Byron would have followed Harrison to the center of town as long as he received chocolate at the end of the trip. Nevertheless, Harrison still held onto the stun gun. Candy was dandy, but it was no substitute for several million volts of electricity.

He was a bit worried about his boy—boys. On the way to the shed, he'd had a chance to look Byron over thoroughly, and while his body was predictably dirty and scratched from gallivanting around the woods, Harrison had also noted the first signs of incipient decay. Just a few patches here and there, but it meant that his creation didn't have much time left. A week, perhaps two at the most. And as the decay grew worse, so would Byron's hunger, driving him to seek out living creatures and absorb their life energy. Doing so would stave off his decay for a time, but it would only be a temporary stay of execution. Death would inevitably come to him.

"It's such a shame. But look at it this way: you've managed to escape the Drain, if only for a short time."

Neither of Byron's heads looked at him as he spoke. They were too intent on finishing their treats. They ate with messy delight, smacking chocolate-smeared lips in between bites and humming tonelessly in a way that seemed to Harrison almost like purring.

He had complied with Conrad's demand to fetch Byron, but that was as far as he intended to cooperate with the ancient alchemist. Conrad had never told Harrison who he really was, but it had taken no great effort to find out. For pity's sake, he hadn't even changed his name! A quick Internet search did the trick. Nevertheless, even given who Dippel was and the terrible knowledge that was his to command, Harrison wasn't afraid of him. The old man had enjoyed a nice long run, but it was time for someone else to take over. Someone like Harrison. And Byron was going to help him do it. When Conrad returned, Harrison would serve him to Byron for lunch. All he had to do was figure out a way—

The shed door opened.

"Hello, Harrison." Conrad, impeccably dressed as always, stepped inside and Harrison stepped back to make room. His gaze focused on Byron, and while his nose wrinkled in disgust—Harrison had to admit his boys didn't smell their freshest at the moment—he seemed pleased. "Excellent work."

"I pride myself on my customer service," Harrison said. "It is, after all, at the heart of the funeral industry."

He hadn't expected Conrad to return so soon, and the man's appearance had taken him by surprise. He took a quick glance around the shed, casting about for anything that he might be able to use for a weapon, but aside from a coiled length of hose, a rusty lawn sprinkler, and an old bag of peat moss, the shed was empty. When Byron had first started sleeping there, Harrison had removed everything that might prove a danger to him. So no sharp garden tools, no hammers, no axes.

As a businessman, he believed in the value of a carefully thought out plan. It was, after all, one of his primary sales tools. He'd even paid for a billboard out on the highway with a cartoon of a grinning man standing up in a coffin, hands held high above his head with enthusiastic joy, and above him in large letters this slogan: "Preplanning is Fun!" Beneath the coffin in smaller letters: "Put your mind at rest before you're laid to rest. Brauer Legacy Center." But as important as having a plan was, sometimes you just had to improvise.

Harrison turned to Conrad, jammed the stun gun against the side of the man's neck, and activated the device. There was a loud crackling sound, accompanied by the stink of ozone and scorched flesh. Conrad's body jerked and shuddered, and Harrison kept the stun gun pressed to his neck, giving him an extra-strong dose of juice. When he figured the man had enough, Harrison pulled the gun away, grabbed hold of his arm, and shoved him toward Byron. Conrad stumbled toward the creature, lost his footing, and fell onto the floor directly in front of him. Alarm crossed both of Byron's faces, and he began hooting in surprise and fear, sounding like a pair of frightened apes.

"Drain him!" Harrison shouted. "Suck him dry!"

Byron's second head—the one Harrison had added to the original body and which hung at an odd angle—looked at him blankly, but the original head's eyes narrowed with cunning. That side of the body dropped what was left of its chocolate bars and slapped its hands on Conrad. The second head finally figured out what was happening, and it too dropped its treats and grabbed hold of Conrad.

Harrison grinned with cruel satisfaction. This was working out even better than he'd hoped. It would all be over within moments, and then he'd be rid of that arrogant prick once and for—

Conrad, looking a bit disheveled but by no means panicked, reached into the inner pocket of his suit jacket and removed an envelope. He opened it and flung the contents in Byron's faces. A fine yellow powder spread outward in a small cloud, and both of Byron's heads inhaled it. The second one sneezed.

"Stop," Conrad said.

Byron stiffened.

"Release me."

Byron removed all four hands from Conrad's person. Conrad pulled himself to his feet, smoothed out his pants, and adjusted his tie.

"It was a valiant effort, Harrison, but electricity, against me? Please! I was working with electricity before Benjamin Franklin was a spark in his daddy's eye." Without glancing at Byron he said, "Stand," and Harrison's creature did. But then, Harrison supposed it wasn't his creature anymore, was it?

"How did you put it, Harrison? Oh yes." Conrad gave the mortician a slow, wicked smile. "'Drain him. Suck him dry.'"

Byron started forward, and Harrison knew that he

was finally going to find out what death was like. He was surprised to discover he wasn't looking forward to it as much as he'd anticipated.

NINE

The Winchester brothers traipsed through the woods behind Lyle's house in search of the Double-Header. Now that they had a better idea what they were up against, they'd come better armed. Dean carried both his Colt and the Winchester 1887 shotgun, and Sam carried his Beretta and the Baikal sawed-off double-barreled shotgun. Both had back-up pistols as well as KA-BAR knives and plenty of extra ammo. In addition, they each carried several flares. Frankenmutt had gone up like a pile of dry kindling, and while they didn't know if the Double-Header would be as flammable, they figured the flares were extra insurance. *Besides,* Dean had pointed out, *maybe he'll be afraid of fire, just like in the movies. You know, "Fire bad!"*

As they walked, Sam fought like hell to keep from yawning. He didn't want Dean to worry about him, and he knew his brother was watching him. Despite what he'd told Dean about his weariness being no big deal, Sam was starting to wonder if something more was going on with him than simple exhaustion. No matter what he did, he couldn't manage to fully wake. Neither sleep nor copious amounts of caffeine seemed to help. He felt slow, not just physically, but mentally, too, like he had molasses running through his veins instead of blood. If they did find the Double-Header, Sam worried that he wouldn't react fast enough, and he'd end up getting his brother killed. To add to all that, the place where Frankenmutt had bitten him had started to hurt again. The wound throbbed with every step he took, and it was an effort to keep from limping. He hadn't examined the wound yet—he couldn't very well do so with his brother around, not without alerting him that something was wrong—but he had the feeling that it wasn't looking too good.

He thought about what Dean had said earlier, about how his crazy might have turned inward, which was why he'd been having nightmares about Trish. If that was true, maybe both his weariness and the pain in his leg were additional symptoms of the crazy. The bite on his leg had stopped hurting, and looked like it was healing normally, so why should it suddenly start up again? What if he was having hallucinations, but instead of *seeing* things this time, he was *feeling* them?

Forget it, he told himself. *One problem at a time. First we gank the Double-Header, then I can worry about my leg.*

"I hate hunting new monsters," Dean said. "Too unpredictable."

"On the bright side, a two-headed, four-armed naked guy ought to be easy enough to spot." Sam said.

"That's another thing: couldn't the mad scientist who made the Double-Header have been considerate enough to at least put a pair of shorts on him? I really don't want to see his monster dork swinging in the wind when he charges us."

They'd considered trying the same technique they used to lure Frankenmutt—using Sam's phone to simulate a crying baby—but had decided against it. For one thing, the Double-Header had just had a nice big meal of Lyle's life energy, so there was a good chance he wouldn't be hungry again for a while. For another, unlike Frankenmutt, the Double-Header was human, or at least he had been, and it was hard to say how intelligent he was. From what Lyle had described, it sounded as if the creature was acting at least partially animalistic— why else would he be digging through Lyle's trash looking for a snack, and in broad daylight? But he had to retain a certain degree of cunning, at least, and without a driving hunger to goad him into ignoring his instincts, there was a good chance he'd sense that the baby cries were part of a trap. So they'd decided to do things the old-fashioned way: walking through the woods and offering themselves as a pair of meals that the Double-Header, full though he might be, would find too tempting to pass up.

"He probably has a… a…" Sam struggled to recall the word he was looking for. It was increasingly becoming an effort to think clearly. "…a *lair* somewhere close by. It gets pretty chilly after dark this time of year, and he'd need somewhere to hole up for the night."

Dean frowned at him, and Sam knew his brother had noted his verbal hesitation. "Probably not a cave. This isn't really cave-y country. I vote for an old barn or maybe an abandoned house."

"Sounds good. I say we keep our eyes out for—"

A branch snapped behind them. The sound wasn't loud at all, and anyone else might have ignored it, but Sam and Dean's instincts had been honed to a razor-sharp edge over the years. The two of them whirled around, shotguns raised and ready to fire…

…only to find themselves looking at a wide-eyed and very surprised rabbit.

The stare-down lasted only a few seconds before the rabbit turned tail and scurried off, running in a zigzag pattern through underbrush and scattered leaves.

Dean turned to Sam and grinned. "Why do I suddenly feel like Elmer Fudd?"

Sam was about to reply when his instincts kicked in again, screaming a warning. He started to turn, but he was too slow, and something struck his chest with pile-driver force. The impact sent him flying backward, and he landed hard, losing his grip on his shotgun in the process. Stunned and feeling as if he'd just gone ten rounds with Godzilla, Sam struggled to sit up. He saw Dean fighting with the Double-Header, the creature no doubt responsible for knocking Sam off his pins. With its top pair of hands the Double-Header had grabbed hold of the barrel of Dean's shotgun and was pushing it this way and that, preventing Dean from getting a good shot. With the bottom pair, the creature had grabbed Dean under the arms and lifted him into the air as if he was a child. Cussing a blue streak, Dean repeatedly kicked the Double-Header in the gut, and lower, but if the creature felt any pain as a result of the blows, he didn't show it. One of his heads grinned, the other laughed, and drool ran from the corners of both mouths. As a hunter, Sam had seen some truly disturbing things over the years, but this scene ranked near the top of his personal Most Freakish list.

Sam knew he should do something, but his head was still reeling from the blow he'd taken, and his chest burned like fire. He figured he had a cracked rib or two at the very least. Normally, he would have been able to push past the pain and disorientation and go to his brother's aid, but added to the deep weariness that had taken hold of him, it was too much. He couldn't think straight, and although he wanted nothing more than to get off his ass and go help his brother, he had no idea what he should do.

The Double-Header started shaking Dean as if he were a shotgun-toting rag doll, and both heads laughed in delight. As Sam watched, shadows appeared on the pair of the creature's arms that were holding Dean off the ground, the darkness roiling and seething as if alive. The shadows, which looked something like animated black tattoos, slithered down the arms until they were concentrated in the hands pressed to Dean's sides. Dean let out a cry that was half shout, half moan, and renewed his exertions, desperate to break free of the Double-Header's grip.

The Double-Header was draining Dean's life force. Dean's energy was waning fast, and within seconds he was moving more slowly, the fight leaving him along with his strength.

Fighting against his lethargy, Sam moved into a crouching position, drew his Beretta, and fired. His aim was off, and instead of hitting the darker right head dead center at the base of the skull as he planned, the head's right ear vanished in a spray of red mist and splintered cartilage. Still, the wound had the desired effect. Startled and in pain, the Double-Header released its grip on both Dean and his shotgun, and whirled around to see who had hurt it. Dean crumpled to the ground and lay there, dazed but alive.

The creature reached up with one of its hands to gingerly touch the ragged bloody ruin where the ear had been. When he removed his hand, the fingers came away slick with blood. He examined them with two pairs of eyes, both heads seeming puzzled, as if they couldn't quite comprehend what they were looking at. Then it must have hit them, for one head wailed in despair and the other started crying.

They're like little kids, Sam thought. *Toddlers trapped in one huge, monstrous body.*

He felt sorry for the Double-Header, and was reminded of the way the Frankenstein monster was sometimes portrayed—as a childlike innocent who had never asked to be reborn as a freakish abomination, and who only wanted to be left alone.

Both heads looked up at Sam, expressions twisting into masks of hate. Two mouths bellowed in single rage, and the creature charged.

The time for sympathy was over. Sam squeezed off three more rounds as the Double-Header ran toward him. On any other day, Sam would have put all three into the creature's heart, but right then it was an effort to hold the gun steady, and his vision was blurry around the edges. The first round only managed to take off the last two fingers on one of the hands. Painful, but hardly a kill shot. The second round struck the left shoulder, but while the impact made the Double-Header stagger for a second, it didn't slow it down. Better, but still not good enough. The third round was, as the saying goes, the money shot. It hit the right head—which Sam thought of as the main one, since it appeared to be original to the body—and tore away a good chunk of the skull in a spray of red.

The Double-Header, or maybe it was the One-and-a-Half-Header now, came to a halt only a couple feet away from Sam. It swayed on its feet, the fingers on all four hands twitching spastically. The wounded head lolled on its neck, eyes wide and staring. The second head turned to look at its companion, gaze dull and uncomprehending. The hands on the second head's side of the body tried to reach up, probably intending to touch the wounded head, just as the creature had explored the ragged ear stump a moment before, but the limbs jerked and spasmed, flailing the air as if the Double-Header was having some kind of seizure.

Sam thought he knew what was happening. The second, fairer head was wired into the body's overall nervous system, but the connections weren't as strong as they could be. The first head was the dominant one, responsible for primary control of the body. Without it, the second head struggled to do the job on its own. Sam kept his Beretta trained on the Double-Header. If he could have trusted his aim, he would've put a round into the second head to end the creature's misery, but as it was, he decided to hold off firing for a few moments. It was possible that the second head would be unable to keep the heart and lungs functioning by itself, and the creature would die soon. If that was the case, all he would have to do was wait for it to collapse, and it would be game over.

Sam watched the Double-Header lurch and flail, moving like a marionette whose puppeteer was having an epileptic fit.

He caught more movement out of the corner of his eye, and turned, swiveling the Beretta toward whatever new threat presented itself. He expected it to be another creature, but instead what he saw was a slender man wearing a suit and tie standing near an elm tree. It looked as if he'd been hiding and had stepped out of concealment to get a better look at what was happening. He raised his right hand—Sam saw it had some kind of black mark on the palm—and gestured. Sam wondered if this could be the hazy figure he'd glimpsed several times since arriving in Brennan, finally come into sharper focus.

He didn't have time to wonder long. The Double-Header gained a modicum of control over its uncooperative body and took a single lurching step forward. Then it took a second step.

The surviving head glared at Sam, murder in its eyes, and it stretched all four hands toward him. Writhing black shadows appeared on the creature's arms, and Sam knew that the Double-Header planned to drain his life force to avenge the death of its companion.

Sam swung the Beretta back around, aimed at the creature's heart, and fired.

He'd aimed too low, and the round entered the Double-Header's midsection. The impact caused the creature to double over, but it quickly straightened. Blood ran from the wound, but the creature ignored it and continued toward Sam.

He aimed for the heart again, taking his time, trying not to look at the dark energy swirling around the creature's hands, trying not to think about how close it was, and how much closer it was getting, but before he could squeeze the trigger, he heard his brother's voice.

"Yippee ki-yay, mamasita!"

A shotgun blast sounded like thunder, and the once Double-Header ended its strange second life as a No-Header. The creature pitched forward and hit the ground like a slab of lifeless meat—which was exactly what it had become. Sam looked up and saw Dean lower his shotgun. He had dark circles under his eyes, and he looked exhausted, but he was alive, and that was all that mattered.

"Mamasita?" Sam said.

Dean shrugged. "Trying to cut back on the swearing."

Sam struggled to his feet. "Admirable, but it lacks a little something in the tough guy department."

He remembered the man in the suit, and turned in his direction, ready to fire, but the man was gone.

"Don't worry," Dean said. "I saw him, too. Moves pretty fast for an older guy."

Sam caught another flicker of movement, this time in the opposite direction. He turned and saw the familiar hazy, shadowy figure that he'd seen before, standing about a hundred yards away. He pointed toward it.

"How about that one?" he asked.

Dean looked in the direction he indicated. "Sorry. That

one I don't see."

Sam squinted, trying to bring the figure into clearer focus, but it was no use. A second later, it was gone.

He sighed. At least the guy in the suit hadn't been a hallucination.

He tucked his Beretta into the waistband of his pants, retrieved the sawed-off shotgun he'd dropped when the Double-Header had sent him flying, and together he and Dean approached the creature's corpse.

Dean kicked it a couple times to make sure it was dead. In their line of work, you never knew if something you put down was going to stay down. The creature didn't move.

"I guess it's officially the Double-Deader now," Dean said.

Sam gave him a weak smile. "Okay, that one's kind of funny." His smile faded. "How are you feeling?"

"Like I could sleep for a week, but otherwise, I'm all right. I don't think he managed to siphon too much out of my tank."

They turned their attention to the dead monster and rolled it over so they could get a better look at it. Now that they were able to examine the body closely, Sam could see that it had scar lines similar to Frankenmutt's, only they were confined to where the extra head and arms had been joined to the main body. The Double-Header had been made from fewer pieces than Frankenmutt, and his scar lines were flesh-colored instead of white.

"NuFlesh?" Dean asked.

"I think so. But there's something wrong about these scars." Sam crouched down and rubbed at the line around the base of one of the extra arms.

"Careful," Dean said. "You don't want to catch Frankencooties."

Sam held up his fingers for Dean to see. "Someone covered up his scars with makeup. That's why they aren't as obvious as Frankenmutt's." He frowned. "He's got patches of decay on him, too. They're not very big yet, but they're definitely present. It looks like he was starting to rot, just like Frankenmutt."

"At least he doesn't smell as bad yet," Dean said. "Not that he's a rose or anything right now."

Sam wiped his fingers off on the ground before standing.

"Guess we didn't need the flares," Sam said.

"They still might come in handy," Dean said. "What do you think the odds are that there are only two patchwork monsters in town?"

"Not very good," Sam said.

"C'mon, let's gather some wood and torch this son of a bitch. Then see if we can figure out who Mr. Suit-and-Tie is." He yawned. "After we go back to the hotel and take a nap."

Seeing Dean yawn made Sam do the same. "That's the best idea you've had in a long time."

The brothers, both moving slow as a pair of zombies, got to work.

Conrad moved through the woods far more swiftly and silently than was humanly possible, but that was only to be expected, as he hadn't been human in three centuries.

He wasn't pleased by the creature's failure to slay the two

men. If he hadn't already killed Harrison, he surely would have done so now. In fact, he was tempted to bring the fool back to life just so he could deprive him of it once again. The encounter had been far from a total loss, however, for he had gained some valuable data.

He now knew who the two men were. Not their specific identities, those hardly mattered, but he knew what their profession was. They were *hunters*. Given the nature of the experiments Conrad had conducted over the previous three hundred years—not to mention the results—he had encountered their kind before, and while they'd usually managed to destroy his creations, none of them had ever come close to killing him, and he intended to, in current parlance, keep his streak alive.

That wasn't the most important piece of information he'd learned from the failure of Harrison's two-headed monstrosity, though. Something else had been observing the proceedings, and while to all other eyes this observer would have gone unseen, Conrad's special status—not dead but technically not alive—allowed him to perceive what others could not. This day a Reaper had been present in the woods. A Reaper!

During his long existence, Conrad had learned much. He was a master of the ancient art of alchemy—perhaps the only one left in the world—and he was well skilled in the runic magic practiced by the Norse people. He had also picked up a great deal of supernatural lore during his time, and he knew that Reapers were beings who appeared to humans at the moment of their deaths and ushered their souls into the afterlife. They were, in a very real sense, the Death Force personified, and a Reaper, or more accurately, the power it contained, could be the final piece of a puzzle he'd been trying to solve for the last three centuries.

He needed to return to the bicycle factory and consult his mistress at once. She would know the best way to lure and capture a Reaper. After all, was she not an aspect of Death as well? Of course, if he expected her to grant him such arcane knowledge, he would need a sacrifice of more substance than a mere piglet. He thought of the farmer who had sold him the animal. The man was in his fifties, but he was still healthy, strong, and hardworking. He'd do.

It looked like he would be making a stop before returning to Kingston Bicycles.

Conrad didn't question the Reaper's presence. He assumed it was following the hunter, the one who'd been bitten by the dog and infected with the creature's taint. The boy was dying slowly, and the Reaper was like a vulture, circling and waiting for its meal to finish the business of expiring before swooping down to claim it. He hoped the boy would survive for a while yet. The longer he took to die, the longer the Reaper would remain, giving Conrad a better chance to capture it.

He was more excited than he had been in decades. At last, victory was within his grasp!

Soon, my lady, you shall tread upon the face of the Earth, and all who behold you will marvel at your beauty and wail in despair. It shall be glorious!

He ran faster.

Daniel walked through the woods, trailing the Winchester

brothers at a discrete distance. Sam had seen too much of him, and he wanted to make sure to remain out of sight, at least for the time being.

Daniel's kind didn't worry, at least not in the way mortals did, for they had a different perspective on existence. What mortals saw as terrible tragedies were more like skinned knees and bloody noses to Reapers, momentary pains that had no lasting significance in the face of Eternity. Nevertheless, Daniel had to admit to being... concerned.

He'd been drawn to Brennan because of Conrad Dippel. All beings who defied the natural order and lived beyond their years were violating the ancient pact God and Death made before the birth of the universe. In order for Creation to be a living, growing thing, there had to be Time, and if there was Time, then there had to be a way to mark its passage. For every Before an After, for every Beginning an End, for every Life a Death. Daniel was charged with ensuring this balance was maintained, and he supposed that made him a hunter, too, in a sense. The "undead," demons, and their ilk usually weren't so much defying death as continuing to exist in a different way, but a creature like Dippel was a very special, very dangerous case. Even then, it wasn't Dippel himself that concerned Daniel as much as what he was attempting to do.

The Winchesters had been of assistance so far, destroying both the monstrous dog and the two-headed man that Dippel's dark combination of magic and science had wrought (even if technically neither creature had been constructed by his own hand), but the brothers still hadn't figured out that Dippel's was the mind behind the patchwork abominations.

As long as they were unaware of his identity—or for that matter, that he even existed—how could they do anything to stop him? Dippel might simply pull up stakes and move his operation somewhere else. He could be vengeful and cruel, but ultimately he was a practical man, and if it became too much trouble to continue working in Brennan, Dippel would move on. Daniel would be able to track him wherever he went, of course. The necromantic energy that Dippel gave off was like a blazing beacon to him. But the Winchesters would likely be unable to locate Dippel again, at least not without some serious effort on their part, and right now they didn't have the time to devote to an extensive search. Daniel knew they had more pressing matters to attend to, namely Dick Roman and the Leviathan. Considering how busy the ravenous monsters had kept the world's Reapers since their release from Purgatory, Daniel would be relieved when—or maybe that should be *if*— the Winchesters defeated the beasts.

As a Reaper, Daniel was forbidden from manifesting in the physical world, but he was permitted to communicate with the living, provided they were close enough to death to perceive him. The very old, those dying from incurable diseases, those who'd had a near-death experience and survived—he could speak to any of them, and try to convince them to act as his agent in the realm of the living. Because Sam Winchester had been infected with a necromantic taint as a result of being bitten by Dippel's monster hound, he was dying, and Daniel hoped he would be able to communicate with the hunter soon. He would tell him, and by extension, his brother, about Dippel, and lead them to the ancient alchemist. However, it was a plan Daniel might not be able to enact. For all the battering Sam's mind and spirit had taken, his mental defenses were still far stronger than an ordinary person's, and his subconscious was shutting the Reaper out, denying his existence, allowing Sam only shadowy glimpses of him. As long as Sam continued to fight like this, Daniel wouldn't be able to communicate with him. The hunter's resistance would erode the stronger the dark taint within him became and the closer he drew toward death, but if he became too weak, there was a possibility he might die before Daniel could speak with him. He supposed he would just have to keep following the Winchesters and gamble that Sam lived long enough to help him take out Dippel.

Dippel himself might be an issue, too. Daniel wasn't certain, but he thought Dippel might have gotten a glimpse of him while the Winchesters were battling the two-headed creature. Daniel didn't know if the alchemist possessed the ability to perceive Reapers. He thought it a strong possibility, though, and if that was the case, if Dippel was aware that a Reaper was watching him, who knew what he might do? At the very least, Daniel would have lost the advantage of surprise.

He sighed. Sometimes working for Death could be a real pain in the ass.

"So, was I right?" Trish whispered. "Isn't this an *awesome* place for a haunting?"

Dean had to admit, the house looked pretty damned spooky, and from the expression on Sam's face, he knew his brother felt the same. It was located a couple miles from the cabin where Trish lived with her father, not far from a small lake. The latter had served as Trish's excuse when she told her dad that the three of them wanted to leave the cabin.

I thought we could take a walk by the lake, she'd said, all innocence. *Maybe skip some rocks or something.*

No swimming, her dad had said, eyeing Sam and Dean. They might be younger than Trish, but they were still boys, and it was clear that Walter Hansen didn't like the idea of them seeing his daughter in a swimsuit.

Trish had rolled her eyes and given him a look. *Da-dee!* she'd said, drawing out the word, her voice dripping with embarrassed disapproval. She'd gotten permission, and they'd left, but their real destination had been this house.

The structure was an old two-story, the wood light gray and mottled with greenish mold and dark areas of rot, the paint long worn away by time and the elements. A section of roof had collapsed, and half of the house sagged, as if the foundation was crumbling beneath it on one side. Dean didn't know much about architecture—okay, he didn't know *anything* about it—but the house looked ancient, like it was built in the 1930s, and maybe even farther back than that. It was narrower than modern houses, the windows smaller, and instead of a porch it had three stone steps leading up to the front door. The steps were cracked, the door hung half off its hinges, and the windows no longer held even shards of glass. Dean was surprised the house hadn't fallen down by now. It looked like a dilapidated house in a cartoon, the kind that barely holds together and collapses the instant a tiny bird lands on top of it. The land around the house added to its impression of age. Trees had grown up close around it, not as tall as others farther away, but tall enough to indicate how much time had passed since anyone had lived there. There was even a tree growing out of the hole in the roof. The underbrush was thick, and if there had ever been a roadway or path to the house, it was long covered over.

Yet the aura of spookiness the house exuded wasn't due to its appearance—at least, not solely. There was a feeling in the atmosphere, a cold tingling that had nothing to do with the early spring air. It made the skin on the back of Dean's neck crawl, and set his stomach to roiling. He remembered something important his dad had told him once.

You know when a place is bad, son. And I'm talking really bad. You can sense it, same way an animal senses danger. We're animals, too, deep down, and we still have those instincts within us. All we have to do is listen when they try to warn us. Promise me you'll always listen, Dean.

Dean had promised, and he listened now. He turned to Trish and kept his voice low as he spoke.

"Your dad may not be a hunter, but he knows plenty. Why hasn't he ever told any of them about this place?"

"He doesn't believe the stories people tell about this place. The old Herald House."

"Harold?" Sam said. "Like the man's name?"

Trish shook her head. "Herald as in 'Hark, the herald angels sing.' I guess it's the last name of whoever lived here." She shrugged. "I don't really know."

"What kind of stories?" Dean asked. He was beginning to

fear they were in serious danger of getting in over their heads, *way* over. When Trish had told them that there was a haunted house not far from her cabin and asked if they wanted to go there and "bust some ghosts," both Dean and Sam had agreed, trying to act as if it was no big deal, like they were veteran hunters despite their age. That was because they didn't want to lose face in front of Trish. Dean figured the "haunted house" would turn out to be nothing but a rundown, abandoned building that kids talked about when they wanted to enjoy a shiver or two. He hadn't expected there to be any *real* ghosts here. He knew enough about vengeful spirits—and those were the ones that usually stuck around after they died—to know that they were about as far from Casper the Friendly Ghost as it was possible to get. If they were angry enough and could muster sufficient energy, they could affect the physical world. That meant they could kill.

"A long time ago, the man who lived here killed his whole family," Trish said. "He didn't have any reason, at least no reason anyone was ever able to find out. One night he just went crazy, got out of bed, went downstairs, grabbed his hunting rifle, went back upstairs, and ordered his family to get up. He marched them downstairs at gunpoint—his wife, son, and daughter—and then forced them outside into the cold night. He told them he was going to hunt them, but if they could run fast enough and managed to get away, he'd let them live. They cried and begged him not to do this, but he fired his rifle at the ground near their feet to prove he was serious. They screamed and took off running.

"The man didn't go after them right away. He wanted to

give them a sporting chance. He waited five minutes or so, and then he started after them. He found his little girl first. She hadn't gone far before climbing into a tree to hide. Most people figure her mother told her to do it because she didn't think the girl would be able to run fast enough to get away. She was sobbing and begging for her life when her father killed her with a single shot. He found his boy next. He was running from tree to tree, trying to use them as cover. It took the man three shots before he hit his target. His wife had heard the shots and knew her children were dead. She picked up a large rock and approached her husband from behind, intending to kill him for what he'd done. But quiet as she was, he still heard her. Maybe she let out a sob just as she was about to bring the rock down on his head, or maybe she just stepped on a twig. Either way, he spun around and fired his rifle point blank at her. At the exact same moment she smashed the rock into his head. They both died. Not right away, but they were gone before the sun rose. It was almost a week before the wife's sister got worried because she hadn't heard from them. She and her husband came out to investigate, but there wasn't much left of the bodies by then. The animals had picked them clean."

Dean looked at Sam. He thought maybe the story had disturbed his younger brother, but instead of looking upset, Sam looked thoughtful.

"If the whole family died, then how does anyone know what happened?" he asked.

Dean hadn't thought about that. He'd been too caught up in listening to the story. Still, he found himself coming to

Trish's defense, for no other reason than because he wanted her to like him. *Really* like him.

"The police probably figured it all out later," he said.

Trish gave him a grateful smile, and Dean felt his cheeks flush. Sam scowled with obvious displeasure at his big brother having scored points with Trish.

Too bad you'll never be as smooth as your big brother, Sammy-boy! Dean thought.

"So where does the haunting come in?" Sam asked.

"As the years went by, people began reporting encounters with an armed man out here, and stories began to circulate that the area was haunted. People came out to investigate, and soon they began turning up dead. No one could ever locate the shooter, and eventually folks just stayed away."

Too bad we aren't as smart as them, Sam thought.

"Over the years, the Herald House ghost became a local legend," Trish continued. "Sometime in the nineteen fifties people nicknamed him the Rifleman after some old TV show, and the name stuck. Hardly anyone ever comes out this way anymore. Every once in a while a hiker or a hunter—a regular hunter, I mean—goes missing. Sometimes the body is found, sometimes it isn't. When it is—"

"It's got a bullet hole in it," Dean finished.

"Usually several," Trish corrected him. "Who knows how many people he's killed over the years? He's got to be stopped, and I figured since you guys have been hunting with your dad before, you could help me get rid of him."

Dean exchanged glances with his brother. Sam had an annoying tendency to be honest at the most inconvenient times, but he said nothing now. Dean was almost disappointed. Part of him was beginning to think being here was a bad idea, and he would have liked an excuse to leave, even if it made them look like jerks in Trish's eyes. He could have backed out on his own, he supposed, but he wasn't the backing-out type. He was the charge-ahead-and-hope-things-didn't-go-all-to-hell type. Especially when there was a girl involved.

"You ready?" he asked Sam.

Sam pulled a gallon-sized plastic storage bag out of his jacket pocket. It was filled with table salt. He nodded.

Dean held an iron poker he'd borrowed from Trish's fireplace. Maybe they'd never really gone hunting with their dad, but they'd picked up a few bits and pieces of lore from him. Salt could be used to temporarily disperse a ghost. Iron did the same thing. If you could find a ghost's bones, you could pour salt on them, set them aflame, and the ghost would be banished to wherever it was ghosts went. Dean had no idea how something so simple as a little salt and fire could do that, but if it worked, it worked, and that was all that mattered to him. He had a container of lighter fluid and some matches in his jacket pocket, so they were good to go. He hoped.

He turned to Trish. "You should probably stay behind us."

She scowled. "Why? Because I'm a girl? I've got a bag of salt, too!" She removed the bag from her pocket and shook it in front of Dean's face for emphasis.

"No, because you've never done this before," he said. Although the truth was, he had wanted her to stay back because she was a girl. It was what all the tough-guy heroes in the movies did. But he could tell that wasn't going to fly with her, so he'd go with the other excuse.

It mollified her somewhat anyway, and she nodded, although she didn't look happy about it.

Dean and Sam stepped in front of Trish and began walking toward the Herald House. Dean made sure his younger brother stayed behind him, but as they drew closer to the front door, he couldn't escape the feeling that he was making a terrible mistake. He was supposed to watch out for Sam. Their dad had drilled that into his head over and over throughout the years, and it had become so deeply ingrained that it went beyond a mere feeling of responsibility. It had become an important cornerstone of Dean's identity. So what the hell was he doing leading Sam toward a house haunted by a trigger-happy ghost? Was he out of his mind? Neither of them was prepared for this, and impressing a girl—no matter how hot—was not worth putting his brother in danger.

He stopped walking and turned to face Sam and Trish. "I'm sorry, but I don't think—"

There was a loud crash as the front door burst off its remaining hinge and flew through the air, barely missing them. Dean spun around in time to see a man walk out onto the top step. No, not walk. He emerged from the darkness within the house, pulling himself free from the shadows, almost as if they had given birth to him.

When Trish had first told them about the Rifleman, Dean had imagined the ghost as a cadaverous, chalk-fleshed scarecrow of a creature, with empty dark hollows where his eyes should be, but the man that stood on the front stoop of the Herald House looked almost disappointingly normal. He was of medium height—shorter than Dean, but a bit taller than Sam—and a paunch sagged over the front of his belt. He wore a white button shirt with the sleeves rolled up, black pants with suspenders, and black shoes. His cheeks held a touch of red, he sported a pencil-thin black mustache, and his short black hair was combed and neatly parted in the middle. It looked wet, as if he'd slicked it down with something. His face appeared human enough, all the parts present and arranged in the proper configuration. Of course, his features were contorted into a mask of raw hatred, and he carried a rifle. And there were bloodstains on his shirt... bright red, as if they were still fresh.

Despite appearances, Dean could sense right away that the figure wasn't human. Not anymore, anyway. There was the way he'd appeared... the word manifested came to mind, but it was more than that. Dean could feel the wrongness emanating from the Rifleman, rolling off of him like waves of heat rising from coal-black asphalt in July. He was unnatural, plain and simple, his existence an insult to life itself. Dean could almost feel the woods around them drawing back from the apparition, recoiling from the presence of something worse than death.

The brothers didn't hesitate. Dean hurled the poker at the same instant Sam flung the contents of his plastic bag. Iron and salt struck the ghost, and the Rifleman's mouth opened in a silent scream of rage as the substance of his body dissipated into wispy shreds like fog.

Before he vanished, the ghost managed to get off a single shot, his gun booming loud as cannon fire.

Dean felt a rush of elation. They'd done it! They might not have banished the ghost for good, but they'd driven it off. Not bad for their first real hunt!

His excitement left him when he remembered the Rifleman had managed to fire his gun before disappearing. He was all right, but…

He turned to Sam, who was staring at the now empty doorway, an expression of awe on his face. "Are you okay?" Dean demanded.

Without taking his eyes off the doorway, Sam nodded.

Relieved, Dean turned to Trish. "So, what do you think about—"

He saw her lying on the ground, eyes wide and staring, the front of her sweater soaked with blood.

Dean sat up in bed. Darkness surrounded him, and for an instant, he didn't know where he was. He realized he was holding something in his right hand, and it took him a second before he recognized the Colt. He must have grabbed it from under the pillow as he awoke. Damn good thing he hadn't fired it.

He sat still for a time, skin slick with sweat, as his pulse and breathing slowly returned to normal. He could hear Sam's breathing, slow, soft, and steady, coming from the bed next to him. He was glad he hadn't woken his brother. As wiped out as he'd been lately, he needed all the rest he could get.

Dean remained there, thinking about Trish Hansen, until the sun rose.

TEN

Sam opened his eyes, yawned, and stretched. He didn't feel rested by any means, but he didn't feel as if he was going to slip back into unconsciousness any second either, and he figured that was an improvement. He sat up and saw Dean sitting at the table, working on the laptop.

"Maybe we should switch roles. How about you do the research from now on, and I fix cars and chase women?"

"In your dreams," Dean muttered. He grimaced then, as if regretting his choice of words. "Coffee's on your nightstand. It's probably cold by now."

"As long as it's got caffeine, I don't care." Sam picked up the cup and took a sip. "How are you feeling this…" He glanced at the clock on the nightstand. 9:34. "Morning?" he guessed.

Dean nodded. "I should be asking you that question."

"I wasn't a snack for a two-headed energy vampire yesterday."

"I've got to admit I'm dragging a little, but I'll be okay. I figure losing life force is like losing blood. You have to give your body time to build the supply back up."

"Yeah. You're probably right." Sam had gone to bed in a T-shirt and sweat pants the night before. Both he and Dean had showered before turning in, and he couldn't smell any traces of Frankenstink in the room. Then again, his senses had been dulled lately, so the room could reek, and he might not know it. They'd stuffed their funkified clothes into a plastic garbage bag, tied it tight, and then stuffed that into another bag and tied that one even tighter. They'd then tossed the clothes into the car's trunk. When they had time, they'd hit a coin-operated laundry, or maybe just burn the damn things and be done with it.

Sam moved to the foot of the bed and sat cross-legged while he sipped his tepid coffee. "So what game did you bring back from the darkest jungles of the Internet, oh mighty hunter?"

Dean gave him a look. "You must be feeling better if you're cracking jokes that bad. But since you asked…" Dean entered a series of keystrokes, then turned the laptop around so Sam could see the screen. "Look familiar?"

Sam got off the bed and walked over to the table for a closer look. The image on the screen was an ink drawing of a man. Only his head and shoulders were visible, but from what Sam could see of his outfit, he guessed the man had lived in either the seventeenth or eighteenth century. The longish curled hair—which Sam thought might well be a wig—helped date the image.

"Actually, he does. That's the guy we saw after we fought the Double-Header, right?"

The resemblance was uncanny. Aside from the hair, they could have been looking at a photograph instead of a drawing.

"You're looking at Johann Conrad Dippel, a German theologian, physician, and alchemist, born 1673, died 1734."

"Sounds like our guy," Sam said. "What led you to him?"

Dean smiled. "Check out *where* he was born."

Sam leaned closer and read the text that accompanied the image of Dippel.

"He was born at Castle *Frankenstein*? You've got to be kidding."

"Nope. Turns out Castle Frankenstein's a real place in Germany. No mad scientists lived there, though. Not unless you count our boy Dippel." Dean leaned closer to the screen as he skim-read. "According to this, he was fond of dissecting things. He even carried out experiments to try and transfer a soul from one dead body to another. Then he wrote about it in a dissertation called *Maladies and Remedies of the Life of the Flesh*, in which he also claimed to have discovered the Elixir of Life. Eventually he set up a lab somewhere in west Germany. A local minister accused him of grave robbing, experimenting on corpses, and—naturally—consorting with the Devil. It doesn't say if he was ever run out of town by pitchfork-wielding villagers, but it does say his 'controversial theories' got him banned from countries like Sweden and Russia. Historical records get patchy after that, but shortly before he died—or at least was *presumed* dead—he announced he'd discovered a potion that would make him immortal. That's it. I'd say that makes him Suspect Number One, wouldn't you?"

"Hell, yeah. So, what, Mary Shelley heard about Dippel and used him as inspiration for her novel?"

"That's what the Interweb says, although it also says there's no definite proof. But given what we've seen—not to mention smelled—over the last couple days, I'd say it's a good bet."

"So I guess, in a way, we really *are* looking for Dr. Frankenstein."

"Pretty cool, right?"

"Yeah." Sam sipped more coffee as he mulled over the information Dean had related to him. "Any idea why an immortal German alchemist is creating monsters in modern-day Ohio?"

Dean shrugged. "The cost of living is cheaper here?"

"Probably easier to keep a low profile in a small town. That way if one of your experiments breaks loose, it's less likely to be noticed."

"It would be kind of hard for something like Frankenmutt or the Double-Header to stroll down a street in New York without raising a few eyebrows."

Besides, it fit a pattern Sam and Dean had become very familiar with over the years. While large cities had their share of supernatural entities, for the most part monsters and malicious spirits tended to inhabit out-of-the-way places so they could keep a low profile while hunting their prey. The Leviathan were, of course, a notable exception to this modus operandi. Given their shape-shifting abilities, they preferred to hide in plain sight.

"I don't suppose the 'Interweb' said anything about how to kill an immortal alchemist," Sam said.

"Not a word. But I figure we can try any of the standard ganking techniques, with decapitation being at the top of the list."

"Fire might be good, too. Both Frankenmutt and the Double-Header caught fire easily enough and burned fast. Whatever Dippel did to their bodies to bring them back to life, it made them extra flammable. It stands to reason that he used a similar process to extend his own life—the same chemicals and mystic rites—and if so…"

"He'll burn as easy as dry grass," Dean finished.

"Let's hope so. Now all we have to do is figure out how to find him."

Dean shook his head. "What a name, huh? *Dippel*. Not as cool or scary as Frankenstein. Kind of dorky, actually. What are the chances the man has changed it after three hundred years?"

"You've seen the Frankenstein movies," Sam said. "No matter which actor plays the doctor, what's the one thing that always stays the same about him?"

Dean answered right away. "Ego. Frankenstein always thinks he can play God."

Sam nodded. "A guy like that, I'm betting he'd never change his name. He's too proud."

"Makes sense. So, about finding him. I have an idea. Every Dr. Frankenstein needs an Igor, right? An assistant to help him carry out his unnatural experiments. I think we may have already met Dippel's Igor."

"Dr. Martinez," Sam said.

"Mr. NuFlesh himself. Looks like Dippel's decided to blend a little twenty-first-century know-how with his sixteenth-century alchemy."

"Two great tastes that taste great together," Sam said.

Dean raised his eyebrows. "That one wasn't bad, Sammy. Almost made me crack a smile."

Sam finished the last of his cold coffee. He was already starting to feel tired again. He fought back a yawn.

"Let me hit the bathroom and get ready real quick, and then we can head over to—"

The motel room spun crazily around him. The next thing he knew he was lying on his back looking up at the ceiling. Dean was patting his cheek, and not gently, either.

Sam pushed his hand away. "How long this time?"

"Too friggin' long," Dean growled. "I took a look at your leg while you were out. That bite wound's not looking too good—and that's an understatement."

Sam glanced down the length of his body and saw that Dean had rolled up the leg of his sweat pants all the way to his knee. The skin where Frankenmutt had bit him had turned black, and dozens of ebon threads had spread out from the wound, covering that side of his leg from knee to ankle.

"You had to have seen this when you took a shower last night," Dean said, accusation in his voice. "Unless you're a prude who showers with his eyes closed because you're embarrassed to see yourself naked."

Sam struggled to sit up, and almost fell back again. He would have, too, if Dean hadn't reached out to steady him.

"Yeah. It's worse today, though."

"Why the hell didn't you say anything? I know your brains are thoroughly scrambled right now, but I refuse to believe you've become that stupid!"

Sam couldn't help smiling. "For a second there, you sounded like Bobby."

"Don't change the subject. We've got to do something about this infection, or whatever the hell it is, before it—"

"Kills me?" Sam finished.

"Or turns you into something like Dippel."

"What *can* we do? I was bitten by a monster dog created by an undead alchemist. Big Pharma doesn't make a pill for that. Whatever this infection is, it's at least partially magical in nature, so science alone isn't going to cure it. If Cass was here, he could wave his hand and make me all better, but he's not, so we're just going to have to keep charging ahead and see what happens."

"What *happens*? Take a real good look at your leg. I can tell you what's going to happen—that black crap's going to continue spreading until it covers your whole goddamned leg. And after that… well, whatever happens after that, I guarantee you neither of us is going to like it."

"You're just lucky the Double-Header used his hands to drain your battery," Sam said. "If he'd bitten you, we might both be in trouble."

"Look, forget Dippel for now. We'll take care of him after we get you fixed up. There's got to be something in the lore about how to counteract this. All we have to do is find it."

"There's only one man who understands what's happening to me, and that's Dippel. Once we find him, maybe he can tell us what to do to counteract the infection, and if he won't cooperate, maybe he'll have some notes or journals we can look through. Maybe he's even upgraded to a computer by now."

"Oh, he'll cooperate all right," Dean said. "I'll make sure of it."

His face was stone, his tone like ice, and Sam knew he was remembering the time he'd spent in Hell learning the secrets of torturing the damned. Dean rarely spoke of that time, and when he did, he never went into any real detail, but Sam knew his brother recalled every horrific moment he'd spent in Hell, and that included everything he'd learned there.

Sam almost felt sorry for Dippel.

He decided now wasn't a good time to tell his brother about the other effect the… death infection, for lack of a better term, was having on him. During the battle with the Double-Header, Sam had seen shadow energy swirling around the monster's arms as it attempted to drain Dean's life force, but Dean hadn't mentioned seeing that. He hadn't seen the shadowy figure either, though he *had* seen Dippel watching them. Sam had initially thought they were hallucinations, but he'd since come to a different conclusion. He had Frankenmutt's taint inside him now, and it had altered his perception, giving him a kind of death vision, allowing him to perceive the dark energy the Double-Header had summoned. Sam now thought the shadow figure was real, but Dean couldn't see it. Only he could. He didn't know what the figure was. Maybe nothing more than a local ghost drawn by the death energy released by Dippel's creations like a moth to a flame. He supposed it was one more thing they'd have to figure out as they went.

He was afraid Dean would dismiss his death vision as

another symptom of his "scrambled brains," or worse, he'd see it as a sign the infection was more advanced than he feared. Better to keep it to himself for now, Sam decided, although he knew Dean would be pissed when the truth eventually came out. He usually was.

Dean took hold of Sam's arm and helped him to stand. "Does it hurt to put any weight on it?" he asked.

Sam shook his head. "Actually, it's mostly just numb."

"That's not as comforting as you think it sounds. All right, you hit the john—or maybe I should say the Johann—and then we'll go see what we can shake loose from the Phantom of the Strip Mall."

Sam was about to chide his brother for making light of Dr. Martinez's appearance, when his sense of smell, dulled these last couple days, suddenly kicked in. He sniffed the air and frowned.

"Do you smell smoke?"

Conrad stood in the parking lot of the Wickline Inn, no more than a dozen feet from the hunters' door. Thanks to the gift from his lady, he had no trouble tracking them. This close, the rune engraved in his palm burned with a cold so intense it was almost unbearable. But bear it he would, for it was a boon granted to him by his dark mistress, and thus the agony was not a burden, but an honor.

He could have gone after the hunters at any time, but his long years had taught him not only the value of patience, but also of planning. So after the pair had slain Harrison's two-headed beast, Conrad had returned to the bicycle company—a far cry from the castle where he'd been born, but serviceable enough—and proceeded to think.

He'd spent the better part of the night developing and discarding one plan after another for ridding himself of the hunters. Some plans were too complex and presented numerous possibilities for failure, others left too much to chance, while still others would draw too much attention, and that he wished to avoid at all costs. He was the closest he'd been to achieving his goal in three centuries, and he didn't want to abandon the town, and Catherine, unless he had no other choice. In the end, as the first rays of dawn pinked the horizon, he finally decided. The plan was a simple one—which was why it had taken so long to occur to him, he supposed—but there was an elegance to it as well, along with an irony that he found as delicious as he did irresistible.

In alchemy, everything came down to the four basic elements from which all creation sprang: Earth, Air, Water…

And Fire.

He withdrew a glass vial from his jacket pocket and pried out the wax stopper. Inside was the mummified body of a tiny lizard-like creature. He'd been saving the little fellow for a special occasion, and it seemed that it had finally arrived.

He shook it out gently onto his left hand, the one unmarked by his lady. He held it up to his mouth and gently breathed on it. Instantly, its parchment-dry skin became a bright crimson, the flesh swelling with liquid, becoming soft and moist. It stirred in his palm, tiny ebon eyes blinking in the morning light.

Conrad raised the creature close to his lips once more and

whispered a single word.

"Hunters."

The salamander's body temperature began to rise, and by the time Conrad crossed the distance to the motel room door, its heat had become almost as painful as the cold blazing from the rune on his other hand. He knelt, lowered his hand, and gently deposited the creature onto the ground. It scuttled forward and pressed its nose against the surface of the door. Conrad could feel waves of heat rolling off its body as if it were a blast furnace instead of a tiny lizard. A second later, the wood at the base of the door where the salamander's snout touched it began to blacken and smolder, and the creature pushed itself forward, burning a tunnel as it went.

If all went as he planned, Conrad would leave with more than the satisfaction of knowing the two hunters were dead, sweet as that would be, he would have obtained the last element necessary to fulfill the promise he'd made to his dark mistress so many long years before. All he needed to do was wait and for the Reaper to make an appearance. If a couple deaths didn't bring one of his kind out of the woodwork, what would?

Feeling more cheerful than he had in decades, Conrad whistled an old German drinking song as he withdrew to a safe distance to watch the fun.

At first Dean thought maybe Sam was beginning to hallucinate smells on top of everything else, but then he smelled it, too—and it was getting stronger. It smelled different than regular smoke, with a chemical tang that made Dean think of a combination of gasoline and sulfur. He looked around for the source, but it was Sam who spotted it first.

"Look!" Sam pointed toward the door.

Dean turned and saw a widening scorch mark at its base, wisps of smoke rising from it as if the wood was being burned from the inside.

What the hell?

As the brothers watched, scorched wood flaked away to black ash and something pushed its way into the room. At first it was covered in soot, but crimson flames flared bright, burning the black stuff into nothing, revealing the body of a small red lizard no longer than one of Dean's pinkies. The lizard came further into the room, leaving a trail of tiny blackened footprints in the carpet.

"What's that?" Dean asked. "A fun-sized dragon?"

"I think it's a salamander," Sam said, a worried tone in his voice. "And not the kind you find next to a pond. It's a mythological creature that—"

Crimson fire burst outward from the salamander in all directions, and it scuttled toward the brothers, coming at them like a mobile campfire.

"Does that," Sam finished.

Daniel had been keeping an eye on the Winchesters since they'd fought the two-headed monster in the woods the day before. He'd even tried communicating with Sam that night after the brothers had showered and collapsed into bed. Given the right circumstances, Reapers could make contact with humans while they slept. The sleep state was in certain ways akin to death anyway—one of the reasons some sorcerers and psychically gifted humans were able to travel astrally while sleeping—and since Sam was already infected with the dark taint which was spreading and growing stronger with each passing hour, Daniel thought there was a good chance he might be able to contact him, or at least plant a suggestion into his subconscious. But he'd had no luck. Sam had been too weary, his slumber too deep. So Daniel had withdrawn from their room, passing silently through the door—physical barriers meant nothing to his kind—and taken up a position next to their vehicle, where he remained throughout the night. His kind did not tire, and they possessed almost limitless patience. It was a trait they shared with their master.

That morning, Daniel had sensed Dippel's approach long before the alchemist appeared, and since he was still uncertain whether or not the man could perceive him, he retreated to the room next to the Winchesters'. He was relieved to find it empty.

He didn't have senses, not in the way humans understood them, so he didn't smell the wood burning, but he could detect Sam and Dean's muffled voices, and their tone of alarm was unmistakable. Given the fact that this coincided with Dippel's arrival, Daniel didn't need to be a genius to know that something was wrong.

He hesitated less than a second before stepping through the wall between rooms. He emerged into the Winchesters' just in time to hear Sam speak the word "salamander." Daniel knew how dangerous salamanders like this—supernatural creatures of an age gone by—could be. He moved toward the creature, hoping that he would be able to reach it before…

Flames burst forth from the salamander's tiny form, crimson, hot, and terrible to behold. Daniel knew the mystical fire could burn through anything, and nothing could extinguish it, not even a lack of oxygen. It would continue to spread, devouring everything in its path until the magic that fueled it was expended, and no power on Earth—and few powers beyond—could force it to do otherwise.

Daniel could do nothing about the flames that the creature had already kindled, but he could ensure that it generated no more. He moved past Sam and Dean, the former gasping as he saw Daniel go by, and crouched in front of the salamander. He reached through the corona of flames surrounding it— the fire feeling hot even to his fleshless substance—and touched his index finger to the lizard's head.

A Reaper's task was vital in a cosmic sense, but ultimately a simple one: to be present at the moment of a human's death and serve as escort to, and if necessary, advisor about, the afterlife. Death's servants had many supernatural abilities to help them perform their duties, and one of the simplest was also one of the most powerful: when they wished it, their touch could kill.

Despite its diminutive size, the salamander was a creature endowed with powerful magic, and it fought the Reaper's influence, but in the end, no matter how hard the struggle, all must bow before Death. The salamander shuddered once, curled into a ball, and grew still. Its magic fled with its death, and since it was no longer protected against its own flame, it was instantly cremated.

With the salamander destroyed, there would be no new flames, but those that had already been released were spreading rapidly. Daniel knew he'd only managed to buy the Winchesters some time.

Without turning to gauge Sam's reaction to what he had done, Daniel stepped toward the burning door and passed through it. No longer would he hide from Dippel. It was high time he did something about the alchemist. He didn't know the full extent of the man's dark powers, but in the end he would surely prove no match for one of Death's chosen.

"Greetings, my friend."

Dippel stood outside the door, as if he had been waiting for Daniel. The alchemist held a polished dark blue stone in his hand, and with a cold smile he thrust it toward Daniel. The two were so close that Dippel's hand entered Daniel's chest, burying the stone deep within his ethereal substance. Daniel had never known pain. If he had, he would have known that this wasn't a pain of the flesh, a simple series of signals transmitted along a network of nerves, this was a pain of the soul, and it washed away Daniel's very self and swept him into darkness.

Conrad held the Lapis Occultus up to his face and peered into its dark blue depths. He couldn't see the Reaper's spirit, of course, but he could sense its power pulsing within, and he felt a swell of triumph. He heard a woman's voice whisper through his mind, cold as an arctic blast. *You have done well, my servant. Now complete the task you embarked upon so long ago.*

Conrad was disappointed. He would rather have remained

to watch the hunters burn in the salamander's unquenchable flames. He couldn't remember the last time he'd had the opportunity to use one of the incendiary lizards, and he'd really been looking forward to enjoying the resulting holocaust. Still, one had to tend to business before pleasure. Especially when said business was done in the name of a goddess of death.

He inclined his head. "Thy will be done, my lady."

He tucked the Lapis Occultus—which idiot scholars had long mistakenly referred to as the Philosopher's Stone—into his jacket pocket and headed for his car. The Lapis Occultus possessed many useful properties: turning base metals into gold, healing illness, and prolonging life. And with the right adjustments, it also made an extremely effective prison for a Reaper.

Conrad had one stop to make before presenting the Reaper's spirit to Catherine. He needed to acquire more NuFlesh, and he owed Peter Martinez the unguent he'd promised him. Conrad Dippel was many things, almost all of them unpleasant, but a breaker of vows was not among them.

Beautiful clouds of crimson-tinged smoke billowed into the sky as he got into his car and pulled out of the motel's parking lot. He was concerned that Martinez might be tempted to over-apply the unguent once he got hold of a fresh supply. If so, the results would be… unfortunate. Still, what did it matter? After today, Conrad would have no more need of Martinez or his NuFlesh. Soon his mistress would be free to walk the Earth, and devastation and despair would follow in her wake.

It was going to be glorious.

* * *

Sam didn't know if it was his proximity to the shadow figure or the worsening of his condition, but he was able to make out some details of the being's appearance this time. Not much, just a suggestion of body shape and facial features, enough to make him think the figure was a shadow *man*. He watched it step toward the salamander, crouch down, touch it, and then straighten and walk through the blazing door as if it and the fire that was rapidly devouring it wasn't there. Sam wasn't certain what the shadow man had done to the salamander, but as near as he could tell it was dead, burnt to a crisp by its own flame. The fires it had already produced continued to rage unabated, however.

The room's smoke alarm began shrilling a high-pitched warning that was as annoying as it was unnecessary.

The door was aflame, as were the curtains around the window and the legs of the table. Sam lunged forward—nearly losing his footing thanks to his numb leg—and snatched up the laptop before the fire could claim it. Although he didn't come in contact with any of the flames, the heat that emanated from them was intense, and his skin stung as if he'd received an instant sunburn. He stepped back, closed the laptop, and tucked it under his arm. He'd been just in time. The blazing curtains fell onto the tabletop, igniting it.

"Let's try for the window," Dean said. "If we break it, we can jump through. We might get a little singed in the process—"

"No good," Sam said, shaking his head. "This is magic fire. If even a single small flame touches us, the fire will spread across our bodies until we've been reduced to ash!"

Sam felt as if his brain was running at near-normal speed again. Amazing how the threat of immediate incineration focused one's concentration.

The room was rapidly filling with acrid smoke. The air had an oily texture, and breathing it in was like inhaling ground glass. Sam thought it would be a race to see which would kill them first: the flames or the poisonous smoke.

"Get your gun." Dean ordered.

Sam didn't question his brother. His gun was still underneath his pillow, while Dean's rested on the nightstand next to his bed.

Gun in hand, safety off, Sam said, "Now what?"

"Motel walls are notoriously thin, right? We concentrate our fire on one spot and shoot our way through to the next room."

"But what if someone's—"

Dean shouted, "Look out!" and fired a round high into the wall, so if it went all the way through, the odds of it hitting anyone on the other side were small. He waited a moment, then said, "That ought to do it." He began firing at the center of the wall between the two beds, and Sam joined him.

The Winchesters were practiced marksmen, and more importantly, they had a great deal of experience shooting under adverse conditions—like when some monster or other was trying to rip their faces off. Their aim was steady and true, and plaster flew out of the wall in large chunks. They both emptied their clips, but while they'd chewed away a good-sized hole, could even see into the next room, it wasn't large enough to crawl through. Ammo spent, both brothers reflexively tucked their pistols into their waistbands. The gun metal was hot, but it was nothing compared to the flames at their back.

Sam could feel the flames, almost as if he was lying on a frying pan with the heat turned to high. He could almost feel his flesh back there starting to blister. He figured they had seconds left, if that, before the salamander's fire engulfed them.

Dean rapidly cast his gaze around the room. If anyone else had been present to witness him do this, they might have thought it a sign of panic, but Sam knew his brother's mind was working at warp speed, trying to come up with a way out. Dean usually put up a front, acting as if he was a regular everyday Joe whose most intellectual pursuit was watching foreign porn movies on pay-per-view. In reality he was highly intelligent, and a master of strategy and tactics. If anyone could find a way to escape this death trap, he could.

"Hit it!" Dean shouted.

Before Sam could ask what he meant, Dean ran toward the hole they'd shot in the wall and threw himself at it, shoulder first. He thudded against the wall in a shower of plaster and white dust, grunted, then stepped back to try again. Sam joined him this time, and after two more blows, the wall crumbled under the impact, and the two of them tumbled into the room next door.

Sam moaned. His shoulder screamed with pain, and he thought he might have dislocated it. At least he wasn't burning to death. He gave the laptop a quick glance. He'd done his best to shield it with his body as they broke through the wall, and as near as he could tell, it had survived the trip intact. The two of them, however, were covered with plaster dust and bits of wall insulation.

He looked at Dean. "Hit it? That was your big plan? What if there'd been a support beam in the way?"

"It worked, didn't it?"

Luckily, the room was empty. For an instant, as they broke through, Sam had feared they'd find someone there, lying on the ground, bleeding from a dozen bullet wounds.

Dean got to his feet, reached down, and helped Sam to his. Sam cradled his right arm to his chest to guard the shoulder, and looked back at the hole. The fire had spread to the rest of their room, and was already coming their way. A cloud of harsh-smelling smoke billowed through the hole, setting off the smoke alarm in the room, and Sam knew if they didn't get out of there fast, they'd be charbroiled.

They headed for the door, opened it, and plunged into the parking lot and the blessedly smoke-free air.

Dean wanted to head straight for their car, hop in, and go gunning for Dippel, but Sam dissuaded him.

"We have to help get everyone to safety," he insisted.

Sometimes being good guys really sucks, Dean thought, but he knew Sam was right, and they spent the next fifteen minutes running around, pounding on room doors and shouting "Fire!"

They found less than a dozen people, including cleaning staff. As it was close to ten a.m., most of the Wickline Inn's patrons had already checked out or left for the day on whatever business had brought them to Brennan. By the time a fire truck and EMT van arrived, Dean was confident that they'd managed to get everyone out of the motel and a safe distance away from the blazing structure. He and Sam watched the firefighters do what they could to put out the flames, but mere water had no effect on salamander-fire, and within a short time, the motel was nothing but a blackened, smoking ruin. One good thing: when the motel was gone, so was the fire. As Sam had predicted, once their power was spent, the flames burned themselves out. It seemed that whoever—or whatever—had created salamanders had been smart enough to realize that a creature that generated unstoppable devastating flame needed some kind of off switch. Lucky for them.

When they were certain the firefighters and emergency medical personnel had everything under control, Sam and Dean headed for the car, got in, and pulled out of the parking lot. One good thing about the place being destroyed: at least they didn't have to settle the bill.

"I'm glad you managed to save the computer, but we lost all the other stuff we had in the room, including our extra clothes. All we got left is what we got on, which smells like smoke, and the crap we bagged up in the trunk, which smells like Frankenrot. I guess no matter what we do, we're going to end up stinking until we can find time to hit a department store."

"I'd rather stink than be stuck in a burn ward," Sam said.

"No kidding." A thought occurred to Dean. "What happened to the salamander? It looked like it died right after it burned its way into our room. Are they supposed to do that?"

Sam didn't reply right away, and Dean wondered if his brother had slipped into another one of his mini-comas again.

But when he glanced over at him, he saw his eyes were open.

"There's something I haven't told you."

Dean's stomach dropped. He hated it when Sam did this to him. Both of them had a tendency to play things close to the vest at times, but Sam was the proverbial still waters that ran deep. When he finally felt compelled to confess something, it was usually because whatever it was had gotten so bad he could no longer keep it a secret. Dean steeled himself for whatever Sam was going to say next.

"I have death vision."

Dean stared at his brother for a long moment.

"Say what?"

ELEVEN

On the way to NuFlesh Biotech, Dean pulled into a coffee shop drive-thru and Sam ordered a large coffee with five shots of espresso. Then he changed his mind and got seven shots instead. Dean ordered a large pumpkin-flavored drink with whipped cream on top. When Sam raised an eyebrow at his brother's choice of beverage, he said, "What? They only have pumpkin in the fall." As far as Sam was concerned, Dean might as well have gotten a milkshake, but to each his own. Besides, he wasn't one to be lecturing anyone about making healthy choices. His caffeine intake was verging on insane, and it still barely kept him functioning.

Dean had taken his revelation about possessing "death vision" fairly well, all things considered. Probably because he was planning to force Dippel to tell them how to cure the infection spreading through Sam's body. Dean always felt better when he had a clear course of action to follow. But even though Sam had been the one to bring up the possibility in the first place, he wasn't confident that Dippel would know of a cure, or if he did, that he'd share it with them. As old and powerful as Dippel was, they'd be lucky to kill him, and there likely wouldn't be any time for questioning beforehand. There was a good chance this would be Sam's last hunt, and while he had faced death on numerous occasions—even experienced it a few times—he knew this time it would stick. There was no Cass to heal him at the last minute with angelic powers, no mystic artifact, spell, or potion in their possession that could counteract the death-infection. Even if they had such an item, Sam wasn't sure he'd want to use it. Magic that powerful came at a high cost, and it often had unexpected— and tragic—side effects. Like with Trish.

Sometimes death is better, Sam thought. *A lot better.*

The brothers shared a guest room in the Hansen cabin, just down the hall from Trish's room, but neither of them got any sleep that night. Before, when they'd had trouble sleeping, it was because of Trish's proximity. It was hard not to imagine her lying on her bed snuggled beneath the covers, and even harder not to wonder what she slept in, or if she slept in anything at all. But she wasn't in her room that night, and she never would be again. Each of the boys had his own twin bed, and Sam lay on his, staring through the darkness up at the ceiling, or at least in the direction where the ceiling was. Heavy curtains blocked all light from coming through the window, rendering the room as black as the inside of a cave. Sam wondered if this was what it was like for Trish right now, surrounded by darkness and silence. Only in her case, morning would never come.

It wasn't totally silent in their room, though. He could hear Dean breathing, and he knew from the volume and rhythm of the sound that his brother was awake. He had a pretty good idea what he was thinking, too. As the older brother, he viewed it as his responsibility to take care of Sam, and by extension, of anyone around him. He'd seen himself as the leader of their ill-fated expedition to the Herald House, and therefore responsible for how it had turned out. That meant he blamed himself for Trish's death. Sam felt that he was equally responsible. After all, both of them had pretended that they'd gone hunting before, that they'd encountered ghosts and knew how to handle them. True, Sam had mostly kept his mouth shut while Dean lied, but he hadn't contradicted his brother, and as far as he was concerned, that amounted to the same as lying. Some hunters they turned out to be. All they'd managed to do was dispel the ghost for a time, to wound it temporarily and make it retreat to wherever it was ghosts went when they weren't manifesting on the material plane. It would be back, as deadly as ever.

Sam wanted to say something to make his brother feel better, or at least let him know that he didn't blame him for what had happened, but he was afraid that anything he might say would be stupid and end up making Dean feel worse. So he lay in the dark and said nothing.

They'd carried Trish's body back to the cabin, Dean holding her beneath the arms, Sam gripping her legs. It was the first time either of them had touched her, but Sam took no pleasure in it, and he knew Dean didn't either. Trish was lighter than he'd expected, almost as if some part of her had departed when she died, leaving behind only an empty shell. Her father had been sitting at the kitchen table when they arrived, waiting for them, as if he'd sensed that something had happened. Something bad.

Sam and Dean carried Trish inside and laid her gently on the couch. When Walter Hansen saw his daughter's body, the front of her sweater tacky with drying blood, he stood and stared at her for nearly five minutes without speaking. Several times Dean tried to say something, but each time Walter held up his hand to forestall him. Then without a word or even so much as a glance at either of them, he picked up his daughter, carried her out of the living room, into the kitchen, and then down into the basement. Sam and Dean trailed behind, unsure what to do. They stood in the kitchen, not daring to violate the sanctity of Walter's workspace, which they'd never been invited into, and waited. A couple moments later, they heard the sound of Walter's boots on the stairs. Sam had thought that this was it. Walter was going to come bursting through the door, yelling at them for having gotten his daughter killed. Then he heard the lock on the basement door engage, and a second later, Walter went back down the stairs.

Not knowing what else to do, they sat at the table and remained there until long after the sun went down. They didn't speak, didn't eat or drink. They didn't do anything but sit and stare at the closed and locked basement door. Eventually, Dean stood up and headed down the hall to their bedroom, and Sam followed. They crawled into bed without brushing their teeth or anything, and they'd been lying there ever since, awake and silent.

In his mind, Sam saw the Rifleman's horrible expression as he emerged from the darkness within Herald House, watched him raise his rifle, heard the thunderous sound of his weapon discharging. Replaying it once, twice, three times…

The next thing Sam was aware of was the smell of bacon frying, and he realized he must have fallen asleep. Some people drifted off while counting sheep, but he'd zonked out counting gunshots. If that didn't make him a prime candidate for the funny farm, he didn't know what did.

The room was still dark, thanks to the curtains, but he had the sense that Dean was sitting up on his bed.

"You smell that?" Dean asked.

"Yeah." It was freaking him out, too. In the entire time they'd been staying with the Hansens, Walter had never made breakfast. Trish always had. Sometimes pancakes, sometimes French toast, sometimes eggs, but no matter what she made, she always fried bacon to go with it. Always.

"What should we do?" Sam asked.

"Check it out," Dean answered, although he didn't sound confident about his answer.

Sam didn't blame him. The skin on the back of his neck was crawling, and he could feel a cold heaviness in his belly, as if he'd swallowed a hunk of lead.

Dean stood up and walked to the door, feeling his way through the dark. When he reached the door, he found the light switch and flipped it on. The overhead light came to life, and Sam squinted against its glare. He wanted to stay right where he was, but Dean was being brave, and that meant he should be brave, too—even if he didn't want to. He climbed out of bed and joined Dean at the door. They'd both gone to bed in their clothes, so they didn't need to change. Too bad. Sam would have appreciated any delay, no matter how small.

Both boys ran their fingers through their hair in an attempt too make it look at least a bit less mussed, and then Dean opened the door and they stepped into the hall. The smell of bacon was stronger here, and despite the situation, Sam found his mouth starting to water, and his stomach gurgled. He felt immediately ashamed. How could he be hungry after everything that had happened? But he couldn't help it. Then Dean's stomach rumbled, making Sam feel a bit better.

They walked down the hall into the kitchen. Walter sat at the kitchen table, sipping a mug of coffee, an empty plate before him. He looked up when they entered, and he smiled.

"Good morning, boys! Pull up a seat!"

He sounded cheerful, but his face was haggard and drawn. The flesh beneath his eyes was puffy and dark, and the lower half of his face was dotted with stubble. He didn't smell too good, either, and he was wearing the same clothes he had on yesterday. Sam wondered when Walter's last shower was. The man could definitely use one. But odd as it was to be greeted pleasantly by the father of a girl you'd gotten killed, odder still was the figure standing at the stove.

Sam froze when he saw her. From the back, she looked like Trish. Same height and build, same hair, same clothes she'd been wearing when they'd hiked to the Herald House yesterday. She was lifting bacon out of the frying pan with a fork and depositing it on a plate covered with a folded-over paper towel to soak up excess grease. Instead of a deep brown color, the bacon was charcoal-black, and Sam knew she—whoever she was—had burned it. When the plate was filled with bacon, she dropped the fork to the floor, as if now that she longer needed it, it had ceased to exist for her. Then she picked up the bacon plate and without bothering to turn off the burner, turned and walked toward them.

Sam's gaze was drawn to the dark stain on her sweater first. It was dry now, and almost black, like the bacon she carried. Then he raised his eyes and forced himself to look at her face.

It *was* Trish. Her skin had a sallow cast to it, and her features were slack, utterly void of expression. And her eyes… they were wide and staring, and they looked glassy-hard, like marbles.

When Sam had been younger, he and Dean had taken a trip with their father. He couldn't remember where to or for what reason. Just another long car ride, and another few nights in a hotel with only Dean to take care of him while their father was out doing whatever he had gone there to do. Somewhere along the way, they'd stopped for gas at a small out-of-the-way station. Sam had needed to use the bathroom, so Dean took him while their dad paid for the gas. The restrooms were located inside the station, and as Dean escorted him through, Sam was startled to see a fox standing on the counter. At first he'd thought it was real, the owner's pet, maybe. Then after a second he saw that it stood perfectly still, and he realized it wasn't a real fox, or rather, it had been real once, but it was no longer alive. It had been stuffed and mounted. It was kind of creepy, but also kind of cool. When he was done peeing, Sam made sure to walk by the counter so he could get a good look at the fox. Close up, he could see that some of the fox's stitching was coming loose, and a fine coating of dust had settled onto its fur. But the worst part was its eyes. Glossy black and lifeless, they were like doll eyes, only worse, because someone had removed this animal's real eyes and glued the fake ones into the sockets.

That's what Trish's eyes looked like now. Dead doll eyes.

He looked to Dean and saw his brother staring at Trish with an expression of shock. Sam was sure he looked the same. Neither of them made a move to take a seat at the table with Trish's father.

She carried the bacon-filled plate to the table and stood there, staring off into space. She made no move to serve it.

Walter saw the brothers staring at Trish, and gave them a smile and a wink. "Where there's a will, there's a way— especially when you work with hunters. A lot of them can't afford to pay me in cash, so they settle their bill the old-fashioned way: with barter. I've picked up all kinds of interesting objects over the years. Sometimes I sell them to hunters who can use them, but most of the time I just put them away, figuring maybe I'll find a use for them someday." He reached into his pants pocket, withdrew an object, and set it on the table. It was a small obsidian statue of a dog-headed man wearing an ancient Egyptian headdress.

"Recognize this fellow? It's Anubis, the Egyptian god of the dead. He's not much in the height department, but he kicks ass when it comes to bringing folks back from what Shakespeare called 'the undiscovered country.'" He looked up at Trish and smiled. "Isn't that right, sweetie?"

Trish opened her mouth as if she intended to reply, but all that came out was a thin stream of drool that fell onto the bacon.

Walter turned back to the brothers and grinned. "So, who's hungry?"

From the outside, the NuFlesh Biotech office looked the same as it had yesterday, but as Sam and Dean got out of the car and headed for the door, it burst open and Dr. Martinez's office assistant came running out. The slender woman looked absolutely terrified, and without realizing where she was going, she ran directly into Dean. She didn't have a lot of meat on her, and the collision sent her stumbling backward as if she'd run full force into a brick wall. Dean managed to reach out and grab her arms in time to stop her from falling on her bony posterior.

"What's wrong?" he asked. "Has something happened?"

He groaned inwardly. He hated it when people in horror movies asked stupid questions like that. *Of course* something had happened! Why else would she be running as if she had a pack of Hellhounds on her tail?

At first her gaze refused to focus on either Dean or his brother, and her lower lip kept quivering. He was beginning to fear that she'd taken the last exit to Loonyville, but then she spoke.

"It's Doctor Martinez. He's… he's not well."

She tore free from Dean's grip with surprising strength for such a petite woman and ran into the parking lot. If she had a car there, she didn't bother with it. She just kept going until she reached the sidewalk and was gone.

"I'd say that definitely qualifies as a bad sign," Dean said.

"You think?"

The brothers drew their pistols—both weapons reloaded and ready to go—and entered NuFlesh.

The reception area was empty, which made sense, as its usual sole occupant had just high-tailed it for the hills. Dean held up his hand for Sam to stop for a moment, and the two of them listened. At first Dean didn't hear anything, but then he was able to make out a voice singing softly.

"The worms crawl in, the worms crawl out, the worms play pinochle on your snout…"

"That's a little creepy," Dean whispered.

"More than a little," Sam replied.

Together the brothers headed down the hall toward Martinez's office. The singing grew louder the closer they got, the same phrase, repeated over and over in a childish singsong tone. Martinez's door was half open, and Dean debated the merits of calling out to the doctor or going in silent, guns at the ready.

He didn't have to make the choice, as the door opened the rest of the way and Martinez stepped into the hall. He stopped when he saw the Winchesters. If he noticed they'd drawn their pistols, it didn't seem to bother him.

"Hello, agents! I didn't expect to see you again so soon. What can I help you with?" His voice was a thick, liquid burble, almost impossible to understand.

Dean and Sam could only stand and stare. They'd seen

some genuinely awful things in their lives, but this qualified for the top ten, easy.

Martinez's skin had taken on a bright pink color that reminded Dean of the nasty slime fast-food burgers were made from, and it sagged from his bones like melting wax. The flesh had drawn away from his eyes and mouth, giving his face a skull-like aspect, and his hair had slid down the left side of his face like a toupee that refused to stay put. His ears dangled from thin pink strands that hung from his head like braids, and his fingers stretched all the way to the floor. The flesh from his legs had run out of his pants cuffs to overflow his shoes, making it look as if he had thick pink stumps instead of feet. His chin had become a long tendril that stretched past his chest and wobbled horribly when he spoke.

Dean turned toward his brother. "Sam, remember when I said this job reminded me of *Frankenstein*? I changed my mind. We are way into *Reanimator* territory here!"

Martinez went on as if Dean hadn't spoken. "I hope you haven't come for any samples of NuFlesh to compare with what you found on that nightmarish beast you showed me yesterday." He spoke almost cheerfully in his burbling voice, as if nothing was wrong. "I'm afraid I traded the last of my supply to a special customer of mine. He provides me with a special unguent that relieves the itching caused by my burn scars and—"

That was the last word Martinez got out before his lower jaw detached from his skull and tumbled to the floor. It landed with a plop in the widening pool of pink goo that spread outward from his feet, and Sam and Dean scooted back to avoid contact with the disgusting substance. Dean had seen the *Blob* movies, and he knew how dangerous nasty goo could be. Pinkish slime continued running from Martinez's skeleton, flowing like syrup, and individual bones came loose without muscles, ligaments, or cartilage to hold them in place. His form began to lose shape and fold in upon itself, though his eyes remained unaffected, darting back and forth in confusion, as if he'd finally come to realize that something was terribly wrong but wasn't able to determine what. Then Martinez lost what little solidity remained to him, and his skeleton collapsed, leaving nothing but a pile of bones, his clothing, and a mound of watery goo. Only his eyes remained, housed in the skull, which sat lopsided atop the pink mound. They looked up at Sam and Dean, whatever emotion they might have held unreadable, until at last they too melted away to nothing.

"I'm never going to eat ice cream again," Dean said. "Or chew bubble gum."

Sam looked as if he might lose the gallon or so of coffee he'd drunk so far that morning. "I'm right there with you, brother."

"I've been using the basement as a lab for weeks now, and I still haven't gotten used to how chilly it is down here. Sometimes I feel as if I should be wearing a parka instead of a lab coat. But the cold's good for you, isn't it, sweetie?"

She smiled down at her daughter. Bekah lay naked on the table, a white sheet covering her from the neck down. Even though it was just the two of them, Catherine wanted to give Bekah her dignity. Catherine might be her mother—not to mention a doctor—but Bekah was a teenager, nearly an adult, and her body was her own. The last thing Catherine wanted to do was treat her like a piece of meat.

Like you treated that poor dog? she asked herself.

That was different. That creature was a test subject, its only purpose to help Catherine determine how effective NuFlesh—with Conrad's special "enhancements"—was at fusing body parts from different donors. Both Bekah and Marshall's bodies had suffered severe damage in the accident, and it had been necessary to replace numerous organs, tissue, and in a couple cases, entire limbs. A good half of Bekah's face had needed reconstruction, and only one of her original blue eyes remained to her. The other was now brown. Beneath the sheet, her body was crisscrossed by faint scar lines of NuFlesh indicating where Catherine had operated on her. She'd taken far more care with Bekah than she had with the dog, so the scars were hardly noticeable. She'd been even more careful with her daughter's face, working diligently to ensure that the skin looked as smooth and natural as possible. When Bekah was… well again, Catherine wanted her to like what she saw in the mirror.

During the last few weeks Catherine had often felt more like a sculptor than a doctor, though with her medium being flesh instead of clay. Conrad had encouraged her to view her work that way.

We want strong, healthy bodies for your family, he'd once told her. *That is, of course, the ultimate goal. At its best the human form possesses an elegance and beauty unrivaled in nature. So we want to make sure that not only are your loved ones restored*

*to life, but that the bodies that house that life are worthy of the
gods themselves.*

Conrad often spoke like that, almost as if he was a poet
instead of... whatever he was. Catherine didn't see her work
in such lofty terms, but she wanted Bekah and Marshall to
be comfortable with their restored bodies, wanted them to be
able to go out in public without drawing attention. Simply
put, she wanted them to be as normal as possible, given the
circumstances. She certainly didn't want them to turn out to
be freakish monstrosities, like the dog. But then, she hadn't
been concerned with aesthetics when she'd made it, only in
testing the efficacy of NuFlesh. And, of course, in proving
that Conrad's resurrection techniques worked.

At least she didn't have to worry about the dog anymore.
Conrad had let her know that the beast had been disposed
of. He'd provided no details, and she'd asked for none. One
of the key aspects of their working relationship was that she
didn't press him for information, and he didn't tell her things
that she'd prefer not to hear. It was better that way.

Bekah's long hair was a deep rich brown, and Catherine
loved to brush it. The action reminded her of when Bekah
had been a child, unable—or truth to tell, unwilling—
to brush her own hair. Even when Catherine had finally
managed to get the girl to go into the bathroom and brush,
she always "forgot" to do the back, leaving it to Catherine to
finish the job. Bekah had grown out of that phase eventually,
and Catherine had been surprised to find herself missing it.
She'd enjoyed the sweet intimacy of touching her daughter's
hair, of running the brush through it, of chatting with Bekah

about this and that while she worked.

She was tempted to get a brush and spend a few minutes grooming Bekah's hair now, but she resisted. She hadn't removed Bekah from the freezer and laid her out on the table so she could play Mommy. She had work to do. She'd begin with the head.

Many were the wonders that Conrad had shown her during the course of their collaboration, and although she was a rational woman, she had come to believe that there was, if not magic in the world, far more to science that she'd ever suspected. One of the most amazing things he had taught her was the formula for creating a chemical mixture that could reverse the cellular damage caused by decay. In and of itself it did not restore life, but it prevented dead bodies from rotting, which given the amount of time Catherine had needed to have Bekah and Marshall out of the freezer and on the table so she could work with them, was vital. However, the treatment wasn't permanent, and when it wore off, not only did decay return, it did so with a vengeance, accelerating exponentially until the subject was nothing but a fleshless skeleton, as she'd learned from observing numerous test subjects. Rats, mostly, and in one case, a stray cat Conrad had brought her. The results of accelerated decay were unpleasant to observe, to say the least, and it was a fate she was determined to avoid for her husband and daughter. So every few days Catherine checked Bekah and Marshall to make sure they hadn't begun to actively decay once more. If she'd had an unending supply of the treatment, she'd use it on them every day, but the ingredients weren't easy to come by, and the process for creating the mixture was quite involved. A mistake at any step along the way would render the result useless. So Catherine made sure to employ the treatment only when it was absolutely necessary.

The results were almost beyond belief. When Bekah had been little, many was the time that Catherine had crept into her room at night, ostensibly to check and make certain she was all right, but in reality because she simply loved watching her daughter sleep. She was always so still—no restless sleeper, she—and her breathing was so gentle that Catherine had to lean down close to hear it. Now, looking at Bekah lying on the table, her features awash in the harsh glow of fluorescent light, Catherine had no trouble imagining that she wasn't dead, that she was merely sleeping as sound as ever, waiting for her mother to rouse her.

In a way, she supposed that was true.

Enough woolgathering. She had work to do. She began her examination with Bekah's feet.

She lifted the sheet and began searching for any discoloration on the skin. Finding none, she drew the sheet back further and moved on to the legs. She was in the process of examining the torso when she heard footsteps on the kitchen floor overhead. Conrad had arrived.

She rearranged the sheet to cover her daughter's body once more, then leaned close to Bekah's ear and whispered, "Don't worry. I know you don't like it when he looks at you. We'll finish the examination later, when he's gone."

She heard the basement door open, and she straightened and took a step back from the table. She saw nothing wrong in talking to her daughter, but she never did so in front of Conrad. She wasn't worried that he'd think her crazy. He was a bit odd himself, to put it mildly. But her conversations with Bekah—one-sided though they might be—were private, meant to be kept between mother and daughter.

He came down the stairs, moving gracefully despite being burdened with a large cardboard box. It looked as if it was heavy, but he carried it with ease. She wasn't surprised. She'd long known he was stronger than he looked.

"More supplies?" she asked.

Conrad reached the basement floor and walked to one of the counters where he set the box down on one of the few empty spaces to be found. He removed his lab coat from the hook on the wall where it had been hanging, slipped it on over his suit jacket, and then joined Catherine by Bekah's side.

"More NuFlesh," he said. "We're going to need it."

"Good." She'd finished restoring Bekah's body for the most part, but there were still a few things she wanted to do to Marshall's. Then she frowned. "Wait, what do you mean, 'We're going to need it'? You sound as if you have something special in mind."

Conrad smiled. She disliked it when he did that. He had a habit of giving her a smile that she imagined a cat might show to a small rodent an instant before pouncing.

"I do indeed! Feast your eyes, my dear, upon *this*." He removed a small object from his jacket pocket and held it out for her inspection.

At first, it didn't look like much to her. It was an oblong stone of deep blue, its surface polished smooth. Then she realized that instead of catching and reflecting the light, the stone seemed to absorb it, and not gently. It grabbed hold of the light and dragged it down into whatever untold depths lay within.

She blinked. For a moment, she'd felt almost hypnotized by the stone, and it took an effort to tear her gaze from it and focus on Conrad once more.

"What is it?" She kept her tone neutral, but inside she was burning with excitement. She could sense the power the stone exuded, and she knew that Conrad had indeed brought her something special today. Very special.

"It's called the Lapis Occultus," he explained. "A token of great power."

"Can I… hold it?" She was almost afraid to ask. The longer she looked at the stone, the less distinct its outline became, as if it radiated some kind of energy that distorted the air around it.

"Of course." He held it out to her, and she took it with trembling hands. It was then she caught a glimpse of Conrad's right palm and saw the black X marring the flesh.

She frowned. "What happened to you?"

"It's nothing of consequence. The materials we work with can be dangerous, as you well know, and I wasn't as careful as I should have been. It will heal in due course."

The symmetrical shape of the mark made it look deliberate. If the affected area hadn't been raised, she might've thought it was a tattoo.

Before she could think on the matter further, her attention was drawn back to the object she held. The Lapis Occultus,

Latin for dark stone.

It was cool to the touch, and seemed to almost vibrate in her hand, as if it was charged with power. In fact, the longer she held it, the more she had the sense that it was somehow alive. She thought she could even hear a voice, so faint it was almost imperceptible, calling to her as if from a great distance. A man's voice, she thought, but she couldn't make out what it was saying.

Conrad took the stone from her hand, and the voice was cut off. Catherine felt momentarily disoriented, as if she'd just awakened from a dream. She shook her head as if to clear it. No doubt about it, she needed to get more rest.

She forced herself to look away from the stone and meet Conrad's gaze. "What does it do?"

"It is the final piece of the puzzle, Catherine. With it, we can ensure that your husband and daughter's bodies will be completely resistant to decay once they are resurrected."

She stared at the stone in Conrad's hand, unable to believe what she'd heard. The problem of decay was the one impediment to successful resurrection of the dead. You could restore them to life, even create a new being from separate parts, but regardless of how careful you were, the resurrected would eventually begin to decay, sometimes sooner, sometimes later, but it was inevitable. She had observed this in one test subject after another. It was almost as if they had a force eating them away from the inside. The effect was more pronounced when pieces from separate donors were joined, most likely due to tissue rejection. NuFlesh helped slow the process of decay a great deal, but it could only forestall it so long.

If the Lapis Occultus could do what Conrad claimed, then there was no reason to wait any longer. They could begin resurrecting Bekah and Marshall right away! But if the stone didn't function as Conrad promised, she would be restoring her husband and daughter to life only to condemn them to a slow, painful second death.

"I can see the hesitation on your face," Conrad said. "When I first came to you, you were skeptical of what I claimed I could do, but have I not proved myself to you time and again? I know to one such as yourself, schooled in the ways of modern science, the Lapis Occultus must appear to be nothing more than a mere gem. Pretty enough, but certainly not capable of performing miracles. Yet you held it in your hand, Catherine. You *felt* its power. You cannot deny the evidence of your own senses."

She had felt the stone's power. She didn't understand it, but she knew it was real. And Conrad had been able to deliver on every promise he'd made so far, no matter how impossible it might have seemed at the time. Surely he'd earned her trust by now. Beyond all that, though, was the fact that she missed Marshall and Bekah so very much. They'd been separated too long. It was high time they were a family again.

"All right." Now that she'd accepted the Lapis Occultus as genuine, she could feel her excitement rising. "Bekah's body is complete, and she's already on the table. I'll give her a thorough examination to make sure she's ready and then—"

"Perhaps we should begin with your husband."

Catherine had already turned toward Bekah, intending to get to work right away, but Conrad's words stopped her. She turned to look at him, frowning. "Marshall isn't ready. He still needs a few finishing touches. Bekah—"

Conrad stepped forward and reached out to touch Catherine's arm. Even through the sleeve of her lab coat and the sweater beneath, she could feel how cold his hand was.

"I understand your eagerness to proceed, and in my own way I share it."

There was something in his tone of voice that made Catherine think there was a hidden meaning to the last part of his statement, but Conrad went on before she could consider it further.

"I have every confidence that the Lapis Occultus will function properly, but I must admit that I have never used it before. Not in this way, at least. I think it might be prudent to test it first."

"You want to use *Marshall* as a test subject?" The thought horrified her.

"If he was alive, and this were a more… mundane medical procedure that both he and your daughter needed, a procedure that carried with it a certain amount of risk, what do you think he would do?"

Catherine knew exactly what her husband would do. The same as she would under similar circumstances.

"He'd insist on going through the procedure first to make sure it was safe."

Conrad's face betrayed no reaction to her words, but she felt a sense of satisfaction from him, as if he'd won an important battle.

"How long do you anticipate it will take to ready your

husband's body for the procedure?"

She considered. "All the major organs are in place and properly connected. The nervous system could use more tweaking, but it's essentially finished. Really, all that's left are mainly cosmetic touches. The nose isn't as straight as I'd like, he's still missing several teeth—and there's the tongue, of course. That's what will take the most time. But with the new… donations you acquired the other night, along with a fresh supply of NuFlesh, I'd say Marshall could be ready to go in two, maybe three hours."

Conrad smiled. "Excellent. Shall we begin?"

TWELVE

After Dr. Martinez had, as Dean put it, turned into a "soft nougaty center," the brothers split up and searched through the NuFlesh offices, looking for any clue to the location of Conrad Dippel's home base. As they moved from room to room, they had to be careful not to step in Martinez's liquefied remains pooling in the hall, which were beginning to smell almost as bad as Frankenmutt's. When they were finished, the brothers compared notes in the reception area.

"There was nothing on Martinez's computer or in his desk," Sam said. "He left his phone in his office, but there was no number or address in it for Dippel. No texts or emails, either."

"Same with Ms. Speedy Gonzalez," Dean said. "Both her computer and desk were fresh out of Dippel, too. Did you see anything with your, uh, death vision?"

Dean still didn't know how he felt about Sam's latest revelation. If it was true, it meant that his brother's infection was worse than he'd suspected. If it wasn't true, it meant that his hallucinations were starting up again. Hell, it could be both: the infection might be causing such a strain on his system that it was provoking hallucinations. That was the thing about being a hunter. When you lived in a world where the impossible not only existed, it wanted to tear your throat out and feast on your insides, real was a slippery concept at best.

"I found this in his office trash." Sam held up an empty glass vial. The inside of the glass contained residue of some thick, greenish-yellow substance.

"Dippel's special unguent," Dean said, then frowned. "What the hell is an *unguent* anyway?"

"Kind of like a medicinal cream," Sam said.

"Looks more like snot. Can you imagine the TV commercial for that stuff? 'Side effects may include sudden goo-ification.'" He paused as a thought occurred to him. "You think maybe Dippel messed with the formula to make sure it killed Martinez?"

"Maybe, but why would he off the only supplier of NuFlesh in the world?"

Dean shrugged. "Maybe he's learned how to make it for himself. Or maybe he just doesn't give a damn. He *is* an immortal psychopath, after all."

"I suppose. But it could've been an accident, too. Maybe Martinez used more than the recommended dose."

"If that's the case, then given what happened to him, I'd say he used *way* more."

"So what do we do now?" Sam asked. "Go check out Martinez's home, see if there's any info on Dippel in his home computer?"

"I doubt he'd have Dippel's address stuck to his refrigerator door. Whatever we do, we'd better step on it. Once the local police see Martinez's remains—such as they are—they're going to freak. They'll put another call into the CDC, maybe even fax some pictures of Martinez's bones-and-pink-goo-stew, and once that happens…"

"Brennan will be crawling with CDC personnel."

Dean nodded. "I wouldn't be surprised if they dropped a giant plastic dome over the whole damn town. If the CDC shows up in force, Dippel will go to ground or get the hell out of Dodge. Either way, we'll have a tough time finding him after that."

Sam yawned. "We could get rid of the goo, so there's nothing for the police to find."

"Now I know you're half asleep. You'd never suggest anything that stupid when you're on your game." Dean started counting points off on his fingers. "For one thing, I'm not touching what's left of Martinez. We don't know just how toxic that goo is. For another, even if we could find a safe way to move that crap, it'll still leave residue for the cops to find, and the CDC after them. And remember, the receptionist saw Martinez when he was in the process of melting, so we could only conceal what happened to him for so long. Hell, she may have already reported his condition to the cops. So, if we move Martinez's goo-mains and the cops find out, they're going to start thinking some kind of conspiracy's going on in their town, which could end up bringing in the real Feds, or maybe Homeland Security. Either way, the heat would get turned up real high, real fast."

"Yeah. I see what you mean. Sorry." Sam stifled another yawn.

Dean was really starting to get worried. If Sam's infection continued spreading, his reflexes could be dulled to the point where he might not be able to defend himself in a fight. After that, how much longer would it be before he didn't have enough energy to move? He might even slip into a coma. They needed to track down Dippel if they were to have any hope of finding a cure for Sam's condition. Otherwise, Dean was afraid his brother wasn't going to make it. Dean wasn't about to let that happen. They'd been through too much together—life and death, Heaven and Hell, and everything between. Dean wasn't going to let his brother down. He'd die—again—first.

"Maybe Dippel has another Igor," Sam said.

Dean had been so caught up in his thoughts that Sam's words didn't register with him at first. "What?"

"Martinez supplied Dippel with NuFlesh, and in turn Dippel gave him the anti-itch cream. Martinez described it as a trade, which suggests it wasn't a medical collaboration. If Dippel had help making his creations, he probably wouldn't go to a biochemist anyway. He'd want someone with a medical background. A physician or maybe even a veterinarian."

Dean smiled. "Maybe you've still got a few functioning brain cells left after all. But if there is another Igor, how do we find him or her? We can't just look up every doctor in the Brennan area, drop by their office, and say, 'Excuse me, but have you built any monsters out of dead body parts lately?'"

"Dippel would need to find someone shady to work with, someone he could blackmail, if necessary. We need to find out if there are any doctors or vets in town who've got a sketchy reputation, maybe even been in trouble with the law."

"Looks like we need to pay a visit to Brennan's finest," Dean said. They'd already spoken to the sheriff when they'd first begun investigating the strange deaths in town. They could easily claim they'd returned to follow up on some unspecified leads they'd gathered. "Let's go."

Dean started toward the door, but before he reached it, Sam said. "On the way, can we—"

Dean sighed. "We'll stop for coffee, don't worry."

"What do you think she's doing? Is she sleeping or just lying awake and staring at the ceiling?"

Dean didn't want to talk about it. He kept his mouth shut and hoped Sam would do the same. They were in their room at the Hansens' cabin, Sam sitting cross-legged on his bed, Dean sitting on the floor, his back against the wall, legs stretched out in front of him. There was a lamp on top of a dresser between their beds, and the light was on. Neither brother had said anything, but they didn't want to be in the dark, not with Trish—or whatever she'd become—in the house. Dean had also locked their door. He had no idea if it would keep Trish out if she wanted in, but even a little protection was better than none at all.

"What do you think she is?" Sam asked. "Is she a zombie?"

"Zombies are made by voodoo," Dean said in a tone that indicated this was the most obvious thing in the world. "You saw that little statue her dad had. It was Egyptian."

"So she's like a mummy, only with no bandages?"

"I don't know *what* she is!" Dean snapped. Sam recoiled as if he'd been struck, and Dean felt instantly ashamed. Sam was scared, that's all. Truth was, so was he. When he spoke again, he did so quietly, in a voice that was little more than a whisper. "Whatever she is, she's not Trish anymore."

The day had been one of the most bizarre that Dean had experienced, and given his dad's job, that was saying something. Trish hadn't spoken a single word, and her face never displayed emotion—or any expression at all, for that matter. At first, Dean had thought she didn't blink anymore, but after a while, he realized she did, only far more slowly than a normal person. He'd read somewhere that people blink an average of once every five seconds. Trish blinked once every minute. She didn't move much, only when her dad asked her to do something. When she did move, she did so with precise, economical motions, like a machine that had been programmed for maximum efficiency. When she wasn't doing anything, she was so still she might have been a wax figure created in the image of the real Trish. And she never sat. She always stood, and if she was in the way, you had to go around her. Not only didn't she step aside, there was nothing in her eyes or expression to indicate that she was even aware of another presence.

Walter Hansen didn't seem to notice that there was anything wrong with his daughter. Dean had heard the phrase "in denial" before, but this was the first time he'd seen it in action. Normally, Walter spent most of the day down in his workshop, preparing documents for his clients, but today he remained upstairs, keeping up a running one-sided conversation with Trish. He spoke about things they had done back when her mother was alive, holidays they'd celebrated, trips they'd taken… He spoke about plans for the future, too. Places they'd never gotten around to visiting that they'd go to soon, renovations he wanted to do to the cabin, changes he wanted to make in their lives. Maybe they'd get a cat or a dog. Trish had always wanted a dog, hadn't she?

Trish stood there, motionless, never speaking. Dean had no idea if she heard her father's words, or if she did, if she understood them.

Whatever command Walter gave her, she obeyed, and after having her make breakfast, he had her do a series of chores around the cabin. She ran the sweeper, dusted, and did several loads of laundry, and all the while Walter followed her around, talking. In the afternoon, Walter had the four of them sit down and watch TV. Well, three of them. Trish remained standing. Walter put on a rerun of an old sitcom, and he joined in with the laugh track, laughing loud, as if the show—which Dean had seen before and didn't think was all that funny—was the most hilarious thing he'd ever viewed. There was an edge of hysteria to Walter's laughter that Dean found just as creepy as Trish's immobile, stone-faced presence, and after a while he couldn't take it anymore. He told Walter that he and Sam were going to go out and gather some firewood, despite the fact that there was a healthy supply already stacked up next to the cabin, and Walter said, "Sure, sure. Good idea." He didn't take his gaze off the TV screen as he answered, and Dean and Sam lost no time in getting the hell out of there.

They didn't bother pretending to get firewood. Instead, they wandered through the woods around the Hansens' cabin, not speaking, just walking. Each alone with the guilt that was eating them up from the inside.

They stayed out past dinner—no way did they want to suffer through another meal prepared by maybe-a-zombie, maybe-something-else Trish—and they finally came in around nine. They went straight to bed, but before they could hole up in their room, Walter told them to make sure they got a good night's rest.

"Tomorrow we'll go fishing at the lake," he said. "Then later, we'll head into town for ice cream and a movie. How does that sound?"

Like a nightmare, Dean had thought. "Sounds good," he'd said. Then he and Sam hurried to their room, closed the door, and locked it.

That had been two hours ago. For most of that time the boys had remained silent, listening to the drone of Walter's perpetual one-sided conversation with his undead daughter. Eventually, Walter decided to go to bed, but not before leading Trish to her room, and—Dean presumed—tucking her in. He wondered if Walter gave her a goodnight kiss, maybe on the forehead, maybe on the cheek. If so, did her skin feel normal, or was it cold and waxy? The thought made him shudder.

"What are we going to do?" Sam asked in a small voice.

This was the question Dean had been dreading all day. He was the older brother, and with their dad away, it was only natural that Sam would look to him for guidance in this situation. It was his responsibility to look after his brother—as their father had made abundantly clear to him on many occasions. He had nearly failed in that responsibility yesterday, when he'd been dumb enough to lead Sam to the Herald House. He'd thought he was so smart, that he was a big-time hunter, just because he'd picked up one or two things from listening to his dad. Trish had paid for his arrogance with her life, but it could've just as easily been Sammy who'd taken a spectral bullet to the heart.

Once, in some hotel room or other, when Sam had been asleep, their father had turned to Dean and said, "Son, there's not a lot of advice that I can pass along to you about life. Real life, I mean. Not the kind of life hunters lead. But I know this: never let the little head do the thinking for the big head."

That had been a few years back, and Dean hadn't been exactly sure at the time what his dad had been trying to tell him. But he understood now. Boy, did he understand! Everything that had happened had been his fault, and all because he'd wanted to act like a big man and impress a girl. An amazing girl who had died and been brought back to some grotesque semblance of life by her grief-stricken, and more than a little crazy, father.

Dean didn't know if he believed in souls. He knew ghosts were real, and if he hadn't known it before, he surely would have after the previous day's encounter with the Rifleman. But he thought ghosts might not be the consciousness of a person that continued to exist after death so much as some kind of psychic energy that was left behind. Energy that took on the shape and behavior of the person who created it, but wasn't literally that person. If that was true, then Trish—her mind, her spirit, her essence—hadn't been brought back, only her body. She was an empty shell, little more than a puppet for Walter to command. If there were souls, though, then it was possible that Trish's had returned with her physical form, but was trapped within, unable to do more than passively observe, a prisoner in her own body. *It would be,* Dean thought, *the very definition of a living hell.* And it was all his fault.

"The first thing we do," he told Sam, "is find some weapons."

They moved silently through the cabin. Both Walter and Trish's bedroom doors were closed, but Dean knew that didn't mean either of them was asleep. Especially Trish. It was very possible that she didn't need to sleep anymore, that she was—as Sam had said—just lying on her bed, eyes open and staring, blinking only once per minute.

They entered the kitchen, and each selected a large knife from the block on the counter. They searched through the drawers, careful to open and close them slowly so as not to make the contents rattle, but all they found were a couple screwdrivers in a junk drawer. Dean took the Phillips, Sam the flathead. What Dean really wanted to find was a gun. Their dad had made sure that both of them knew how to shoot, and even if neither of them was a highly skilled marksman, they could do more than merely hit the broad side of a barn. If they found more than one gun, Dean wouldn't have let Sam carry one, though. Sam was an okay shot, if not as good as him yet, but if their dad ever found out he let Sam use a gun without his express permission… Well, Dean would rather face an entire town full of vengeful ghosts than John Winchester when he was angry.

"Should we go down into the basement and look?" Sam asked. "If Walter has any guns, he might keep them down there."

Dean found himself feeling proud of his little brother. He was obviously scared, but not only was he keeping himself together, he was thinking strategically. Dean knew Sam was smart—smarter than him, that was for sure—but sometimes he forgot just how smart.

Dean thought it over. If Walter sometimes let hunters pay him in trade, he probably did have a few guns somewhere, and his workshop seemed like a logical place to keep them. He could have other things down there, too—items more powerful and dangerous than firearms. He'd said the Egyptian statue he'd used to bring Trish back had come from one of his clients. He might have other magical objects in the basement, maybe even something that could reverse the spell that had resurrected Trish.

Don't be an idiot, Dean told himself. *It's not like any items Walter has will be labeled and come with a set of instructions.* If Walter did have any more magic goodies downstairs, they would be extremely dangerous to use, assuming he and Sam could even get them to work in the first place. They were better off sticking with simple weapons, ones that wouldn't backfire and turn you into a pile of ash, or worse. But they really could use a gun. Dean didn't know what sort of creature

Trish had become, but he figured that they should avoid getting too close to her. He'd seen *Night of the Living Dead* maybe a dozen times, and the last thing he wanted was for Trish to sink her teeth into either him or Sam and turn them into flesh-eating zombies. Knives and screwdrivers were only good for close-up fighting, but with a gun, they could deal with her from a distance.

Listen to you! You're thinking about killing a girl you had the hots for yesterday!

Dean thrust the thought away. He'd learned from watching his father that sometimes a hunter had to put his emotions aside in order to get the job done. Despite the fact that they were in this situation because of his screw up, he was determined to live up to his father's example and do the job right.

"Okay, let's go check the basement. But we've got to be quick. There's no telling—"

He broke off as he heard sounds come from down the hallway: a soft creak followed close by another, and that followed a muffled click. Dean felt his gut turn to ice.

"Trish left her room," Sam whispered, "and went into Walter's."

That's exactly how Dean saw it. No time to look for guns now.

They left the kitchen and hurried down the hallway, Dean's instincts screaming for him to move faster. They carried their weapons down at their sides so they wouldn't accidently injure themselves or one another, and when they reached Walter's door, they stopped. Enough light spilled into the hall from the kitchen for them to see that Trish's bedroom door was open. The interior was dark, which only made sense. Why would she need light anymore?

Dean shifted his knife to his left hand, with the screwdriver. He then reached out and tried the knob of Walter's door. He wasn't surprised to find it locked. He returned his knife to his right hand, then turned to Sam and whispered, "Get ready."

He'd seen cops break into locked rooms on TV and in the movies, but he'd never tried to do it himself before. *There's a first time for everything,* their dad always said. Dean stepped back, raised his right leg, and slammed his foot against the door next to the knob. He had to repeat this maneuver twice more before the door finally burst open and swung inward.

Dean entered first, Sam right behind.

Walter's nightstand light was on, and in its dim glow, Dean could see the man sitting up in bed, Trish crouched on the mattress next to him, her face buried in his neck.

He smiled weakly, his face pale. "It's okay. She just wanted a snack. A little something to tide her over until morning." He reached up a trembling hand and stroked Trish's hair. "Wouldn't want my girl to go to bed with an empty belly now, would I?"

In the future, when Dean would remember this moment, several horrible details would stand out. One was that despite what his daughter was doing to him, Walter didn't cry out in pain. How detached from reality did you have to be not to feel someone tearing into your flesh with their teeth? Then there was the blood. Despite Trish's best efforts to swallow as much as she could, blood stained the front of Walter's T-shirt and soaked the sheet drawn up to his waist. Another was the wet smacking sounds that Trish made as she nuzzled at her father's neck, sounds more like those of a baby animal suckling from its mother than an undead thing chewing on living meat. She'd been silent all day, but now sounds of satisfaction rumbled softly in Trish's throat, almost like a cat's purring. As bad as all these details were, though—and that was damned bad, make no mistake—the absolute worst for Dean was the look in Walter's eyes. In them, Dean could see that, at least on some level, the man knew exactly what his daughter had become and what she was doing to him. Yet still he loved her, deeply, fiercely, and he would give her whatever she needed, even at the cost of his own life.

It was at that moment that Dean realized that as awful as hate was, love, unthinking and unrestrained, could be far more terrible.

Trish drew away from her father, ropey strands of blood stretching from her mouth to the ragged mess that had been his neck, and turned to regard Sam and Dean.

Dean thought there'd be hunger in her gaze, or rage, or maybe even sorrow, because deep down somewhere inside that cold, dead body she was still Trish, and she was horrified by what she had become, by what she was driven to do, but what he saw in her eyes was far worse. Her gaze was empty of all thought and emotion, bereft of the slightest sense of identity. Her eyes lacked even the basic self-awareness that an animal possesses. They were as empty as the largest subterranean caverns, as cold as the deepest arctic waters. Dean knew he was looking at something far worse than simple evil in her gaze. He was looking at nothing.

"Dean…"

"It's all right, Sammy." He knew damn well that it wasn't, that after this nothing would ever be all right again, but he said it because he was the big brother, and it was the kind of thing you were supposed to say when things were bad. And he couldn't imagine things getting much worse than this.

Trish began crawling toward them across the bed, her father's blood dribbling from her mouth, pattering on the comforter like thick drops of crimson rain.

Dean wished to God he had a gun, but he didn't, he had a knife and a Phillips screwdriver. And he had what his dad had always told him was the most important weapon of all. Himself. He switched the screwdriver to his right hand and took the knife in his left. Then, before he could reconsider, he ran toward Trish, took aim, and rammed the point of the screwdriver into her left eye, shoving the metal deep into her brain, all the way up to the handle.

He heard Sam gasp and saw Walter's eyes widen with shock. Trish didn't react at all. Instead of blood, clear liquid trickled around the screwdriver protruding from her socket. She remained like that for several moments, crouching on all fours atop her father's bed, expressionless, wounded eye leaking liquid, her mouth still dripping with Walter's blood. Then suddenly, as if she was a machine whose power supply had been cut off, she slumped over, rolled off the bed, and thumped to the floor.

Dean could only stand and stare at Trish's unmoving body, right hand slick with the clear goo that had spurted from her eye when he'd jammed the screwdriver in. A moment later, he felt Sam move to his side and put his arm around Dean's shoulders. That simple gesture did more for Dean than any words his brother might have spoken.

Walter showed no reaction at first, and Dean feared that he'd lost so much blood that he wasn't fully aware of what had happened. Then he let out a howl of anguish, jumped out of bed, and knelt next to his daughter's body. He tried to pick her up and cradle her, but he was too weak and only managed to lift her partway before she slipped from his hands and fell back to the floor. A second later, tears streaming down his too-pale face, Walter collapsed beside her.

The brothers tried to revive Walter, but he'd lost too much blood. So they dug two graves in the back yard, beneath a large old oak that Trish had loved, and buried father and daughter, saying what words they could think of over their graves. They did their best to clean up the mess in Walter's room, then searched the cabin and found the statuette of Anubis down in the basement in one of the drawers of Walter's desk. After a brief discussion, they left it alone, along with a number of other artifacts Walter had stored in his workshop. When they were finished, they went upstairs, locked the basement door, and waited for their father to come get them.

It would be the better part of two weeks until John Winchester returned.

"You guys were out at the motel during the fire, right?"

Sam looked at Dean, unsure how to answer the sheriff's question.

She smiled. "Nothing personal, but you smell like you've been to a week-long bonfire."

Dean grimaced. "I'm really getting tired of stinking up the joint wherever we go."

The sheriff raised an eyebrow in curiosity. Amanda Kopp—who no doubt had long ago grown tired of hearing jokes about her surname—was in her mid-forties, with short brown hair, minimal makeup, and a thin white-gold wedding band on her ring finger. She was friendly, but projected an air of complete professionalism, the latter undercut somewhat by the Hello Kitty cover on the smartphone sitting on her desk in easy reach of her hand.

Sam wondered if she was one of those people who was so addicted to her phone that she felt anxious if she was too far away from it.

"It's been a long few days," Sam said, hoping she'd let it go at that.

"Tell me about it." She let out a sigh. "I've got four people dead from some kind of mysterious wasting disease, in addition to the two from last week, and now to top it off, a whole motel burns down so fast it was like it was hit with goddamned napalm. That's why I'm sitting on my ass in my office. I'm waiting on a call back from the CDC."

Sam and Dean exchanged glances. It was just as they'd figured.

"We understand how busy you are, Sheriff," Sam said, "and we really appreciate your taking the time to speak with us again."

Although it had only been a couple days since they'd first

spoken with Sheriff Kopp, she looked as if she'd aged ten years in that time. The lines on her face were more pronounced, and her eyes were red and sore-looking, much like Sam figured his own did. Unfortunately, Sam was far too used to seeing law officers suffering from stress and lack of sleep, not to mention the frustration of knowing something bad was happening in their town and having no idea what was causing it or how to stop it. Most of the time, he and Dean couldn't tell the local authorities the truth, no matter how much they might want to. Almost always, in their experience, telling the authorities resulted in one of several increasingly negative scenarios. Best case, they'd think they were crazy and stop cooperating with them. Or they'd decide they needed to be held in custody for a psychiatric evaluation. In the worst case, the authorities would believe Sam and Dean, because then they would want to help, and that would put them face to face with dangers that they were in no way trained to deal with. It had worked out okay a time or two—like with Jody Mills in Sioux Falls— but those were the exceptions to the rule.

There was a reason why hunters tended to work alone or in pairs. The fewer people that had to risk their lives, and often more than just their lives, against the dark things that lived in the world's shadows, the better. He thought of Trish Hansen. If he and Dean hadn't let her talk them into taking her ghost hunting…

Dean frowned. "Wait a minute. Did you say there were *four* disease victims this week? I thought there were only three."

"There were. Until Harrison Brauer turned up dead. He's a local mortician, and he was due to meet with the wife of one of his... clients. Is that the right word? Anyway, when she got there the door was open, but she couldn't find anyone, so she started calling Brauer's name and wandering around his place, looking for him. Eventually, she wandered downstairs into his embalming room, and that's where she found him, looking like all the others."

Sam gave Dean a nod to say, *Nice catch*. As fuzzy-headed as he was, the detail had slipped right by him. Sam hadn't considered that Dippel might have been using a mortician as his Igor, especially as it was unlikely the man would have the necessary medical background, but he supposed it was possible. If so, the mortician's death could mean that Dippel was closing up shop in Brennan and preparing to move on. For all they knew, he might already have left town, in which case they'd have a hell of a time locating him. Sam doubted Dean would have the patience to even try. With Dippel gone, Dean would want to return to figuring out a way to take down Dick Roman.

Dean's thoughts must have been running along similar lines, for he gave Sam a look that said, *Why are we wasting our time here?*

"Sorry I didn't call you guys," the sheriff said. "Between trying to get hold of the CDC and dealing with the fire, I've had my hands full."

"No problem," Dean said. Sam thought he was going to tell the sheriff thanks, but they no longer needed her help. Instead he took a deep breath, and said, "But if you could answer just a few more questions for us..."

"Sure thing. It's not like I'm doing anything at the moment

besides sitting here waiting for my phone to ring."

Sam wondered which she'd used. Her office phone or her smartphone. Maybe the latter, if for no other reason than to make sure no one else in the department could pick up their extension and listen in. If she believed she was dealing with some sort of contagion, the last thing she would want to do was cause a panic, especially among her own people.

"We're exploring the possibility that someone with a medical background might be involved in these deaths," Dean said.

Sheriff Kopp's eyes widened. "You mean, someone did this on purpose? Like, some kind of *terrorist*? You think I should contact Homeland Security?"

"We're just trying to cover all the bases," Dean said. "At this juncture, we don't have any evidence that would indicate terrorism. If we did, we'd be sure to tell you."

The sheriff looked skeptical at the idea that federal agents would place a high priority on keeping a local like her in the loop, but she just said, "So what do you want to know?"

"Have there been any problems involving doctors or nurses in the area?" Sam asked. "Maybe even a nurse practitioner, a physician's assistant, or a paramedic?"

"Problems?"

"Patient complaints," Dean said. "Legal trouble. Strange behavior. Anything out of the ordinary."

"You mean like a scandal?" she asked.

"It doesn't have to be anything that major," Sam said. "It could be something small, something that no one would think too much about in ordinary circumstances."

She considered for a moment. "I'm sorry, but nothing's coming to mind. Up until the last couple weeks, Brennan's been a pretty quiet town. Usually, all we ever have to deal with is petty crime, marital disputes, and traffic violations." She paused, and from the expression on her face, Sam knew she'd thought of something. "This might not be anything, but a few months back we had a father and daughter killed by a drunk driver. The girl was only fifteen, and just starting to learn how to drive. It was a damned shame. Anyway, the mother wasn't with them when it happened, but she's a doctor here in town. After the accident, she became depressed. Who wouldn't, right? She started seeing fewer and fewer patients, until she finally stopped altogether. As far as I know, she hasn't officially closed down her practice, but she might as well have."

A grieving widow and mother who was also a doctor? Dippel would find her an irresistible candidate for an Igor. Not only did she have the knowledge of twenty-first century medicine he needed, but she had a compelling reason to want to work with him. Two reasons, in fact. Her husband and daughter. Sam thought of Walter Hansen, and he knew that if a grief-stricken parent had the opportunity to restore a dead child to life, he or she would be unable to resist taking it, regardless of the consequences.

Dean must have been thinking the same thing, for he gave Sam a quick nod before turning his attention back to Sheriff Kopp.

"We need the doctor's name and address."

THIRTEEN

Catherine gave Marshall's body a final check. The tongue looked good—the NuFlesh had done its work, bonding the organ into place almost as easily as gluing two pieces of paper together—as did the new teeth. A couple of them weren't as straight as she'd like, but she told herself not to be overly critical. Besides, human beings weren't meant to be perfectly symmetrical. It was the imperfections, slight as they might be, that gave a man or woman character.

While she continued her examination, checking the spots where Marshall's limbs—both original and new—had been fused, Conrad busied himself setting up the resurrection equipment. The procedure was primarily a chemical one, and the cart that Conrad wheeled over to the table where Marshall lay contained what at first glance appeared to be a simple arrangement of IV bottles, plastic tubing, and needles hanging from a metal framework. Chemicals of various colors filled the bottles, with tiny glints of illumination that resembled glowing flecks of multicolored metal floating within. Catherine had once asked Conrad what those flecks were, but he'd only given her a thin-lipped smile and said, "It's an ancient secret." At first she'd thought he was making a joke, but after everything she'd seen since starting to work with him, she'd come to accept that he was telling her the truth. An ancient secret, and no doubt one as dark as pitch, but she didn't care, not as long as it returned her husband to her. There were enough chemicals in the bottles to treat both Marshall and Bekah today—assuming all went well with Marshall's resurrection, that was.

Catherine knew the formulae for Conrad's chemical mixtures, save for that one ingredient. Perhaps if she had a stronger background in chemistry, she might recognize the flecks, but she doubted it. Whatever they were, she didn't think they were the sort of thing you could simply order from a chemical supply company.

Conrad wheeled a second cart over to Marshall that contained an external automated defibrillator—*Much more convenient than waiting for lightning to strike,* he'd once told her—along with strips of cloth that had been chemically treated and coated with more of those mysterious flecks of metal. She knew from their previous experiments that Conrad would wrap the strips around Marshall's chest, leaving a section bare so the defibrillator's electrodes could make contact with his skin. His head would be wrapped in the cloth, too, down to the neck. The one new element in the procedure this time was Conrad's stone, the so-called Lapis Occultus. She had no idea what it was and would have dismissed it as pure nonsense if she hadn't held it in her hand and felt its power for herself. The stone, he had explained to her, would be placed on Marshall's forehead before the procedure got underway. When she'd asked Conrad what the stone's purpose was, he'd been even more vague than usual: *It's to ensure that death is held at bay indefinitely.*

She'd long ago given up doubting Conrad's claims. She'd seen too much, accomplished too much with him. If he said the stone would provide some kind of protection against death, then she believed him.

Satisfied that Marshall's body was ready for the procedure, Catherine double-checked the IV bottles, tubing, and needles. Conrad had no ego when it came to his work. He insisted that Catherine check everything he did to make sure all was in order. The only thing that mattered to him was obtaining his desired outcome. He didn't care who made a mistake, he only cared about finding and fixing it. In another person, she would have found the quality admirable, but in Conrad, she knew it arose from a single-minded obsession with success at all costs, including the sublimation of his own ego. Why he was so hell-bent on success, she wasn't certain, but she sensed his motivation was more than merely intellectual, and it sure as hell wasn't altruistic. He was working toward something, and had been for a long time, and helping her restore her husband and daughter to life was only one more step toward achieving his ultimate goal. She'd never asked him what that goal was, and truthfully, she didn't care, not as long as she got Marshall and Bekah back.

Once she'd determined the chemicals and IVs were in order, she double-checked the defibrillator while Conrad examined Marshall to make sure she hadn't missed anything.

The defibrillator's battery was fully charged, and it seemed to be in perfect working condition. When their examinations were complete, Conrad looked at her.

"Shall we finish?" he asked.

She nodded and together they wrapped the treated cloth strips around Marshall's head and chest, Conrad lifting his body as needed while Catherine wrapped. The cloth needed to be put on immediately before the procedure, because— for reasons she didn't understand—the chemicals it had been treated with lost their efficacy the longer they were in contact with the skin. They'd only used half the strips by the time they were finished. The other half were for Bekah. They checked to make sure Marshall was wrapped tight, and then Conrad took the Lapis Occultus from the cart and gently, almost reverently, placed it on Marshall's forehead.

He stepped back and cocked his head as he regarded the stone's placement. Catherine couldn't see what earthly difference the position of the object made, but Conrad must have, for he reached out, made a small adjustment, then nodded to himself.

"I believe we are ready to begin inserting the—"

Needles, Catherine knew he'd been about to say, but he broke off, a look of astonishment on his face. He raised his hand with the X on it and stared at the mark as if he couldn't believe what he was seeing. The X looked the same to her, but whatever had changed about it had alarmed the usually unflappable Mr. Dippel.

"We need to hurry," he said, tension in his voice. "They're coming."

"Who?"

"Two men. Hunters… Killers. They want to stop us. I thought I'd dealt with them…" He curled his hand into a fist. "…but evidently I was mistaken."

Catherine's head was swimming. "What are they? Police? Hit men? Secret agents, for god's sake?"

"I don't have time to explain fully. Suffice it to say that they will break into your home, come down here, and not only stop what we're doing, but destroy Marshall and Bekah's bodies to ensure they will never rise. Is that what you want?"

Conrad was shouting by the time he reached the end of his words, but it was his emotional intensity more than anything else that convinced Catherine he was speaking the truth.

"What do we do?"

"I can try to hold them off, but at this point, I'm not confident in my ability to do so alone. If I had use of the Lapis Occultus… But no, it's needed here. No matter what else occurs, it is vital that Bekah be restored to life."

Just Bekah, she noted. Not Marshall.

Conrad looked down at Marshall's body, still lifeless and waiting for resurrection. A cold sly smile spread across his face.

"If I had your husband's help…"

"No! I'm not going to bring Marshall back only to send him into harm's way. If these men really are as dangerous as you seem to think—"

"I'll ask you the same question I asked regarding which of your loved ones was to be resurrected first. Given the situation, what would Marshall do?"

As before, Catherine didn't have to think about her reply.

"Protect his daughter."

Without exchanging another word, they began inserting the IV needles into various points of Marshall's body.

Daniel raged inside the confines of the Lapis Occultus. To his perceptions, it seemed as if he was floating disembodied within an endless expanse of darkness, and that he'd been there for a very, very long time. Another being might well have gone insane in the same circumstances, but Daniel was a Reaper. Darkness, no matter how vast or unending, didn't scare him. It did, however, seriously piss him off.

He couldn't believe he'd allowed himself to be captured by Dippel. It hadn't occurred to him that the alchemist might have conceived of a way to harness the energy of a Reaper and use it in his obscene experiments. That was something Daniel needed to prevent at any cost. The question was, how? He'd tried translocating, a common ability for his kind. Normally, he could move from one location to another simply by willing it, but no matter how hard he concentrated, no matter how much power he summoned, he was unable to break free of the darkness. He'd tried reaching out to any other Reapers that might be in the vicinity. Considering how many deaths had taken place in Brennan lately, there were bound to be a few around. Yet although he strained to stretch his thoughts outward, he was unable to penetrate his prison's walls. That left him with only one option—the last option, as far as any Reaper was concerned—calling the boss.

Death was a strong believer in delegating. When he assigned a task to one of his servants, he expected it to be carried out, and if any problems arose, he expected them to be dealt with. What he did *not* want was to be bothered every time some little thing went wrong. Whenever Death was disturbed for something trivial—and given what he was, almost everything was trivial to him—he was not slow to express his displeasure. But Daniel didn't see any other choice left to him. If Dippel succeeded in incarnating Hel, as bad as it would be for the humans on Earth, it would be far worse for him. Death would make certain of it.

Daniel had no eyes to close in his black prison, but he imagined himself performing the action anyway. He concentrated and called out to Death—

—and received no answer.

Daniel was shocked. There was no place in existence that Death couldn't reach. All worlds, all times, all dimensions were part of his inconceivably vast domain. Yet Death hadn't heard him.

Whatever this stone was, it had been created by magic far greater than Daniel had anticipated. Perhaps Hel herself had taken a hand in its construction. She was nowhere near as powerful as Death, but as a goddess of death (with a lowercase d) her power could easily counter Daniel's.

He was on his own, trapped in a magic artifact, his energy to be used to pave the way for an ancient Norse goddess of death to enter the world of the living. There was nothing he could do but wait and hope the Winchesters found a way to succeed where he had failed. Which didn't do anything to improve his mood.

* * *

Dean drove past Catherine Luss's house, then pulled the car off the side of the road onto the shoulder. Catherine lived out in the country. There were no sidewalks, and he didn't want to park in her driveway. The last thing the brothers wanted to do was announce their presence. Dean turned off the engine.

Then he looked at Sam. "What did you do?"

"I-don't-know-what-you-mean," Sam answered quickly, speaking so fast his words ran together.

"Yeah, you do. Ever since we stopped at that gas station so you could hit the head and get rid of all that coffee you've been drinking, you've been suspiciously wide awake and full of energy."

Sam shrugged.

Dean noted his brother's bouncing leg and tapping fingers.

"Maybe-the-caffeine-finally-kicked-in," Sam offered in his too-rapid voice.

"*Something* kicked in," Dean said, "but it sure as hell isn't caffeine. What did you do? Steal some pick-me-up pills from the med kit?"

Hunters tended to get banged up pretty good on the job, and even if there was a hospital in the area, they preferred to patch their own wounds whenever possible. Fewer questions that way. So every hunter had a fully stocked medical kit with its own mini-pharmacy. Dean figured that while he'd been busy buying some snacks—extra-hot jalapeno tortilla chips and crème-filled chocolate snack cakes—Sam had grabbed some stimulants from the kit and taken them in the restroom.

At first Sam looked as if he intended to deny it, but then

he sighed.

"You know the weird black veiny marks on my leg? They've spread."

Dean didn't like where this was going. "How far?"

"Basically, my whole leg is covered now. I can still walk, but it's numb all over. If there's any chance of fixing whatever's wrong with me, it lies with Dippel. I can't afford to sit this one out, Dean. Not if I want to survive."

"I could—"

"And I'm *not* letting you face the real-world equivalent of Dr. Frankenstein on your own."

Dean didn't like it. In fact, it pissed him off something fierce. It didn't help that he knew he would have done the same thing if their situations had been reversed.

"How large a dose did you take?" Dean asked.

"Large enough. Let's go before it starts wearing off."

Sam got out of the car before Dean could say anything else. He sat there for a moment, struggling to deal with his anger.

"Sam, if you die because of this, I'm going to force Dippel to teach me how to resurrect the dead, and then I'm going to bring you back so I can kill you myself!"

He let out a long sigh of frustration and got out of the car. Sam already had the car's trunk open and was gearing up. Dean joined him, nose wrinkling at the stink of their plastic-bagged clothes. Was there any substance on the planet that could contain the Frankenstench?

They selected the same weapons they'd carried during the hunt for the Double-Header. Dean armed himself with his Colt and the Winchester shotgun, and Sam chose his Beretta and the sawed-off double barrel. They each took a pair of KA-BAR knives and some flares. They hadn't had a chance to use the latter against the Double-Header, but they could still come in handy. This time, they brought something new, one of their standard pieces of equipment that they rarely got to use: a homemade flamethrower constructed from a container of kerosene, various lengths of pipe, and a control button to regulate the release of fuel. It was capable of producing a flame about fifteen feet long, but the kerosene wouldn't last forever, so you had to make sure every blast counted.

Sam started to speak, but Dean cut him off.

"Given your condition, there's no way I'm letting you use this thing, so don't even ask."

Sam scowled, but he didn't protest.

Dean slipped the flamethrower's straps over his shoulders, then stood for a moment to get a feel for the weight. Carrying the flamethrower always made him feel as if he had a bomb on his back that was ready to go off at any time. *Fun, fun, fun!*

"Once more into the breach, eh?" Dean said.

"Unto," Sam said. "The correct quote is 'Once more unto the breach, dear friends, once more.' It's from Shakespeare's *Henry V*."

Dean sighed. He should've known better that to try and get literary on Sam.

"How about this? Let's go kick some Frankenass."

"That'll work," Sam said with a smile, and together they headed for the house.

* * *

Catherine had attached the electrodes of the automated external defibrillator to Marshall's chest. Normally the sensors in the electrodes sent data to the AED's computer, which would determine whether someone was experiencing sudden cardiac arrest and required an electric shock. The computer would then use voice prompts to guide whoever was using the device, but Catherine had deactivated that function, as it was for people without medical training. Besides, at the moment Marshall had no heartbeat, and therefore there was no data for the computer to pick up. In a normal situation, this would mean the device wouldn't deliver a charge, but she'd paid a local computer repairman a sizeable sum to bypass those safety features for her, and to keep his mouth shut about it. This AED was one of the early models and was capable of delivering a shock of up to four hundred joules. More recent models gave two sequential shocks of only one-twenty to two hundred joules, as that was now considered safer for the patient, but Catherine didn't need safe. She needed a strong enough charge to, as Conrad had put it, "galvanize the chemical admixture." Four hundred joules had been sufficient to do that for the dog. She prayed it would be enough for Marshall.

"I believe the moment is at hand," Conrad said. He stood by the cart containing the IV bottles, monitoring the amount of chemicals that had passed into Marshall's body.

Catherine nodded. She had gone through this procedure a number of times, first with rats and then with the dog. The rats hadn't lasted long, decaying in less than a day. The dog had been more successful, but it too had succumbed to tissue degradation in the end. She hoped that Conrad's magic stone would make the difference, but there was only one way to find out.

Each time she'd gone through this, she was amazed at how unremarkable it all was. No Van de Graaff generators crackling with electricity, no crazed hunchbacked assistant's mad cackling, no spooky gothic music swelling in the background, just a few chemicals quietly entering the bloodstream and then a single button to push. Bringing the dead back to life should be a spectacular, monumental moment. Instead, it was no more dramatic than any other medical procedure. Of course, the results were a different story.

She stepped over to the defibrillator, said, "Clear," more as a precaution than from any real worry that Conrad might be in physical contact with Marshall's body, and pushed the button.

Marshall's muscles tightened and his spine arced as electricity coursed through his body. She'd inserted a plastic mouth guard between his teeth to make sure he didn't bite his new tongue. After all the work she'd put in to attaching the organ, she didn't want anything to happen to it. The Lapis Occultus was dislodged from his forehead, but before it could tumble to the floor, Conrad's hand shot out and snatched it from the air, moving with inhuman speed. As far as she could see, the stone hadn't done anything special, but Conrad held it close to his eyes, examined it, then nodded as if satisfied.

Once the charge had been delivered, Marshall's body collapsed back onto the table and lay still once more. Catherine knew that what she had witnessed was a reflex action, not any sign of life, but she still couldn't help being encouraged. Just to see him move again after all these months, even if it was just a reflex, filled her heart with joy.

"Check the defibrillator's battery," Conrad said. "We need to make sure there's enough charge remaining for Bekah."

Catherine didn't want to take her eyes off Marshall, but she did as Conrad said. If he was right about the two men who were coming, they didn't have any time to waste. She checked the readout and saw there was enough power remaining for at least one more charge, maybe two.

"It's fine," she said.

She turned back just in time to hear Marshall draw in a gasping breath of air, his first in months.

"Remove the bandages!" Conrad said.

They each grabbed a pair of surgical scissors and began cutting the cloth strips away from Marshall, Conrad cutting those around his chest, Catherine those around his head. When the bandages fell away from his face, she saw that his eyes were open and looking up at her. She had been afraid she would see the same glassy expression that the dog's eyes had held—dead eyes with no hint of life or recognition in them—but his eyes were alive and intelligence shone in them. He mumbled something, trying to speak around the mouth guard. She gently removed it, and Marshall said, "Caff… rinn?"

His voice was a deep phlegmy rumble, unlike his normal tenor, and his mouth couldn't form the syllables quite right, the sounds too soft and mushy, but it was Marshall speaking. The first word he'd said had been her name.

She felt tears trickling down her face and realized she was crying. "Yes, sweetheart. It's me." She took his hand and gave it a squeeze. At first his hand remained limp, and she feared something was wrong, but then he squeezed back, his grip strong—even stronger than she remembered.

"I'm genuinely sorry I have to do this. I'd prefer to give the two of you more time to enjoy your reunion, but as the British say, 'Needs must when the devil drives.'"

She looked at Conrad in time to see him hold a small envelope over Marshall's mouth. Yellowish powder drifted out and floated down to cover his face in a light coating. Without thinking, she lashed out and smacked the envelope out of Conrad's hand, but it was too late. Whatever he'd intended to do was done.

Though Conrad's eyes flashed with anger at having been struck by her, his voice was icily calm as he spoke. "His mind will most likely be confused during the post-regeneration period, and even if he was at his peak mentally, it would take too long to explain the current situation to him. The powder I used will make him obey me without question. I assure you the effect is only temporary."

Catherine didn't like it, not one bit. She especially didn't like Conrad's use of the word obey, as if he were the master and Marshall nothing more than his slave. She forced herself to think practically instead of emotionally, though. It had taken the dog almost a full day to recover from the effects of being reborn. During that time, it had slept, mostly. Perhaps Marshall would recover more swiftly, especially since they'd used the Lapis Occultus with him, but they couldn't afford to wait and find out.

"Very well," she said. "But I expect you to make sure he's as safe as possible."

Conrad smiled. "Of course. Take heart. If he *is* damaged, we'll just repair him."

He looked at Marshall, and his smile fell away. He removed the defibrillator's electrodes from his chest and handed them to Catherine.

"Get off the table."

Marshall did as Conrad commanded, not bothering to wipe the residue of yellow powder from his face. His movements were stiff and uncoordinated, but Catherine knew from previous experiments that he'd soon adjust to his new body. She hoped it would be soon enough to help him fight off the two killers Conrad assured her were coming. She did wish there was time to put some clothes on him, though. She didn't like the idea of sending him out to fight naked, but there was nothing to be done about it now.

Maybe it won't matter to him, she thought. *Maybe he is like a newborn child, innocent and without shame.*

"Stand over there." Conrad pointed to the basement steps. After a second's hesitation, Marshall lurched over to the steps and stood there, a blank expression on his face.

Catherine couldn't stand seeing him look like that. She hadn't brought her husband back to life to become a mindless automaton.

Before she could protest, Conrad said, "Quickly. We must make Bekah ready. I fear you'll have to perform the procedure by yourself, my dear, but I believe you're more than capable."

Catherine wasn't certain about that, but if it was a choice between bringing Bekah back by herself or watching as her daughter's body was destroyed by these so-called hunters, then it was really no choice at all.

"Let's get her on the table," she said.

Sam wasn't sure taking the stimulants had been a good idea. His heart was racing, and his skin was slick with sweat. Worse, his pulse felt erratic, black spots danced in his vision, and he couldn't feel his right leg at all. It wasn't even numb; it just felt like it wasn't there. He had to concentrate extra hard with every step he took to make sure he didn't fall over. The hell of it was, he *still* felt tired. Not sleepy-tired, but physically exhausted, as if his body was on the verge of collapse. To make matters even worse, he'd started hallucinating. Nothing major yet, just ghostly half-images of strange shapes he couldn't identify, but he knew from experience that the hallucinations would soon intensify, and when that happened, he wouldn't be able to tell what was real from what wasn't. Which would be liable to get both him and his brother killed.

Come on, Sam, he told himself. *Just try to hold it together a little longer…*

One benefit of the Luss residence being located outside town was that there were no nearby neighbors to call the police and report a pair of armed men sneaking around to the back of the house. One disadvantage was the amount of trees in the Luss's yard, or rather, all the leaves that had fallen from them. It seemed Dr. Luss had been too busy playing mad scientist to do any yard work, and her property was covered with brown, yellow, red and—above all—*crunchy* leaves. Sam and Dean had to move carefully to make sure they didn't make too much noise, but a certain amount was unavoidable. They'd have to hope that whoever was inside was either too busy to pay attention to any sounds outside, or if they did hear some leaves crunch, would put it down to squirrels or deer. It was dusk, and the fading light would help to conceal them somewhat, but not as much as if it was full night. They'd debated waiting until dark to approach the house, but given the fact that Dippel might be preparing to leave town as soon as possible, they'd decided they couldn't afford to. They would have to rely on a hunter's two best friends: surprise and one hell of a lot of luck.

Sam began shivering, but although the air was chilly, he knew the cold came from inside. If he could examine himself unclothed in front of a full-length mirror right now, how far would he see the infection had spread? Onto his stomach? Maybe up to his chest? How much longer did he have until the dark taint inside him had spread to the point where his body could no longer function? He had no idea, but if he was going to be taking an eternal dirt nap after this hunt, he at least wanted to see it through to the end. He owed Dean far more than that, more than he could ever repay, but it would have to be good enough, for it might be all he had left.

The Luss family had a deck at the rear of their house, with a picnic table on one end and a gas grill set next to a patio door. Sam wondered when the last time was that all three of them—Catherine, her husband, and her daughter—had sat out there and had a meal, talking, laughing, enjoying being in one another's presence. What had it been like for Catherine to come home to an empty house after a long day of seeing patients? Had she looked through the patio window at the picnic table, maybe even stepped outside and sat down at it for a few minutes, crying and remembering? No wonder Conrad Dippel had chosen her to be his ultimate Igor. With the sorrow she carried, she would have been ripe for his psychological manipulation.

The brothers walked side by side, close enough that when Dean whispered, Sam had no trouble hearing him. "I'll go in through the patio door. You stay outside in case anyone tries to get away."

"I don't think so," Sam whispered back. "I'm perfectly capable of going in with you, and since we don't know if there are any more Frankenmutts or Double-Header juniors in there, you're going to need back-up."

Dean didn't look happy about it. "Fine. But you're not in the best shape right now, and you know it. So if—"

Dean was cut off by the sound of shattering glass as a naked man crashed through the patio door. Glass shards scattered across the deck, and blood from fresh cuts on the man's hands and forearms pattered to the wood in thick droplets.

Dean looked at Sam. "He might be naked, but at least he doesn't have any extra body parts."

"True."

Dippel, dressed formally in a gray suit and tie, stepped through the opening in the patio door and onto the deck.

"My apologies," he said, his voice carrying a hint of a

German accent. "It appears Mr. Luss hasn't yet remembered the proper way to open a patio door."

"The naked guy is the doctor's husband," Sam said.

"And it looks like we managed to get here before Dippel skipped town," Dean replied.

Luss stood on the deck, looking at them without expression. He seemed more like a classic voodoo zombie—the kind that was resurrected to serve as a mindless servant of a houngan—than a Frankensteinian creation. Then again, as Sam looked closer, he could see the scar lines where NuFlesh had been used to attach various body parts together, and although they were close matches, they weren't exact. The right leg was slightly longer than the other and had more body hair, while the left arm was thinner than the right, its skin a shade or two darker. As Sam watched, dark energy gathered around Luss's arms, just as he had seen with the Double-Header.

"Do you see that?" he asked Dean.

"See what? The guy's Frankendork hanging out? And by the way, if his wife put him back together, you'd think she'd have given him a little extra in that department, you know what I mean?" Dean looked toward the resurrected Mr. Luss. "Nothing personal!" he called out.

"He's got the same ability to drain life force that the Double-Header had," Sam said.

"Death vision?" Dean asked.

Sam nodded.

"All right. Important safety tip. Thanks." Dean took a step forward and addressed Dippel. "You see we're armed, right? So before any of us goes and does something stupid, let's talk."

Sam glanced sideways at his brother. *What are you up to?* he thought.

Dippel smiled. "What is it you Americans say? We don't negotiate with terrorists." He turned to Marshall Luss. "Kill them."

The man started toward them, ignoring the glass shards on the deck. He cut his feet and left bloody footprints in his wake, but the injuries didn't seem to cause him any more pain than the cuts on his hands and arms did.

Dean cradled his shotgun in his elbow, grabbed a flare from his jacket pocket, pulled off the striking cap, and lit it. A shower of reddish sparks burst forth from the flare's tip. Dean dropped the striking cap and, still cradling his shotgun, held the burning flare out before him and started walking toward the deck.

Marshall stopped at the edge of the deck, blood pooling beneath his shredded feet and dripping from his hands. The dark energy that had been building around his hands faded and was gone. An expression crossed his face at last. It was one of fear.

"Fire bad," Dean said.

"Indeed," Dippel commented dryly. "I would think it doubly true in your case, considering you carry a container of flammable liquid on your back."

"What can I say? I'm just a guy who likes living on the edge."

Dippel regarded Dean for a moment, sizing him up, Sam thought, trying to determine how dangerous he was. Evidently, dangerous enough, for Dippel said, "What did you want to talk about?"

"My brother got bit by your dog, and he picked up some kind of Frankenrabies. You're going to cure him."

Dippel arced an eyebrow. "Is this so? And why, pray tell, would I do something so clearly against my own interests?"

"Because if you do, we'll let you go."

Sam couldn't believe what he was hearing. "Are you nuts?"

Dean ignored him. "And there's one other thing."

Dippel laughed. "You're a bold one, aren't you? Very well, what is it?"

"We need a weapon."

Sam didn't like where this was heading. "Dean, we can't do this. We've both made deals we shouldn't have, with forces we shouldn't have, and it's never turned out well."

Dean kept his gaze focused on Dippel. "You ever heard of the Leviathan?"

Dippel's eyes narrowed. "I've encountered some lore about them in my time."

"Well, they're real and they're loose on Earth. My brother and I are determined to stop them before they turn the planet into their personal all-you-can-eat buffet, but to do that, we're going to need some serious firepower. Something like that fire lizard you sicced on us back at the motel."

"So if I cure your brother and give you a weapon, you'll simply allow me to depart Brennan—*and* you won't attempt to hunt me down later?"

"Oh, we'll come after you eventually," Dean said. "Assuming the Leviathan don't make a meal out of us. But that's down the road. What we're talking about now is what it's going to take for you to live long enough to get out of town."

"I must admit, it's an intriguing offer."

Dippel looked as if he might be considering it, but Marshall's fear of the flare seemed to be fading. He stepped closer to the edge of the deck, and the black energy began to swirl around his arms once again. He no longer looked afraid. He looked angry.

This, Sam thought, *is bullshit.*

He shifted his sawed-off shotgun to his left hand, drew his Beretta, took aim at Marshall Luss, and fired.

FOURTEEN

Catherine stood next to the defibrillator, finger poised above the activation button. Bekah's head and chest were wrapped tight in the treated cloth strips, and the rest of her body appeared whole and unmarred. The IV needles had been inserted at various junctures and had delivered the chemicals into her vascular system, and the AED's sensors had been attached, one to her upper chest, one to her lower. Her flesh showed no sign of decay, and the NuFlesh scars were less noticeable on her than on Marshall. Catherine knew it was sexist of her, but she'd taken more care with Bekah than Marshall because she thought the scarring issue would matter more to a young woman than it would to a middle-aged man. She didn't think Marshall would mind.

She jumped when she heard the distant sound of shattering glass.

It's started.

She knew she should activate the defibrillator, but she hesitated. Had she administered the IV chemicals in the right dosages? Properly positioned the Lapis Occultus on Bekah's forehead? She'd told Conrad that enough battery power remained to operate the AED, but what if she'd miscalculated? What if she had made a mistake somewhere along the line? The smallest error could negatively affect the outcome, and if the procedure didn't work, if Bekah didn't return to life, Catherine feared she might not get another chance. It wouldn't matter if Marshall and Conrad defeated the hunters, not if Bekah's body was so damaged due to her bungling that it couldn't be salvaged. Bekah would die a second death before she could be reborn, and after that, resurrection would no longer be possible.

Catherine felt the temperature in the basement drop, as if the central air had been turned on and the thermostat set to "cold as ice." Shadows gathered from every corner of the room, sliding across the floor toward her like sinuous black serpents. She watched with a mixture of awe and dread as the shadows merged to form a swirling whirlpool of darkness. A moment later a figure rose from the ebon mass, a woman with marble-white skin who wore the shadows around her like a cloak of night. Her eyes were solid obsidian, and her lips the bright red of arterial spray. She was the most beautiful being, male or female, that Catherine had ever seen.

The woman's mouth didn't move, but Catherine heard her speak nonetheless.

Fear not, my daughter. Your work has been exemplary. This body is both comely and strong, and with the aid of the Lapis Occultus, it shall contain the whole of my power without ill effect. It will be the perfect vessel. All you need do is release the tiny lightning, and your daughter will not only draw breath again, she shall truly be reborn, becoming something far more than you ever dreamed possible.

The voice was cold but hypnotic, a winter wind whispering across a snow-covered plain in the dead of night. Catherine felt compelled to obey, and if she noted the woman's use of the word vessel, it did not trouble her. She smiled as she gazed into the limitless dark depths of the woman's eyes, and she pressed the defibrillator's button.

Dean saw blood mist from Marshall Luss's right shoulder the same instant he heard the crack of Sam's Beretta going off. He didn't know what he was angrier about, that Sam had shot before he could negotiate a deal with Dippel, or that he'd missed doing any real damage to Marshall.

His aim's off because he's so sick, Dean thought. *Hell, he's probably lucky he still has the strength to hold the damned gun and squeeze the trigger.* Taking all that into consideration, he supposed it wasn't that bad of a shot after all. Still, it pissed him off, and it didn't leave him much choice about what to do next.

He hurled the flare toward Marshall, and before it could strike him, he switched the Winchester into a firing position and let 'er rip.

Marshall brought up his hands to shield his face and took a step back as the burning flare tumbled toward him. His feet were still slick with blood, and that's what saved his life—or unlife, as the case might be. His feet slid out from under him and he fell backward just as Dean fired his shotgun. Marshall slammed to the deck, glass shards lodging in his back. The flare hit the deck, bounced a couple times, then rolled to a stop six feet from him. The wood beneath the blazing tip blackened and began to burn. Marshall jumped to his feet and pointed at the flare.

"Fy-uh!" he shouted. "Fy-uh!"

He sounded like a four-year-old, maybe younger. Hearing a child's halting attempt at language come out of a grown man's mouth filled Dean with both pity and rage. As much as he hated monsters, he viewed most of them as not much different than animals. They did what they did because it was their nature, but because they preyed on humans who didn't believe in them and had no idea how to defend themselves, hunters like him and Sam—and Bobby and their dad— had to kill them. Demons were a different story, of course, and don't get him started on friggin' angels! But the poor reanimated son of a bitch that was Marshall Luss hadn't asked to become an undead *thing*, and he'd still be resting in peace if it wasn't for Conrad "Just call me the mad alchemist" Dippel. He was the real monster.

"You know, Sam, it's been a while since we had ourselves a good old-fashioned barbecue."

He dropped the Winchester to the ground, took hold of the flamethrower's nozzle, and started running toward the deck. Although the fire stream had a fifteen-foot range, he wanted to get good and close before unleashing hell so he could make every lick of flame count. He could hear kerosene slosh as he ran, and he couldn't wait to empty the whole damned container on Dippel.

Dippel looked less than impressed by Dean's charge. He reached into a pocket of his pants, pulled out a fistful of powder, and tossed it at the flare, barking a few harsh words in what Dean supposed was German as he did so. The powder transformed into water in midair and splashed down onto the flare, dousing both it and the flames around it.

Dippel turned to face Dean, reaching into his pocket for more powder.

Dean came to a halt three yards from Dippel, raised the flamethrower's nozzle, and thumbed the switch.

"Flame on!" he shouted.

A stream of fire shot from the flamethrower's nozzle and arced toward Dippel just as the alchemist hurled the rain powder and shouted more German. But Dean wasn't aiming directly at Dippel. Instead, he aimed at the deck around Dippel's feet, stepping to the side as he fired to avoid the powder—now water—coming at him. Flaming liquid splashed onto the deck, causing Marshall to shriek in terror and leap into the yard to get away from the "Fy-uh." Dean would deal with him later. Right now his primary objective was to cook himself up a little Southern fried Dippel.

He'd forgotten the powder-turned-water was magical in origin, however, and instead of splashing harmlessly to the ground, it changed trajectory in midair and curved toward the flamethrower's nozzle. Before Dean could react, it struck the nozzle and flowed into it, the water moving as if it was alive. The fire cut off at once, and although Dean thumbed the release button several times, all that came out were thin streams of decidedly not-flaming liquid. The flames he'd already ignited on the deck were spreading, but none had reached Dippel yet, and the alchemist was hard at work using more of his magic water-powder to douse the fire.

Some Human Torch you turned out to be, Dean thought.

He caught movement from the corner of his eye and turned just in time to see Marshall Luss running toward him, features contorted into a mask of rage, bloody hands stretched out, fingers curled into fists.

"Fy-uh bad!" he bellowed. "You bad!"

"Sam? A little help?"

No reply. Dean's gut twisted with a cold, sick feeling, he looked over his shoulder to see Sam lying on the ground, still clutching his Beretta, eyes closed, body still. Dean couldn't tell if his brother was still breathing, but he couldn't afford to waste any more time fighting. He needed Dippel's help.

Marshall slammed into him with all the ferocity of a pro linebacker. The resurrected man wrapped his arms around Dean as he hit, and the impact carried them both to the ground. Dean tried to twist out of Marshall's grip on the way down, but the man was strong as hell—probably way stronger than he'd been in life—and he was unable to break free. Dean's breath was forced out of his lungs as he struck the ground, Marshall still holding tight to him. Under other circumstances, Dean might have found it more than a little awkward to have a naked man lying on top of him, but just then he had bigger concerns. The longer it took him to get Sam help, the greater the chance that his brother would die. His thoughts raced as he desperately tried to think of a way to break the man's iron grip. Then he felt a familiar draining sensation, as if the life was being sucked out of him. He remembered Sam telling him that Marshall had the same ability to drain life force as Frankenmutt and the Double-Header. If he didn't get away from Marshall fast, he'd be sucked drier than a juice box on a desert playground at high noon. Dean thrashed and kicked, but nothing he did helped, and he could already feel himself growing weaker. A few more moments, and it would be over. His worst nightmare would have come true. He'd have failed to carry out the charge his father had given him so many years ago: to take care of his younger brother. More than that, he would have failed to kill that slimy land-shark Dick Roman and avenge Bobby's death.

Looks like I'll be joining you in the Happy Hunting Ground, you old grump, Dean thought. *Hope you got a cold one waiting for me.*

He continued struggling, but it was getting harder to move. It would be so much easier to lie back, close his eyes, and allow himself to slip away. No more killing, no more feeling like he carried the whole damn world on his back, like everyone's lives depended on him not screwing up. In a lot of ways, death would come as a relief. All he had to do was stop fighting…

"Hold!"

A woman's voice. No, a teenage girl's.

Dean immediately felt the draining sensation stop. Marshall released him and rose to his feet. Dean was too weak for the moment to do anything but lie where he was and watch.

Dippel knelt on the scorched deck, head bowed. A woman

Dean presumed was Catherine Luss stood next to him, gazing with adoration upon a brown-haired, barefoot girl dressed in a T-shirt and jeans, both black. On the shirt in white letters: *I'm only wearing black until they make something darker.* In her right hand, the girl held a dark blue stone.

She looked at Dean. "My apologies. I would have been here sooner, but I insisted on finding something to wear first. Do you like it?" She twirled around to display her outfit. "To the Norse people, the color black symbolized new beginnings, just as night heralds the birth of day, and winter the birth of summer. I thought it appropriate considering that today is the day of *my* birth, in a sense."

Norse? Dean thought. Then he registered the way Dippel was kneeling before her, like she was some kind of...

He moaned as he struggled to a sitting position. "Don't tell me we're dealing with another friggin' god! I am so sick of you guys! You're nothing but stuck-up monsters with delusions of grandeur."

The girl bristled but maintained her composure. "I am Hel. Just one L. The Vikings worshipped me as the embodiment of death."

"Well, the Vikings were dumbasses then, 'cause I've met capital-D Death, lady, and believe me, you aren't him. But you're not a teenage girl either, are you? You're just using the doctor's daughter as a meat suit. I've seen that trick before, too."

Dean still felt weak as a half-drowned kitten, but he could feel his strength returning bit by bit. He wanted to keep Hel talking to give himself more time to recover. He glanced at

Marshall. The doctor's Frankenhubby stood staring at Hel, an empty expression on his face. Dean wondered if the man had enough beans left in his *cabeza* to recognize his daughter, and if so, somewhere inside his mind, was he shouting in anger at what had been done to her? Not that the good lady doctor seemed upset. From the way she was beaming at the goddess, it looked as if she was ready to join the First Church of Hel, get baptized, and run for Pope.

He glanced at Sam, but saw no change. He still lay there, unconscious or worse. Dean didn't know if he could work a deal with Hel, but despite Sam's warning against making pacts with dark powers, he had to try. His brother's life depended on it.

He was trying to think up a good sales pitch when Hel turned to Conrad and placed a hand on his head.

"You may gaze upon me, my most good and loyal servant."

She removed her hand and Conrad, trembling, raised his head to look at her. He made no move to stand.

"My lady. You are more beautiful than I ever could have imagined." Tears of joy streamed down his cheeks. "To see you incarnated in flesh that will not wither before your dark power is the fulfillment of a dream I have carried for three centuries, ever since the day I first heard your voice as a child in Castle Frankenstein."

She smiled lovingly down at him. "I reached out to many others before you, Conrad, but yours were the only ears that heard, the only mind brilliant enough to understand what I needed, and the only heart steadfast enough to find the courage to keep on striving through all the long years. And now, here we are."

"Yes, my lady. I will never know a moment finer than this."

Hel's smile turned cold. "This is true."

She pointed the stone at him, and a bolt of ebon energy shot forth and struck him in the chest. He stiffened, and his body began to age at a rapid rate, the centuries catching up with him in a second. His flesh wrinkled, became parchment-dry, and drew tight against his bones. His hair became white wisps that drifted away from his liver-spotted scalp and fell, decaying to nothing before they could hit the wooden deck. His eyes sank into his skull and vanished, and his lips pulled back from his teeth, creating a ghastly grin. He fell onto his side, and what remained of his body collapsed into dust. A moment later, that was gone too, and all that remained of Conrad Dippel, the insane alchemist who had inspired one of the most famous horror novels in the English language, along with scores of films, was an empty suit.

"What did you do that for?" Dean demanded. "Not that I'm sorry to see him go, but it's a lousy way to repay three hundred years of devotion. The least you could've done is given him a gold watch or something."

Hel shrugged. "He was a tool I was finished with, so I discarded him. I needed someone to serve as my agent in the physical world, but now that I have a suitable body, I need no one but myself."

Hel continued to face him as she spoke, so she didn't see the look on Catherine Luss's face, but Dean did. The adoration was gone, replaced by confusion. *Mamma can't wrap her head around what her little girl just did,* he thought. If Hel kept going like this, it wouldn't take long for the spell she'd cast over the doctor to break. Once that happened, she was liable to get zapped by that weird blue stone of Hel's and end up like Dippel.

Dean wasn't close to his full strength again, but he thought he might be strong enough.

"You know, I was going to try to make a deal with you to save my brother's life, but I get the feeling you aren't really the dealing type."

"You are correct. If I want something, I take it." She grinned. "It was one of the reasons the Vikings were so fond of me. They thought like I do."

"That's what I figured. In that case…" Dean drew his Colt, aimed for the stone, and fired.

Sam stood on the shore of a vast dark ocean. The water looked like ink, the ground beneath his feet black ash. Fragments of ivory bone poked through in places, most unrecognizable, but Sam saw several skulls, hands, and feet. The sky was a canopy of roiling shadow that stretched from horizon to horizon, but despite the complete lack of illumination, he had no difficulty seeing. Waves rolled into shore, moving thick and slow, more like tar than water, and when they broke they made a sound like sandpaper scraping bare flesh.

The last thing he remembered was taking a shot at Marshall Luss. After that, nothing.

"Am I dead?" he wondered aloud.

"Nearly."

Sam turned to see a man standing next to him. He looked

to be in his mid-thirties, with short blond hair and a kind, gentle face. He wore a light blue button shirt and dark blue pants, and even though Sam had never seen him clearly before, he knew who he was.

"You're the shadow figure I've been seeing."

The man nodded. "The infection you acquired from the bite from Dippel's hound made that possible. But you know that already."

"What are you? A Reaper?"

"Yes."

"So I *am* dead." Sam took in the surreal landscape around them. "I have to say, I've been dead before, and I don't remember it being anything like this."

"The infection combined with the amount of stimulants you took proved too great a strain for your body. However, as I said, you're only *nearly* dead. This..." He spread his arms. "...is a construct of your subconscious. And a most theatrical one at that."

"So you're here to shepherd me to the afterlife. I don't suppose there's any way I can talk you out of it?"

"I have come to take you away from here, but our destination isn't eternity. We both have unfinished business back in the realm of the living."

"Dippel," Sam said.

"Not anymore. He's been... dealt with. Unfortunately, the creature that he's brought into corporeal existence is a far more dangerous threat than he could ever be. She is Hel, the Norse goddess of death, and she is using the body of Bekah Luss as her vessel. I was trapped in the Lapis Occultus, but your brother freed me, allowing me to come to this mindscape you created in order to retrieve you. I can return your spirit to your own body and even counteract the necro-mystical infection that has almost destroyed you, but other than that, I can offer no help. Hel is too powerful for me to confront directly, especially since Dippel used a measure of my own power to resurrect both Marshall and Bekah." The man lowered his gaze to the ashen ground. "My capacity for acting in the physical world is limited, and I'd hoped to... use you and your brother to help me stop Dippel. If I could have thought of any other way..."

Sam didn't quite follow everything the Reaper said, but he got the gist.

"Don't worry about it. You were doing your job, just like we were doing ours. So, any advice for when I get back?"

"I'm only permitted to return you to life this one time because of the particular unnatural power that brought you to the edge of death. So my advice is, don't die again."

Sam smiled grimly. "I'll do my best."

Sam opened his eyes. He felt better than he had in days, wide awake and full of energy, as if he'd just woken from the best night's sleep he'd ever had. He still had hold of his Beretta, and he gripped it tight as he lifted his head slightly to survey the scene. Dippel was gone, nothing but an empty set of clothes to indicate he ever existed. A teenager he assumed was Bekah Luss—or at least her body—stood on the deck, cradling her right hand to her chest, an expression of venomous hatred on her face. Lying near her feet were scattered fragments of dark blue stone. The remnants of the Lapis Occultus, he assumed, whatever that was. Catherine Luss stood close to the creature that now wore her daughter's form, looking lost and confused. Dean was getting to his feet, less than twenty feet away from Sam, facing Marshall Luss. He had his Colt drawn and aimed at the man, but Marshall seemed not to care. He snarled like an animal, but although his eyes blazed with fury, he made no move to attack Dean. The man's hands and arms were no longer swathed in ebon energy—or rather, Sam could no longer see it. The Reaper had been true to his word. The infection was gone, but so was his death vision. He had to assume that Marshall was still capable of draining life force, which meant they had to keep him at bay, out of arm's reach.

Sam took in all the details in an instant, along with one thing more: no one had noticed his restoration to the land of the living.

I'm sorry about this, Bekah, he thought. He sat up and in one swift movement raised his Beretta and fired.

The girl's head snapped back as the round penetrated her skull. Catherine Luss shouted, "No!" and rushed to her daughter's side. But Bekah didn't fall down. She straightened her head, and trained her gaze on Sam, a trickle of black blood running from the new hole in her forehead.

"You seem to have made a remarkable recovery, boy. I wonder if you had help."

She held out her hand, and the bullet popped out of the hole and landed in her palm. She regarded it for a moment before turning her palm downward and allowing it to clatter to the deck.

"This body was created to be strong, and now that it is imbued with my power, it cannot be harmed by such simple means. You cannot stop me, hunter. My new servant will drain the life essence from both of you, then I shall animate your husks and make you the first recruits in my army of the dead."

Dean didn't take his eyes off Marshall as he said, "Nice shot. Good to have you back."

"Good to be back. So we've got another rogue god on our hands, huh?"

"Can you believe it? The damned things are crawling out of the woodwork like cockroaches."

"And it sounds like she plans to take over the world," Sam added.

"Yeah. Big surprise. You ever wonder if these jokers actually give any thought to what they'd do with the world once they've conquered it? It's a pretty big place."

"Be a real bitch to keep clean," Sam said.

Bekah's features tightened with Hel's anger. "I shall not permit such mockery. Marshall—kill them both."

"Bad men!" Marshall growled, and then started toward Dean, hands raised. Although Sam could no longer see it, he knew black death energy radiated from them.

Dean was through fooling around. He fired his Colt twice, putting a round in each of Marshall's legs. The man didn't seem phased by the wounds, but his legs collapsed out from under him, sending him sprawling to the ground. Dean tucked the Colt into his pants and took hold of the flamethrower's nozzle.

"This stuff might be diluted, but I'm betting it's still got

CARVED IN FLESH 293

a spark or two left in it." He thumbed the release button and pumped several streams of liquid onto Marshall. The man squeezed his eyes shut and sputtered as the watered-down kerosene splashed his face. He struggled to rise to his feet, blood pouring from the fresh wounds to his legs. Dean released the flamethrower's nozzle and removed a flare from his jacket pocket. He pulled off the striking cap, lit it, and tossed the blazing flare onto Marshall.

Flames erupted across the man's body, and although he'd seemed unaffected by gunshot wounds, this was a pain he was unable to withstand. He let out an ear-piercing howl of pure agony.

"Oh my god!" Catherine shrieked. "Marshall!"

Hearing his wife's voice, Marshall staggered to his feet and lurched in the direction of the deck. Whatever difference the Lapis Occultus had made in the man's resurrection, it hadn't caused him to be any less flammable than Dippel's other creations. Within seconds, Marshall had become a mobile bonfire, flames roaring and crackling, greasy smoke rising into the sky, filling the air with the gut-churning smell of burning flesh. He cried out in agony one more time before his voice cut out, destroyed by fire.

Catherine tried to go to him, but Hel grabbed her arm and stopped her.

She struggled to pull herself free from the creature inhabiting her daughter's body. "Let me go! I'm a doctor!"

"I fear your husband is beyond all help, medical or mystical." Hel flicked her hand toward Marshall and tendrils of ebon energy extended from her fingers. They struck

Marshall like five black whips, and then retracted back into Hel's flesh. Marshall stood still for a moment, flames burning furiously, then he fell to his knees and collapsed onto his side. He lay still as the fire continued to devour what was left of his flesh.

Hel released Catherine, and she whirled to face the dark goddess. "What did you do?"

"He had no need of what life force remained to him, so I took it. We gods no longer enjoy the high stations we once did, nor do we receive the offerings and sacrifices that are ours by divine right. Because of this, we've learned over the long, lean years not to waste resources. Or as your people would say, 'waste not, want not.'" She smiled. "Of course, all of this will change once my darkness has cloaked your world in everlasting night. There are so many more of you now than there were during my time, and every one of you shall fall down and worship me. And if you refuse…" Her smile turned ice-cold. "…you'll just fall down."

While Hel spoke to Catherine, Dean walked over to Sam. "I don't suppose you brought back any knowledge about how to defeat this bitch with you from the Other Side?"

"Afraid not."

"You think if we put enough rounds in her, she'll go down long enough for us to burn her?"

"I don't know. It might work. If I remember right, the Norse viewed Hel's domain as a realm of eternal ice and cold where those who died of sickness or old age were condemned." When Dean gave him a questioning look, he added, "The Vikings preferred to die a glorious death in battle so they could get into Valhalla, the hall of heroes."

"That's the one where you fight all day and feast all night, right? Doesn't sound half bad. So you're thinking that fire is the opposite of ice, and if we give her a hotfoot, it might take her out. All right, let's reload and put that theory to the test."

"Don't bother."

They looked up to see Hel walking toward them. Catherine remained standing on the deck, watching, eyes filled with despair, sorrow etched on her face.

"I'm not deaf, you know," she said with a smug smile. "While Niflheim is indeed a harsh frozen landscape, I am Death, and what is fire but the ultimate devourer, the ultimate killer? Flames cannot harm me."

"I told you, I've met Death—" Dean began.

"Fine," Hel snapped. "So I'm *a* death, not *the* Death. You may think of me as his little sister, if it helps. Whatever I am, I'm more than a match for a pair of mortals like you."

She stopped when she reached them. "Any last words before I turn you into my undead slaves?"

"I can think of a couple," Dean said, "but I don't think they're appropriate to say to someone underage."

Sam wasn't certain, but he thought he heard a voice whisper next to his ear. It said, *Catherine.*

Sam didn't know what he was supposed to do, or if the voice was real or just another hallucination, so he just started talking and hoped something would come to him. "Catherine, I know you only wanted to bring your family back. The pain of losing someone you love… it's indescribable. And no matter how much time passes, that pain never goes away, not completely. You think if only you could have a little more time with them, you'd say all the things you never got around to saying, do all the things you put off when they were alive. You pray for a miracle, and sometimes, one happens. In your case, Conrad found you, and with his help, you learned how to restore life to the dead. But when people come back, they're not the same. Their personalities, their souls are gone, and what returns is… something else. My brother and I, we've seen it happen before. We knew a girl called Trish…" He trailed off. "My point is we watched someone we loved brought back as a horrible, murderous thing, and we had to—to make it right again."

Catherine's face gave no hint of whether Sam's words had any impact on her, or indeed, if they'd registered at all.

Hel sneered at Sam. "How sentimental." She raised her hands and tendrils of darkness began to emerge from her fingers.

Sam could feel Dean tense, and he knew his brother intended to go down shooting. It might not stop Hel, but it was better than standing there and letting her kill them without a fight. Neither of them had gotten a chance to reload, and he didn't know how many rounds remained in his clip, but he didn't care. Whatever he had left, he'd make sure they counted.

Before the brothers could begin firing, Catherine said, "Wait!"

She stepped off the deck and came walking toward them. She glanced at the remains of her husband. The flames had died away for the most part, leaving behind only a blackened, smoldering husk. Sam thought he saw her lips tighten, but otherwise her expression remained neutral as she joined them.

Sam exchanged a look with his brother. They couldn't shoot now, not without hitting Catherine, too.

"Before this goes any farther, I want you to tell me something, Hel. I understand that you're in control of Bekah's body, and that your spirit is dominant, but is she anywhere inside? And if so, is she aware of what's happening?"

The ebon tendrils slithered back into Hel's fingers, and she turned to face Catherine. "If I say yes, will you follow me loyally and without question? Even though I no longer need an agent in the physical world, I have to admit that Conrad had his uses. You would make a suitable replacement."

"If my daughter is within you, then yes, I will serve you."

Hel smiled. "Of course she's here. Can't you tell?"

Catherine stepped closer and peered into Hel's eyes. She stared for several moments, looking deeply, before finally nodding. "I can see her. She *is* in there." She stepped back. "I am yours, Hel." She smiled. "Till death do us part."

Hel let out a laugh and then turned to face Sam and Dean. Once more the goddess raised her hands, and Sam knew they couldn't wait any longer. They were going to have to start firing and hope Catherine didn't catch a stray bullet.

Catherine reach into the pocket of her lab coat and withdrew something sharp and silvery. Sam had just enough time to realize it was a scalpel before she plunged it into the base of Hel's skull. Hel's eyes went wide, more from surprise than pain. Catherine flicked the scalpel's blade back and forth with a single deft motion. Hel's eyes rolled white. She collapsed to the ground, the scalpel handle still protruding from her skull.

Catherine, Sam, and Dean stood looking down at the body of Bekah Luss for several seconds. Then Catherine spoke in a toneless voice. "If you want to know death, study life. It's why doctors make the best killers."

"You severed the connection between her brain and spinal cord," Sam said.

Catherine nodded. "I don't know how long it will take Hel to heal the wound and restore life to Bekah's body. I left the scalpel in place in the hope it will slow her down, at least a little. But as powerful as she is, she will heal. It's just a matter of time."

"We should burn her," Dean said. "If Hel can't work her mojo, fire should take care of her as easily as…" He glanced at Marshall's charred remains. "…anything else." He reached for the flamethrower's nozzle.

"Not yet," Catherine said. "There's something we should do first—as insurance, if nothing else."

"What's that?" Sam asked.

She raised her eyes and regarded the Winchesters grimly. "Disassembly."

Sam looked at Dean. In unison, they put away their pistols and reached for their KA-BAR knives.

FIFTEEN

"I'm getting tired of digging graves," Dean said.

"Me, too."

The crapmobile cruised through the night on I-70, heading west, Dean behind the wheel, Sam riding shotgun.

After they'd "disassembled" Bekah's body, they'd burned the parts and buried them separately in the Luss's back yard. When that chore was finished, they buried Marshall's remains as well. The sun had long dropped below the horizon by that point, and Catherine invited them in for a drink. They accepted, feeling more than a little awkward. As they stood in her kitchen and drank tap water, she thanked them for their help.

What am I going to do now? Catherine had asked. *I've done terrible things. I never asked where Conrad found the limbs and organs I needed, but I knew where they came from—especially the freshest ones. And the experiment that got loose, the dog... it killed people. Those deaths are on my hands, too. I may not have taken any lives directly, but I'm just as responsible as if I had. I don't even have Dippel's excuse of being manipulated by a dark goddess. I was just a sad, lonely woman who missed her family. I'd go to the police and turn myself in, but what good would it do? No one would believe my story.*

The only physical evidence left was her homemade lab in the basement. She could lead the cops to the remains of Marshall and Bekah, but there was a chance that, like Frankenmutt and the Double-Header, they'd decay to nothing soon. Besides, she didn't want anyone disturbing Bekah's various graves, just in case doing so somehow freed Hel. They had no idea if the goddess's spirit had returned to the realm it had come from—Sniffleham or something like that; Dean couldn't remember—but none of them wanted to take any chances.

Start your practice back up, Sam had suggested. *Return to helping people. Isn't that why you became a doctor in the first place? Besides, what better way to fight death than by preserving life?*

Catherine had thought for a moment. *I think… I think maybe Marshall and Bekah would like that. But should I? Is redemption even possible?*

Dean had taken that one. *Doc, if we didn't believe it is, we wouldn't be able to get out of bed in the morning.*

"Too bad the Lapis Occultus was destroyed," Sam said. "I think it might have been another name for the Philosopher's Stone, in which case it could've made a powerful weapon to use against Dick Roman."

Dean shrugged. "No use crying over shattered mystical artifacts. I'm glad to see you're feeling better, though. You finally manage to fight off that infection?"

Sam smiled. "Looks like it." He crossed his leg and pulled up the cuff of his pants. "See? No more weird black veins."

"That's a relief. We'll save a ton of money on coffee." Dean paused before asking his next question. "You… seeing things?"

Sam tugged his pants cuff back down. "You mean like a strange shadow man? Don't worry. I don't think I'm going to see him anymore."

Something about Sam's tone made Dean think he was missing something, but he decided to let it go. "You think the doc is going to be okay?"

"I don't know. We were raised in this life, and the stuff we go through still messes us up. I can't imagine how much worse it is for a normal person. But if she starts seeing patients again, surrounds herself with life instead of brooding on death, I think she stands a chance."

"In our business, sometimes a chance is all you need."

They drove in silence for a while. Dean almost turned on the radio, but he decided against it. He didn't feel like music just then.

After a time, Sam said, "I've been thinking."

"There's a shocker," Dean said.

"Remember those dreams I had about Trish?"

"Yeah."

"It occurred to me that we never did anything about the Rifleman."

Dean did some quick mental calculating. "It'll only take thirty-five or forty hours to get to Washington State from here, assuming we drive straight through."

"I'm wide awake," Sam said, smiling.

Dean sniffed the air and caught a whiff of stink coming from the trunk.

"Maybe we should stop at a Laundromat and wash our funkified clothes first."

"Let's find a Dumpster to toss them into, and buy more when we get to Washington."

"Sounds like a plan."

The brothers continued traveling through the darkness.